The Demon of

Renaissance Drive

By

Elizabeth Reuter

JournalStone

San Francisco

JournalStone books may be ordered through booksellers or by contacting:

JournalStone
199 State Street
San Mateo, CA 94401
www.journalstone.com

The views expressed in this work are solely those of the authors and do not necessarily reflect the views of the publisher, and the publisher hereby disclaims any responsibility for them.

ISBN: 978-1-936564-25-5   (sc)
ISBN: 978-1-936564-26-2   (ebook)

Library of Congress Control Number: 2011933014

Printed in the United States of America

JournalStone rev. date: November 18, 2011

Cover Design: Denise Daniel
Cover Art: Joey Adams

Acknowledgements

To Mom. Mom *always* has to come first.

Check out these titles from JournalStone:

Shaman's Blood
Anne C. Petty

The Traiteur's Ring
Jeffrey Wilson

Duncan's Diary, Birth of a Serial Killer
Christopher C. Payne

Ghosts of Coronado Bay
J.G. Faherty

Imperial Hostage, Book 1 of the Destruction Series
Phil Cantrill

That Which Should Not Be
Brett J. Talley

Jokers Club
Gregory Bastianelli

Available through your local and online bookseller or at
www.journalstone.com

Chapter

1

As houses in Hell went, Annabelle's was lovely: wide, spacious, tastefully decorated. The large living room windows gave her the same ol' view of fire and carnage and let the stink of burning human flesh drift through her halls, but no home was perfect.

On the day Vinnie came to visit her, Annabelle had been stalking round her house, stomping up and down her stairs, glaring at the walls, jumping on her bed, and occasionally, just to release some tension, opening her front door and shrieking, "I'M BORED!"

Oh, to be reduced to having violent tantrums in her own house that made her servant imps run in terror! Annabelle had lived through illness, war, pregnancy, and drug abuse. She had seen and experienced death and misery, madness and agony. None of those matched up to her torment now, to the sheer, mind-numbing boredom that permeated every second of her miserable life. She was fed up and tired and without a clue of how to fix either problem. Throwing fits was disgustingly undignified for a noblewoman, but when you had lived long enough to experience everything, what was left to do?

Vinnie's cheap suit and mirrored sunglasses assaulted Annabelle's eyes from miles away. She froze in the middle of hurling a Faberge egg, given to her by some lover or another decades ago, into the nearest wall and squeaked in horror as he ascended the rocky cliff-face to her home. Why did Vinnie have to visit her *now*?

Dropping the egg, she ran up carpeted stairs to her bedroom and threw open her closet. The slinky, sexual clothes all succubi favored made up most of Annabelle's wardrobe; she had to dig deeply into boxes of old shoes and rags to find dirty, baggy sweats. Vinnie was just the latest messenger in a long string of them, all coming to ask for the same thing. The sweats would insult him, telling Vinnie that Annabelle couldn't be bothered to look good for him or his master. With luck, it would be all the irritating idiot needed to realize there was no point asking her for anything.

She doubted it, though. Vinnie wasn't the guy one chose for his intelligence.

When Annabelle opened her front door Vinnie stopped short and gaped at her, so she felt confident that he got the message. Instead of leaving, however, Vinnie rallied himself, pasted on a plastic smile, and bowed low.

Annabelle shut the door.

Three-tenths of a second later, Vinnie began knocking in a rapid cadence that continued the entire time he spoke. "Lady Annabelle? Most esteemed Lady, King Bael asks for just a moment of your time."

"I'm sure he does," said Annabelle, but she opened the door again. To offend Vinnie was one thing, but it would be political suicide to ignore King Bael. However much Annabelle hated her life, complicating it with an angry king's wounded ego would hardly improve matters. Even if Bael wasn't technically *her* king, being one of the last succubi in Hell only gave Annabelle just so much political leverage.

So, in accordance with hospitality, Annabelle summoned an imp to get Vinnie a glass of blood—vampires, in her experience, were always thirsty—and invited him to sit down in one of her plush living room chairs. His bony butt sunk into the cushions. Not hiding her grimace, Annabelle sat in the chair furthest from him.

"King Bael greets you, Annabelle, most beauteous and wise of all succubi, and extends an offer he's sure you won't refuse." Vinnie paused and began fishing around his back teeth with his tongue.

"Something stuck back there?" Annabelle asked.

"Old man flesh," said Vinnie ruefully. "I tell you, never eat an old man. Especially an old white man. They're like leather; you can never get them unstuck from—ah, thank you." An imp handed the glass of blood to Vinnie, bowed, and disappeared into a wall.

"Oh yes," Annabelle sighed. "It's just miserable when something sticks to you and won't let go."

Vinnie nodded. Annabelle could almost see her insult flying right past his head. She was impressed in spite of herself. King Bael obviously knew by now how Annabelle played dumb around the more intelligent messengers sent by aristocrats wanting possession of her womb. Trying a different sort of emissary, one she might let her guard down in front of, wasn't a bad idea.

Not that Vinnie was going to be any more effective than all the other messengers who'd lined up at her door, but still.

"In any case, most succulent and splendid creature," Vinnie continued, making a dramatic, sweeping gesture with his arms and dribbling blood on Annabelle's shag carpet, "His Majesty is prepared to offer you your own palace. Aren't you tired of living so far away from civilization, on the edge of a cliff? King Bael will give you a palace, many times the size of this hovel. Your imps will be replaced by the finest servants in King Bael's service. Your, uh, current wardrobe—" Vinnie tried not to look over Annabelle's rank attire and failed, "—replaced by silk and satin. He will appoint you a chef to cook any food you desire any time you are hungry, a masseur to ensure that no stress mars your magnificent flesh or sensuous musculature. You'll not take a step if you don't wish it. If you please, you'll have houses in every city in Hell and can travel to each at your own discretion, without the need to tell anyone you don't want." He said all this very quickly and mechanically, as though reading off a cue-card.

"Even King Bael?" Annabelle asked, surprised.

"Even His Majesty," Vinnie said. He took a sip of blood and swizzled it round his back teeth.

"My! That is a generous offer." Annabelle hocked up a loogey and wiped her nose on her sleeve, enjoying how hard Vinnie tried to hide his shock. "Just think, my own ladies, like I've had in almost every home on Earth I've owned up until now. And a palace! Of course, I've lived in several dozen of those, but I'm sure King Bael's will be much shinier. And naturally, I can already come and go wherever I want from my own house, but knowing that I can do so with His Majesty's approval will make the freedom much more satisfying."

Vinnie's smile widened and faded, widened and faded, as he tried to discern what Annabelle really meant.

"Yes," he said. "Well...what do you say?"

"I can hardly answer without knowing what His Majesty wants in return."

Again, Vinnie looked surprised. "I, uh, I thought that was obvious."

"To an extent," said Annabelle. "But, for example, would he want me to be exclusive to him?"

"Well," said Vinnie uncertainly.

"Then you'd better go back and check with him," said Annabelle, rising to her feet. "I'm eager to know exactly how I can be of service for King Bael."

Vinnie brightened like a light bulb screwed into place. "Really, O brightest and most radiant beauty?"

"Oh, yes," said Annabelle. "I can't think of a single thing I'd rather do with my life than spend it bowing and scraping to a demon with three heads and the legs of a spider."

Again, Vinnie looked confused by the sarcasm. He paused, only halfway up from the chair, empty cup halfway down to the tray an imp held up for him. "Yes, well, it's my honor to do so. But, I'm not supposed to leave without securing an answer—"

"Think how King Bael will feel if you make a deal that he doesn't like," said Annabelle. Vinnie, now standing, froze with fear. Annabelle hurried across the room to pat him on his polyester-clad back.

"Don't worry, Vinnie," she said. "A servant who knows when to ask good questions is appreciated by his master much more than one who leaps ahead when he's not supposed to."

Vinnie squinted in concentration as he tried to untangle Annabelle's words in his head. "I...I suppose so..."

"All right, then!" Annabelle slapped Vinnie's back, hard, forcing him towards the door. "We're clear. You'll go to King Bael and tell him how honored I am by his invitation and come back with more specific information." She opened the front door.

"Yes...yes, of course..." Vinnie could tell by now that he was being had but couldn't quite figure out how. "About how exclusive you would be. To him."

"That's right," said Annabelle. "After all, it would take a lot for one of the last remaining succubi in Hell to sleep with just one creature.

Why, soon King Bael would have more children than his castle had room for, and no one else would get any. Think of the inconvenience."

Vinnie was still nodding as Annabelle pushed him towards the door. Then he stopped. "Inconvenience to whom?"

Standing by her open door, Annabelle smiled.

"Well, thank you for the blood," said Vinnie when he realized she wouldn't answer. He stepped outside and bowed, putting his head back through the doorway. Annabelle resisted the urge to shut the door on it.

"Think nothing of it," she said. "All the best to His Highness, now!" And she closed the door the moment Vinnie straightened up.

Sagging against it, Annabelle squeezed her eyes shut and took deep breaths. More messengers would come, from many different noblemen with bribes and threats. Eight kingdoms in Hell, each with its own king and nobles, and they were chasing after her even when she'd moved to the least inhabited, ugliest space she could find in Emperor Lucifer's domain! How much longer could she put them off?

Furious, she punched her wall, then swore at the resulting pain in her knuckles and rain of plaster.

She had to get out. Not bothering to change, to inform her imps, even to take her keys, Annabelle threw open the front door, letting Hell's burning, acidic air fly into her lungs. She ran into it, embracing it, hoping it would burn her clean.

"I tell you, darling, you just take everything too seriously." Samantha took a thousand-dollar purple hat from the sales lady in front of her, placed it delicately on her fair head, and examined herself in a mirror another Bloomingdale's store clerk held up for her to use. "A little sex, a little labor, and out pops the baby. Really, it's hardly worth making trouble about. Do you think this hat makes my eyes look darker?"

"No, but it dulls your hair," said Annabelle. The sales clerk gave her a curious look before pulling herself under control. "And you don't get to say what 'trouble' is when you're as young as you are."

"The hell I don't, darling. You wouldn't have asked for my opinion if you didn't care what I had to say. And I'm not just going to say what lets you wallow comfortably in your maudlin rut. How about this one?" Now she had what looked like a stack of fruit piling its way from her head to the ceiling.

"Christ, Sam, Marie Antoinette would have thought that was tacky."

The clerk looked decidedly miffed. Sniffing derisively, she snatched the hat back and marched away from the two demonesses with the fruit-pile hat held high.

"You do have a way with people," said Samantha, ignoring the remaining sales lady's stuttered apologies. "We're not going to find anything to buy at this rate."

Annabelle mumbled something even she didn't understand and looked out the store window. The New York skyline was beautiful at night but so ugly and gray during the day. She supposed nighttime covered the defects of chrome and concrete the same way it hid flaws in a person's face. Wrinkles faded away and fat melted into the darkness, leaving a younger, lither figure behind. In the daylight, every harsh, ugly mark lay exposed.

Samantha smacked her arm, hard. "Hey! This is ridiculous. You've become a Byronic hero with tits. Soon you'll be writing bad poetry about suffering beautifully under a rosy sunset. We're here surrounded by yards and yards of gorgeous waste that upholds a racist, elitist class system designed to make everyone on Earth miserable, and you're still not having any fun. Take out the sex, the money, and the smug superiority; what's left of your life?"

"I think that's what I'm asking myself," said Annabelle.

"Well *that's* a disaster waiting to happen."

"I'm old, Sam. I'm reaching my sixth millennia in a few weeks, and I'm so tired of everything." The mirror-holding clerk, repeatedly opening and closing her mouth like a suffocating fish, began backing away from Samantha and Annabelle with the mirror clutched to her chest.

"She must be new to New York," Annabelle commented. Samantha shrugged without looking at the sales clerk. She never bothered to pay attention to servants.

"Anyway, if you're bored, you need to find something new," Samantha said. She grabbed Annabelle's arm and pulled her out the door, soaking up the envious glances women threw her way like a plant feeding off sunlight. "Come on, I want to buy lots of ice cream and eat it in front of dieting women."

"Oh, *Sam*," said Annabelle, allowing her friend to drag her out of Bloomingdales. After the relative quiet inside the building, the New York afternoon seemed like an explosion of sound and color. Gas fumes belched, horns honked, food stands sizzled with dozens of different cooking meats, street-corner prophets predicted Armageddon, homeless veterans begged, vendors yelled for attention, lovers made out against skyscraper walls, performers danced and sang, and Annabelle had seen all of it literally thousands of times before. "Find something new? What's new?"

"To an extent, nothing." Samantha held her hand even on the street as though scared Annabelle would slip away if she let go. "But have you been paying attention to the latest gossip? I bet you haven't, stuck up in that shack of yours. There are some interesting things happening just outside of Dis."

Dis, the greatest city of Hell, the pride and joy of all citizens and the home of Lucifer, the Emperor himself. Annabelle had lived there, long ago. "I designed my 'shack' myself, thanks. And let me guess about Dis: shifting alliances, rumblings of war between some of the kings, talk of Armageddon…again…"

"Well duh," said Samantha. Ducking into a Starbucks, she called to the counter (over twenty-three waiting people): "Oh sweetheart! The cutie with the blue hair? I'll take a drink with enough calories to make Rosanne Barr think twice and a blueberry muffin."

The boy behind the counter turned to tell her off, only to be struck dumb. Looking into his mind, Annabelle saw what he saw looking at Samantha: a short and curvy woman with soft brown eyes and dark blonde hair so long it nearly dragged against the floor. It was the woman of his fantasies, the one he'd thought about while masturbating since seeing her in *Playboy* three years ago. He smelled an exotic scent drifting from her, a touch of sandalwood mixed with ocean spray and something he couldn't identify and desperately wanted to.

Nodding dumbly, he abandoned the customer he'd been attending to make Samantha's drink. Many of the long-waiting patrons in line began complaining and Samantha sat down looking very pleased with herself.

Plenty of stares focused on Annabelle as well; plenty of noses picked up her skin's irresistibly alluring scent. The attention fed Annabelle's pride, though not as much as it once had. She knew magic, not her own charms, drew her admirers in.

Besides, attention didn't ease her boredom anymore.

"Anyway," said Samantha, ignoring an old man who marched over to her and began yelling about young people these days. His complaints withered when he got a good look at Samantha and realized she was the woman of his fantasies: tall and slender with thick blonde hair, so light it was almost white, just down to her shoulders, and beautiful green eyes. "Emperor Lucifer decreed that all illegitimate children of our illustrious kings are ineligible for any rank higher than duke."

"No!" said Annabelle, straightening in her seat. "But of course, it's so obvious—what a way to protect his throne! Is King Belial still the only married king?"

"Yup, and his wife is as stubbornly barren as every other female demon who's not, you know, us. So now it's a scramble for the remaining seven to find wives. They're stuck and they know it. Suddenly hundreds of eligible bastard candidates are as useful as kitchen cooks!" She was still laughing when the counter boy brought her muffin and drink, elbowing aside the drooling old man at her shoulder to get as close to her as possible. "Loads of them have been sniffing around me for weeks. Even a couple of kings."

Annabelle raised an eyebrow in disbelief. Samantha's smile vanished.

"Who knows," she sneered, tossing her hair back and narrowing her eyes into slits, "I think one or two of the lower nobles might even be desperate enough to want you."

Annabelle smirked. Her voice dripped with sugar when she said, "It's not *my* fault you were born to a commoner." She gloried in Samantha's fury; best frenemies forever. Why hadn't previous generations thought of such a marvelous, useful word?

Her good humor vanished when she tried to imagine being married. Perhaps to handsome King Paimon with his beautiful, feminine face and muscled body...? But being the sovereign of kingdoms was not new to her, and the thought of having sex with the same man every night for the rest of eternity made her shiver.

"No good?" said Samantha, licking her straw and waving the counter boy away without thanks. "Oh well, maybe you can get something interesting out of the competition, at least. I've had the most extravagant offers since the whole thing started. Soon I'll need a new room for all the jewelry."

Annabelle thought the new law had already given her a great gift: a lack of violence from any of her recent suitors. They could force her to have sex but not to say marriage vows.

Thinking of Vinnie and his half-baked offer yesterday evening, Annabelle wondered if King Bael had been hoping to summon her to his castle so he could propose marriage himself. Or perhaps his offer had been marriage. Vinnie had only said that what Bael wanted should have been obvious to her. Maybe he'd assumed she knew about the new marriage law. Annabelle cursed Vinnie for having a mind so unattractive as to have made her reluctant to read it and make sure.

"Darling," said Samantha. "I'm terribly insulted that you're not paying me the proper amount of attention. It's just rude."

"Sam, cut me a break," Annabelle snapped, annoyed at being pulled out of her thoughts. "I'm old, I'm worn out, and I'm frustrated."

"No," said Samantha. "You don't age, you're as healthy as any of us, and if you still haven't found a solution to your frustration after so many years of ennui, you're choosing not to."

"Drop dead," said Annabelle, letting her forehead fall onto the table with a *thud*.

Moving from Earth to Hell was somewhat like being reborn. Annabelle would sink into the ground, the earth clutching at her feet and then her legs, her torso, her chest and finally closing round her head. She would feel the pulse of life around her, sliding over her, stroking every inch of her. It was soothing and invigorating at once, a pleasurable sensation that Annabelle was always loath to end. She sometimes considered just not emerging, spending the rest of her days being touched and coddled and feeling her every nerve ending come alive. But then the thought would come to Annabelle that she was inside the Earth, and what if it trapped her? Would she suffocate?

Panicked, Annabelle would fall into Hell shrieking like a madwoman and making a great spectacle of herself.

The last time that had happened, a couple of decades ago, she'd found herself somewhere in Dis with a great crowd of shocked demons staring at her. The memory of that embarrassment was enough to dissuade Annabelle from ever lingering in the soil again.

This time she made sure to travel rapidly and arrived outside Jigoku, the closest city to her home, just before sunset in New York City.

She didn't want to go home and see familiarity too soon, so she walked several miles instead of teleporting. This took her past, among other tortures, Farfarello's sand pits a mile or so from her house.

Farfarello was a giant, floating horror that mired his victims in dark, boiling quicksand. They sank and drowned over and over again, suffocating in muck until they couldn't scream, only to suddenly find themselves above the ground and just beginning to sink once again. As they sank, Farfarello lowered himself to their level, ostensibly to offer them help, only to fly away just as they reached for his black, fly-like legs. Huge boulders, perfect for grabbing, lay perfectly visible and just beyond their reach on the soft, wet ground.

The stench of the pits would have overwhelmed a less experienced creature, even some demons. Bubbling quicksand, burning humans, and the rot of Farfarello's postulant body were driven toward Annabelle by the furious beating of his wings.

"Hey, Farf," said Annabelle.

"'Ey there!" said Farfarello, abandoning his wide-eyed, screaming charges to swoop almost gracefully around her head. Black strands of hair blew into Annabelle's eyes, and she brushed them back into her loose ponytail. "And where've you been, eh? Up and disappeared, you 'ave!"

The strength of his cockney accent made him difficult to understand, but Annabelle got the gist.

"Just needed to relax a bit," she said. "Stressful year, that's all."

Farfarello laughed, his wings spreading wide and sending black shadows over the sand. "All you gotta do is lay back and 'ave orgasms. What's so stressful there?"

And here it came: *rage*, welling up from deep in some corner of Annabelle's soul, encouraging her to rip Farfarello apart, to tear his ugly bat wings from his stinking back. Her hands balled into fists before she could stop them. She quickly lowered her head so Farfarello would not see her expression.

Fortunately, he had never been very sharp. "Oi, you wanna come join me, then? C'mon, I'll let ya dip one o' them boys in the quicksand; it'll cheer you right up." Despite the sticklike look of his limbs, he smacked Annabelle's shoulder with nearly enough power to send her to her knees.

In stumbling, Annabelle could suddenly see below Farfarello's left wing just as a gaggle of dirty little imps dragged a new victim up to the quicksand. From the look of the human, he was being transferred from one torture to another. His face was too vacant for him to be new; in her experience, that empty look showed a broken mind. Glancing into his thoughts revealed a dark whorl, like a television set hit with a baseball bat that now broadcast only static. Perhaps some demon hoped a new horror would bring life, and pain, back to him.

"Thanks," she said, tearing her eyes away from the man just before the imps dropped him to the ground for Farfarello to take care of. "But you know I couldn't, um, take the pleasure from you." Her eyes strayed back to the crumpled man. She felt compelled or perhaps bewitched. Something about him arrested her attention.

No, more than that. It felt as though the world had frozen. All of Annabelle's senses focused on the broken, limp young man just lying on the ground, waiting passively for abuse. Welts covered his pale body from head to toe, spreading to the edge of his hairline and down to each fingertip. Mud and other filth caked his brown hair. His helpless state reminded her of her own, sitting at home, cowering in her bedroom in the oldest, nastiest clothes she could find, waiting for the next loathsome messenger with an unwanted proposition. Empathy bloomed inside her, leaving her heart aching.

"Aw, no trouble, Luv. C'mon, just grab an ankle."

"You know what?" Again, Annabelle had to force herself to look back at Farfarello. "I have an orgasm to experience. You know me, right?"

"Ha! And my quicksand can't compare to that. All right, but I expect to see you back 'ere sometime in the next sodding year, 'ear me?"

"Sure thing, Farf." She waved goodbye. As she'd expected, he launched himself high into the air, showing off for her, trying to leave an impression. To Farfarello, Annabelle was emaciated like an anorexia victim with arms so thin they'd break at the slightest impact. She smelled of waste and decay. This attracted him so strongly he couldn't resist putting on a show.

Annabelle teleported the second Farfarello's eyes turned away from her. She grabbed the naked, broken man just as Farfarello crested in the sky, his face pointed upwards into the blood-red atmosphere. Hugging the man's body close, cursing the platform heels Sam had forced her into, Annabelle dived behind a nearby boulder before Farfarello could turn and see that there had ever been a new soul waiting.

What was she doing? Annabelle scolded herself even as she peeked from behind the boulder, waiting for Farfarello to go back to work so she could run for her house. She would be in so much trouble if anyone found out about this, so much trouble! Emperor Lucifer would crush every bone in her body, if she was lucky.

Yet Annabelle found she didn't care. Exhilaration left her trembling with the desire to move and made her feel alive in a way she hadn't in decades or more. Just looking at the man's unconscious face and thinking of the rebellion she had perpetrated made her giddy. She muffled her giggles and bounced around behind the boulder like a child given a treat, alight at her own cleverness, head spinning with possibilities and joy.

Chapter

2

It didn't take long for Annabelle to realize she had no idea what to do with her guest. She'd ordered her imps to clean him up, a task that had taken two bathtubs worth of water and an entire bar of soap, then put a pair of pants on him. Tucking him into her bed herself, Annabelle watched him alternately thrash about shrieking with nightmares, then lay so still she was sure he had lapsed into a coma. All this worried her, since, as far as Annabelle knew, the souls in Hell did not sleep. If he was in some sort of pain-induced blackout, would that do permanent harm? She'd never wondered how much punishment a soul could take. Then again, she'd never paid any attention to whether or not they slept, so maybe this was normal.

Even without a plan or a clue, Annabelle was determined to take care of him herself. She spent all her time at home anyway, most of it sheer boredom. Hadn't she just complained to Samantha that she wanted something new to do? If she didn't have a clue how to take care of traumatized torture victims damned to Hell, the fun would be in the learning.

Hours later, when nighttime covered Hell as well in a velvet blackness, the man awoke. He sat up in bed with a scream, eyes flying so wide Annabelle was sure his eyeballs would pop right out of their sockets.

"The roaches!" he shrieked. "The maggots! The worms!" A peek into his mind showed Annabelle the same storm of confusion she'd seen at Farfarello's sand pits; he probably didn't know what he said any more than she knew what he meant.

Annabelle checked herself over to make sure nothing was crawling on her body anyway. The man blinked, mouth opening and shutting over and over again as the room came into focus for him. Then he scooted back against the headboard, pulling the covers around his body and shivering. He made himself as small as possible, trying to be invisible and staring at Annabelle as though expecting her to attack at any moment.

She hoped her bedroom provided a calm enough atmosphere for him. She'd ordered her imps to paint the walls a sunflower yellow, something she'd heard soothed the human mind. As the room was already soundproof to give Annabelle relief from the human screams outside, Annabelle just tried to come up with a relaxing scent, digging up a few sticks of incense to lie on a small, marble table against one wall. Judging by the way the man shook against her headboard, however, her efforts had failed. Sitting on the edge of the bed made him flinch.

He wasn't bad looking, with soft brown hair hanging into blue eyes, though emaciation and stress took their toll on his appearance. It was impossible to say how old he had been when he died, given what terrible shape his scarred, wasted form was in now. Perhaps when he recovered a bit he'd tell her.

"What's your name?" she asked him.

He stared at her, eyes wide and full of horrors she saw every day but could never comprehend from his point of view. Fairy tales in her mind entered his and rotted there, infecting his synapses and clogging his neural pathways with filth until it spread through all his body, through all he was.

"I understand," Annabelle said, staring down at her feet. "That's exactly how I feel, too."

Nursing a sick man or demon back to health required patience and care, good food and medicine. Souls, however, did not eat or drink, and neither healing powers nor physical medicines could strengthen them. So, Annabelle concentrated on improving his mental state.

First, she closed and covered her windows so her guest would not see the tortures and demons outside, even from a distance. Then, she talked. She read him books, sang him lullabies, and just chattered about anything she could think of until her throat went dry. Her whole world narrowed to the room, the man, and the sound of her own voice.

In return, he stared at her. He stared and stared as though Annabelle was some sort of interesting movie playing before him. He stayed huddled against the headboard, swathed in Annabelle's blankets, unmoving except to blink those huge, blue eyes.

They fascinated Annabelle, those eyes. They looked somehow deeper than demon eyes or even other human eyes she'd seen.

She stopped answering her door and didn't even check who had visited. The politics, which she'd taken part in just days ago, had ceased to interest her in the slightest, though she knew the consequences for such negligence.

About two weeks after Annabelle first took the soul to her house, he spoke. That day wasn't different to any other; she'd brought an old book of *Grimm's Fairy Tales* to her room and read him the story of *The Fox and the Grapes*. It was one of her favorites; the story that seemed the most true to life. What did a person do when he couldn't have what he wanted, when the pain of longing ripped through his gut and reduced him to tears? Hate the object of that longing, of course. So many times had Annabelle seen that sort of lust-induced anger, she considered that a truth beyond question.

When she paused to take a breath and turn a page, the man spoke so quickly and quietly that she almost missed the words.

"Why did you save me?"

Annabelle jumped up from the edge of her bed where she'd been perched and looked around to see who had just spoken in such a gravely whisper. She assumed someone, tired of waiting for her to end her self-imposed hermitage, had broken into her house.

But no, her room remained just as it had for weeks. The walls stayed bare, the closet to her left hung half open and showed her nothing but clothes. None of the chairs placed around the room had anyone or anything in them.

Slowly, unable to believe her guest could possibly have been the source of actual words, Annabelle turned towards the head of her bed. The man was drawn up against the headboard as always, as pale as the white covers bunched around him, but his expression had changed. Now his blue eyes were expectant, waiting for something instead of passively absorbing information.

"Are you talking to me?" she whispered, somehow worried about startling him, though she'd been reading in a louder voice only seconds ago. His mind stayed obscure to her probing, dark and confused. It seemed impossible that he could speak.

He nodded, very slightly, then pulled the covers higher around his neck.

"Wow," Annabelle said. She was really good, snapping him out of madness in just two weeks!

"Well, I…" Annabelle sat down on the bed again, thinking of how to explain. "I was bored with my life, sitting around and waiting for something, anything, to happen. I saw you sitting there at the edge of that quicksand pit waiting to be hurt, and I felt bad for you."

"You risked so much to help me out because you were bored?" said the man incredulously.

"When you put it that way, it sounds so petty," said Annabelle. She scowled, annoyed at being made to feel stupid. "You know, I did it because I sympathized with you, too."

"No, it's not that," said the man quickly, shrinking against the headboard so it knocked against the wall in the face of her irritation. "It's just, when most people get frustrated with life, they beat their girlfriends or steal money from Mom to buy heroin. I've never heard of a person being nice to someone because they were in a bad mood."

Annabelle laughed. "Well how could I not be? After a million children or so, who wouldn't get sick of a succubus's life?"

The incredulous tone came back. "A *million*? How many demons are there?"

"Living in Hell right now? Our population is a few hundred million, last I checked," Annabelle said. "There are only seven succubi, not including Lady Lilith, so the population increases slowly."

"You mean all of Hell came from just seven mothers?"

"No. There've been a few more succubi over the centuries, and there's the occasional blue moon pregnancy of a demoness who isn't a succubus. But all of us came from just one grandmother before that," said Annabelle. "What of it?"

"It just explains a lot," said the man.

Annabelle considered hitting him but decided he might still be too delicate for that sort of thing. "What's your name?" she asked instead.

"I'm…" the man trailed off and then frowned. "I don't know."

"I've heard of that happening to live humans," said Annabelle wisely. "Trauma. Why don't I give you a name until yours comes back to you?"

"Um." The man looked extremely nervous. "Okay."

"How about…Endymion?"

His jaw dropped open. "*What?*"

"I think it's a manly name."

Silence. Then: "*What?*"

"Fine, then." Annabelle crossed her arms, insulted. "What sort of name do you want?"

"Something really boring," said the man, clutching at the covers and leaning towards Annabelle as though imparting some great secret. "I feel like the luckiest thing that could happen to me right now would be my life becoming dull."

"Dull and boring…well, you're speaking English, and the accent is very middle-America," said Annabelle. "How about Harry? You know, from '*every Tom, Dick, and Harry.*'"

The man smiled, a pitiful, wan expression, but genuine. "Perfect."

"Okay then. Do you know who I am?" It occurred to Annabelle only later what a silly question that had been. Harry hadn't even blinked when she'd mentioned the word "succubus," so he had to have at least an idea of who she was.

Harry nodded. "The noble Lady Annabelle. You're very famous."

Preening, Annabelle straightened up and extended one hand for her guest to shake. "The Noble Lady Annabelle is pleased to meet you, Boring Harry."

Harry jerked back, banging his head against the headboard. His eyes widened again and his voice escaped in a panicked squeak. "Please stay away!"

Annabelle froze. Of all the ungrateful things to say! She abruptly wanted nothing more than to toss him out and never see him again.

"I'm sorry," he said hastily. "I'm sorry, it's just everything's still so strange and I'm so scared…please don't be mad! I'm grateful, really, you've been so kind to me and I'm very grateful, please…"

Ego somewhat appeased, Annabelle relaxed and let her hand drop. But the idea that a male, any male, wouldn't be besotted with her offended her deeply. It was her nature to be perfect to any man. All heterosexual men were attracted to her...though now that she thought about it, she'd never spoken to a condemned soul before. She'd heard that trauma could wreak havoc on a human sex drive, if souls even had sex drives to wreak havoc on. Annabelle now regretted never speaking to one before to find out, but well...they were just so far beneath her notice.

"Thank you," Harry said into the silence. Looking at his wan face and the terror stamped onto it, Annabelle softened. He'd suffered at the hands of demons, after all, and alluring though she was, Annabelle was still a demon.

"You're welcome," she said, feeling charitable once again. "Well, now that you're somewhat coherent, would you like me to show you around my house?"

Harry made the strangest face, excited and fearful at once. He leaned forward and then pulled back again, wrapping his arms around himself.

"What?" Annabelle asked.

"It's just. I really want to. But I'm..."

"Scared? I understand. But this is my home. No one but Emperor Lucifer, who is far away and busy, would dare enter without my permission." Annabelle tried to keep how unsure she was about that statement off her face.

"You really are important," Harry whispered reverentially.

"My mother was the greatest of royalty." Annabelle straightened and preened again. "Besides, without me, Hell has no children to replace demons killed in war or by demon hunters on Earth. Not even a king will risk angering me. If I say you are safe, you're safe."

The grateful way he smiled made Annabelle feel extra magnanimous. She gestured for Harry to follow her and forgave him when he put distance between them as they walked.

For a week, things went very well. Harry thanked Annabelle over and over again, and she accepted graciously every time. She read to him at night or told him stories from the six millennia she had lived. She described past lovers to him; described the rise and fall of dynasties in Korea, Japan, and China; described Hell and the controlled chaos that powered it.

Only in Hell would towering demons dwarf whole cities as they passed while condemned souls cowered in terror below. Bloated green and gray imps skittered about, carrying trays of entrails and eyeballs to their masters as large, horned demons with flesh that looked like vomit lurched over them, sometimes squashing the imps for fun or by accident. Beautiful, elaborate mansions and palaces adorned with gold spiraled so high that dragons scraped their bellies flying overhead; right beside them bubbled pits of muck so pungent even Hell's most sadistic torturers walked by with their noses plugged. Occasionally creatures no demon could identify lifted clustered yellow eyes above the muck's surface as though spying for prey, then ducked back underneath and traveled to unexplored regions of the Underworld. The music of Mozart and Bach drifted through the streets underscored by screams of agony and pleasure from many corners.

Sometimes, the cities shifted around with a will of their own that only Emperor Lucifer fully understood. Dis in particular was never the same city two days in a row.

"Our cities are so much *more* than your human cities," said Annabelle.

"Really?" asked Harry. "Then why did you move to a house so far away from them with a soundproof bedroom?"

Annabelle grinned. Sharp guy. "Because even the most conventionally exciting things don't interest me anymore," she said. "I suppose I've been spending the time searching for something worth doing."

Annabelle enjoyed that time in her home more than she'd enjoyed anything in decades, but some small part of her knew it couldn't last, however much she wanted it to. In days Harry began to babble again, to stare around Annabelle's room with wide and fearful eyes.

"Let me out!" he'd shriek, clawing at the walls until paint and plaster came loose. "I have to get out of here!" And no words of Annabelle's could calm him. She might as well have been Farfarello the way Harry looked at her. It was like he'd never seen her before, like she would rip him apart if she got hold of him.

She wanted to be insulted, but Annabelle understood his feelings too well for that. He had gone from trapped in the fires of Hell to trapped in a comfortable bedroom, but he was still a prisoner. Wouldn't anyone go mad looking at the same walls for too long? Could anyone recover from trauma while mired in hostile territory, fearing for their lives?

No, Harry needed more than a comparatively safe place in which to go mad. Relative excitement was not enough for Annabelle, who longed for total freedom from her dull, monotonous home, so why would relative safety be enough for Harry, who craved security and peace as well as freedom? His need for escape equaled her own, Annabelle knew now.

And she could give it to him. Hell no longer suited her. It had taken Harry falling into her life to galvanize her into doing something about it, but do something about it she would.

They would go to Earth. Permanently.

Chapter

3

Hell would not release one of its last brood mares easily. Annabelle needed a safe place to hide and as far a head start as she could manage. That would require help.

Annabelle thought to appeal to her mother first, but rejected that idea even as it formed in her mind. She shivered with dread, not wanting to think of what asking *her* for aid might mean.

Besides, Annabelle had nothing to pay her mother with, and incurring a debt would be pointless at best and detrimental to her future at worst. Annabelle would have to strike a deal—and she knew just who to bargain with.

King Belial ruled the Northern Territories of Hell. Approaching his castle by land was no easy task; most demon travelers had to cross miles of rocky, mountainous land, and then a wide, acidic moat that stretched all around a small mountain upon which his stone castle perched.

The Lord of lies and guilt, lawlessness and worthlessness, Belial was as old as Lucifer himself. Some whispered he was older, that he might even be Lucifer's father, though never very loudly in Lucifer's presence. Annabelle didn't believe that rumor. Lucifer would never allow a greater power than himself to exist in his own domain, and Belial would never have allowed his own son to surpass or govern him. Annabelle assumed Belial never quashed the rumor because it made people fear him, and that fear could be useful. No one ever questioned his orders.

Teleporting herself past the mountains, Annabelle materialized on the edge of the moat, where the castle guards could clearly see her. Teleporting any closer was not an option, as just appearing on the doorstep would be seen as a threat.

Belial's castle was a dismal place, Annabelle thought, with shadows strangling every surface. The cemented stones pulled darkness over them as Annabelle had pulled on her red traveling cloak before leaving home. Windows lit from the inside penetrated the gloom; when the lights went out, Belial's castle could only be identified by how much darker it was than the shadows around it.

Plugging her nose to block out the fetid stink rising from the moat, Annabelle walked as close as she could, until acid hissed only millimeters from the toes of her boots. Then, taking a deep breath through her mouth, she yelled, "Lady Annabelle announces her presence and seeks an audience with His Royal Majesty King Belial, Ruler of the Northern Territories of Hell!"

For several moments, Annabelle heard only her own cry echoing off the rocks until it disappeared into the sulfuric atmosphere. She knew Belial would make her wait. The Lord of Arrogance kept anyone but Lucifer waiting on principle. She made sure not to move so he would see her determination and patience.

Several minutes later, a small shadow detached from the large, looming shadow that was the castle and flew at Annabelle so quickly she would have screamed and ducked if she hadn't known better.

But she did know better, so she just watched skeletal wings unfurl; in a moment, a gargoyle messenger shot towards the ground. Soon it came close enough for Annabelle to make out red eyes and a swollen belly.

Wind blew through Annabelle's hair as the demon messenger drew to a halt, pumping its wings to suspend itself before her. Annabelle had always thought lower demons like this one much more useful than the imps she had to deal with. Heck, marrying Bael might be worth it just to get one.

"King Belial demands to know your business with him," the flying demon said, its voice like nails dragged over a chalkboard.

Bowing her head, Annabelle said, "Please tell him I have a business proposition. To say more would be to give away secrets he might not wish me to speak."

The flying demon snorted, blowing little puffs of smoke into Annabelle's face, and scrutinized her closely.

Then it said, "Hmph!" and flew away, whipping its tail insolently in her face. Again swallowed by the shadows of the dark castle, it left Annabelle waiting for several more moments. Then a spiked drawbridge, nearly invisible until it moved, lowered over the moat. Careful not to let her heels get stuck between the grains of wood, Annabelle crossed over.

Nothing offered her help getting up the mountain, made of a mass of fused human souls that had been liars in life. Now they begged for freedom and fallaciously swore their innocence, each new untruth adding weight to them so that they crushed themselves and their fellow damned. Annabelle could teleport over them, but even when invited, one didn't just appear in a demon king's castle. He had to see her coming, or he could legally consider her a threat.

Keeping her poker face firmly in place, Annabelle grabbed one screaming face, crushing its front teeth when she dug her fingers into its mouth for a handhold, and ignored its shrieks of pain when she hoisted herself up. Carefully using flailing hands as footholds and bloody eye sockets for her fingers, Annabelle made her way up over cries of agony, false promises of virtuousness, and entreaties for salvation.

Good luck with that, Annabelle thought. They annoyed her, asking others for help when no one in Earth or Hell helped anyone else without getting something for themselves. Anyone with half a brain knew that.

No one greeted Annabelle at the front doors, which opened on their own when she approached, or guided her through the twisting hallways and rooms of Belial's castle. Indeed, the castle seemed empty; not only could she not see anything, but her heels clicking against the stone floor was the only sound. Annabelle couldn't feel anyone when she searched with her mind, though she supposed Belial might be blocking her. Only roaring fires in every room and lit torches hung along hallway walls told Annabelle that the entire place wasn't abandoned. Annabelle didn't know if Belial kept his court and hundreds of servants in another building or if he'd simply ordered them to hide from her, but if he'd hoped she'd get lost in his stone maze of a home, he was going to be disappointed. Annabelle refused to give up until she found him.

"Well," said a voice that echoed around the wide, empty halls, surrounding Annabelle with hostile echoes. "Look who graces us with her presence."

Turning a corner, Annabelle came face to face with Belial's Queen and General, Avaira. Bone-white with as many muscular arms as the average insect, her long, snakelike tongue flickered from between needle teeth to clean a speck of blood from her chin. Probing her mind, Annabelle felt nothing. The Queen commanded a lot of power to mask her presence that way.

"Queen Avaira." Annabelle bowed low, enjoying Avaira's hiss of surprise. She obviously hadn't anticipated submission and respect. "I dearly hope you'll join me as I meet with your lord. My business concerns you, too."

"Does it, now? It wouldn't involve plotting my death so you can take my place, would it?"

Annabelle laughed before she could stop herself. She'd sat out of political wheeling and dealing for so many years, and gotten so used to speaking honestly, that it was difficult to bring herself back to appropriate manners. "No, Your Majesty," she said. "No, of course not. If that was my goal, I'd hardly want you attending the meeting."

"A whore is a whore, even with a fancy title," said Avaira. She walked slowly, gracefully up the hall, radiating menace, threatening Annabelle as clearly as if she'd directly said she planned violence. "You exist to steal husbands from the wives that work so hard to love them!" Her jaw worked furiously, tongue snapping in and out.

"Perhaps if the wives weren't ugly and suffocatingly jealous, their husbands wouldn't need to look elsewhere," Annabelle snapped.

Avaira shrieked, an enraged sound that promised pain. Annabelle knew the Queen had a violent temper, but she'd no idea Avaira was this unhinged.

For the first time, Annabelle felt afraid. No demon with any sense would harm her—to kill one of the last fertile demonesses would mean a death sentence. But a jealous wife afraid for her position wasn't sensible.

"I apologize if I've insulted you in the past, or just now, with my careless words," said Annabelle quickly. She began backing away, not even daring to glance behind herself. "I assure you, I have no intention of taking your lord from you."

"The assurance of a slut!" Avaira reached out and grabbed Annabelle's hair with several arms, yanking her close and shaking her like a bitch disciplining a disobedient pup. "You think you can fool me, do you? You think I'm stupid?"

Annabelle couldn't concentrate enough to teleport to freedom. Avaira yanked hair from her scalp in chunks, forcing tears from her eyes. "Stop!" she cried and kicked out with one pointed boot, miraculously connecting with Avaira's right kneecap. The Queen stumbled and Annabelle yanked herself free, landing on her rear minus a huge chunk of hair and scooting frantically backwards, almost choking herself on her cape.

She wanted to teleport away. Every cell in her body screamed at her to escape. But if Annabelle went home now, Avaira could make up any story she liked for Belial. Annabelle had to find the King immediately, or she'd never get another chance. The thought of losing her possibility at freedom scared her more than even Avaira bearing down on her, all six muscular arms at the ready to pull her limbs off.

So Annabelle got to her feet and ran, not back towards the entrance but past Avaira and further down the hall, dodging grasping claws and that horrible, twisting tongue.

Her cloak spread behind her like a trail of blood as she ran past rooms set up for Belial and Avaira's guests to enjoy. Cushioned chairs with indents from bodies only recently departed sat against most walls. Cups rested half-full on tables and chair-arms; books lay open with bookmarks just to the side. Demons were here, they were in this castle and they'd been in these rooms five minutes ago at the most. Annabelle just had to find them!

Annabelle mentally called one of her imps to her side; a tiny green body was suddenly running alongside her, panting as it struggled to keep up when the top of its head barely came to her thigh. "Mistress?" it squeaked, its long, flat feet slapping against the stone floor.

"Find Belial!" Panic made Annabelle yell. "I'll check this floor and the next, but there's twenty-three floors to this castle and I need to find him *yesterday!*"

A great scream rose from behind, recognizable to Annabelle now as Avaira. "How dare you! How dare you use his name so casually, how dare you! Oh, I'll ground your bones to powder! I'll rip your flesh off and use it to make myself a dress!"

Squealing in terror, Annabelle's imp divided itself so that a dozen imps the size of a thumb scrambled to keep ahead of Avaira and her wrath. They scattered in all directions, disappearing to, Annabelle hoped, higher levels of the castle.

Annabelle next crossed a study with a large oak table against one side. The legs were carved into the likenesses of torture victims in varying levels of agony.

Annabelle went inside and slammed the door shut behind her; she heard Avaira curse and skid to a stop to keep from running into the door. Annabelle leapt up onto a padded chair beside the desk, then onto the desk itself. Avaira ripped the study door from its hinges just as Annabelle jumped upwards and touched the ceiling with her fingertips. In the same way her body sunk through the soil when traveling between Earth and Hell, the stone ceiling sucked her body through it at her mental command, drawing her up to the second floor of Belial's castle.

Almost to the top, Annabelle felt Avaira grab one of her exposed boots, pulling her down and almost breaking her ankle.

No!

Reaching through the stone with the dexterity of a person moving through water, Annabelle undid the bootlaces below the bend of her knee and slid her stockinged foot from it. Clawing at the stone to pull herself up, Annabelle's leg jerked around in the constricting leather and Avaira's punishing grip...looser...and then she slid free. Her feet came safely up, her right ankle sore but unbroken, Avaira left behind.

On her belly, Annabelle kissed the ground.

Groaning and rolling onto her back, Annabelle shut her eyes and took several deep breaths. Her skull tingled where hair had already begun growing back, her ankle *didn't* heal immediately which suggested a sprain, and her heart beat so quickly her head spun from the speed her thundering heart pumped blood to her brain.

She wanted to go home. An easy thing to do. Just will herself there and teleport...

Annabelle gritted her teeth, gathered her will, and stumbled to her feet. When her vertigo eased, she found herself in the castle kitchen. Like the first floor rooms, the kitchen looked like it had been abandoned moments ago in a great hurry. Utensils lay all over, some hanging half-off the counters or dumped awkwardly into sinks. Bowls, some empty, some with food in them, were scattered around and aprons had been hastily discarded in piles on the floor.

After unlacing and removing her remaining boot—checking twenty-two floors with a sprained ankle would be hard enough without hobbling along on one stiletto heel and one flat foot—Annabelle grabbed the largest knife she could find and left the kitchen as quickly as her throbbing ankle allowed. She could only hope Belial hadn't been in one of the rooms she'd been forced to skip on the first floor.

Not long after, Annabelle's imp found Belial on the sixteenth floor. Annabelle teleported up and approached the room her imp pointed at, expecting anything from further attacks to a gathering of the missing denizens of the castle, only to find a scene straight out of *Masterpiece Theater*.

Thick Persian rugs adorned the floor, and a fire crackled in the hearth. A sinfully luxurious chair sat in front of the fire, its back to Annabelle. She saw only a pale, perfectly manicured hand when it reached out and took a crystal goblet of white wine from a small side table.

Annabelle was grateful to be granted a private moment to catch her breath and calm down. Straightening her hair and arranging her cloak so it covered her body completely, she looked around to make sure no one else was in the room before speaking.

"King Belial," she said, pleased to hear her voice sounded smooth and flirtatious rather than angry and frightened, which was how she felt. "I have no words to describe the honor of being in your presence."

A born showman, Belial knew just how much time to take standing up from his chair. He was beautiful with golden hair, delicate features, and huge, blue eyes like an angel; only a pair of fangs gave him away as something less than heavenly. His skin looked luminous in the firelight, and Annabelle didn't think he accidentally dressed in impeccable white clothing at all times. At the moment, he wore a white robe with gold trimming that looked slightly more translucent than was proper. He'd tied his hair back so the flickering firelight could trace every curve of his face.

"Lady Annabelle!" he said. He had a rich, velvet voice known to make anyone in hearing distance stop whatever they were doing to hear more. One of the most famous bits of gossip about him said he once talked a woman to death by so enrapturing her with his voice that she forgot to eat or sleep until she died from malnourishment. "What a delightful surprise, though goodness knows you took your time getting up here. Where have you been? I was told you arrived almost half-an-hour ago."

Annabelle dropped into a deep, formal bow, purposely exposing a flash of leg as she did, though the effect was lessened without heels. "I'm afraid your wife decided to have a word with me before letting me through to see you."

"That woman," Belial sighed, shaking his head. "Her devotion is touching, but I'm afraid she's...overprotective. She didn't give you any real trouble, I hope?"

"Oh, no, my Lord," said Annabelle, just as Avaira herself came running around the bend in the hallway. Seeing the edge of Annabelle's cape in the doorway, she came to a screeching halt and made the rest of the way at a more sedate pace.

"My Lord," she said, dropping to one knee behind Annabelle and looking at only her husband.

Belial smiled and put one arm out in invitation. Avaira's pale face lit up, and she brushed past Annabelle to kneel by her master's side and kiss his hand. The look of adoration she fixed upon Belial disgusted and amused Annabelle, but the King himself clearly enjoyed it. He reached down and began petting Avaira's short, white hair. Avaira was so pleased by the contact that she seemed to forget Annabelle even existed. Leaning her head as close to her husband's body as possible without actively leaning against him, she sighed happily and relaxed. Her eyes unfocused and her muscles went limp.

"Now then, Lady Annabelle," said Belial, giving his wife one last affectionate pat and leaving his fingers tangled in her stiff, white hair as he turned to his guest. "You said you had business to discuss?"

Annabelle considered asking why the castle was empty, but decided against it. It had nothing to do with what she needed and it would just give Belial a chance to play mind games with her.

"First, let me say what a surprise our Emperor's new law on royal succession was to me," said Annabelle.

Avaira visibly stiffened. Belial began stroking her hair again but showed no sign of stress himself.

"Yes," he said. "Given how rare it is for any demoness other than you succubi to give birth, he's putting his kings in quite a bind. Wine?"

Annabelle shook her head and waved away the wine bottle he'd picked up. "Indeed. Why, I can't tell you how many marriage proposals I've received since then. It's been quite stifling!"

Avaira stiffened further, her eyes narrowing. A fine tremble ran through her body, satisfying Annabelle immensely. Judging by the way Avaira had suddenly turned peaceful in front of Belial, she'd attacked Annabelle without his permission precisely because she feared this sort of conversation.

"Well congratulations, Lady Annabelle," said Belial, looking for all the world as though he felt happy for her. "Have you decided on a husband, yet?"

"Oh, Your Grace," said Annabelle, covering her mouth demurely with one hand as she tittered. "I'm just not the marrying kind. In fact, I've come to ask you how you're doing? After all, the thought of never having an heir should something happen to you must be a thorn in your royal side, a pressing problem."

Raising an eyebrow, Belial leaned against his chair but kept a shrewd eye on Annabelle and his free arm on Avaira's head. "Your concern touches me, Lady. But immortality has certain benefits, doesn't it? I have no reason to think I will ever step down."

Liar! thought Annabelle. Belial was famous for cultivating his heirs. He'd personally sorted through bastard children fathered with humans and succubi, hand-picking those candidates he found worthy of succeeding him and training them rigorously. Lucifer had probably made his decree to control Belial in particular.

Aloud she said, "Of course, Your Highness. For who could rival the mighty King Belial? Yet still, wars happen, with humans and…others." Such as the other kings of Hell, though it would be rude to say so directly. Stab an enemy in the back and be admired if you didn't get caught; insult him aloud and be derided for your poor manners. "Think of your people, King Belial. Eighty legions of soldiers, endless servants, loyal nobles, and of course, your gallant wife."

Avaira sneered at her.

Smiling in reply, Annabelle removed her cloak to reveal the black lingerie beneath it: a beaded corset, a matching scrap of fabric passing for panties, and translucent stockings. She dropped the red velvet to the ground in a practiced move, so that it puddled round her feet like a stand for her to preen upon.

Avaira leapt up, but Belial grabbed one of her arms before she could attack. He kept his focus on Annabelle, and though his expression remained polite, his eyes had narrowed. Annabelle wished she dared try to peek at his thoughts, wished he didn't have the power to block her.

"As the child must be legitimate," he said, "impregnating even a woman with your noble pedigree would be useless. As I'm sure you know."

"Why, Your Highness! Do you think I'd come here and try to seduce you right in front of your adoring wife, after all the tenderness she's shown me?"

Belial raised one golden eyebrow and said nothing. Beside him, Avaira vibrated with rage, her demonic energy filling the room. She wasn't the brightest demoness ever spawned in Hell, but she might be the most powerful. Just that inadvertent power slippage almost knocked Annabelle flat—not that she'd ever let the bitch know.

"In fact," said Annabelle, lowering her voice and stepping quietly, gracefully, towards the royal couple as though imparting a great secret, "I'm here to offer you help having your own child."

Even Belial lost his polite façade at that. His hand tightened around Avaira's arm and his eyes widened just a fraction before he composed himself again.

"How dare you!" Avaira jerked free, and this time Belial did not try to hold her back. "To mock us with our greatest wish! Oh, you'll regret coming here!"

"And you'll regret harming me," said Annabelle. "Really, I'm becoming disinclined to help you already."

Avaira hesitated, seemingly fighting with herself. That told Annabelle more clearly than anything just how much the Queen wanted a child.

Belial glanced at his wife. "Avaira," he said, "leave us."

Avaira spun around, gasping with indignation and clearly ready to protest, but Belial had already turned from her again. Indeed, if Annabelle hadn't known any better, she'd have thought he'd forgotten his wife stood not two feet away from him. Avaira turned one way and then the other, looking for an answer from cold stone and burning fire, so bewildered and hurt that Annabelle almost felt sorry for her.

With one last glare, Avaira stomped out the door, making sure to bump Annabelle's shoulder on her way out.

Belial straightened up and waved one arm through the air. Behind Annabelle, the door slammed shut. She could feel and smell the sweat that began to bead on her upper lip, and quickly licked it away so Belial wouldn't see how nervous she felt.

You're not trapped, she repeated to herself, *you can teleport away at any time. He can't hurt you, you're too important. You're not trapped…*

"Now, Lady Annabelle," he said, walking towards Annabelle as she had towards him moments ago, with a sly smile. "It seems we have some important matters to discuss."

"Yes," said Annabelle. "I'll take that wine now, if you're still offering." To her relief, Belial moved away to pour the wine himself instead of just levitating it over.

"You know," she said, cocking her head and trying to look thoughtful, "it occurs to me that what others think is true is more important than what really is true."

"Oh, yes," Belial agreed, closing in on Annabelle again to hand her a crystal wine glass full of red liquid. It smelled cloyingly sweet, and was thick on her tongue when she took a sip. "That's something a ruler must know if he's to lead effectively."

"I can imagine," said Annabelle. She turned and walked towards one of the room's windows, again trying to put some space between them. Belial followed her, however, his presence crawling up her back like a huge, poisonous insect. The wine stuck to her tongue, making it feel clunky and awkward.

"It's just like on Earth," she continued, proud of how steady she kept her voice. "I go to Earth all the time, love it up there. Anyway, on Earth, people believe some of the strangest things. For example, many of them face death at some point in their lives. They're in a car crash, or their home catches fire. Something like that.

"And when they face death this way, do you know what many of them insist?" Caught up in her storytelling, Annabelle managed to face Belial again with a smirk.

With his back to the fire, shadows crawled over much of Belial's face, obscuring it so Annabelle could see only his eyes and strands of hair clearly. Giving her only as much space as courtesy demanded, he said, "What?"

"That God must have some plan for them. That He spared them, protected them."

Belial burst out laughing and Annabelle joined him.

"Of course," she continued, "this is particularly amusing when other people have died in the accident. Apparently it never occurs to these chosen humans that, by their logic, God must have decided to let the deceased die; that He didn't protect anyone other than their special selves from the accident; that the dead must have been worthless to God. They don't ask what made them so special to have been saved but just assume that they are. Special, that is. Not only is it ridiculous, it's really quite offensive to those who didn't make it, both in that accident and every other. Imagine the arrogance! You're one of seven billion humans crawling around, but still, you're special enough to warrant personal salvation from the Almighty. Not like those other useless humans dying from starvation and war all over the planet, no, you're special."

"Do they really think that?" said Belial. "I suppose I'm not too surprised. Arrogance has always been one of their great failings."

"Really, Your Highness, you should know that," said Annabelle teasingly. "You, the Lord and master of all earthbound demons, and yet you know nothing about the humans they interact with."

"Yes, well, one of the best parts about being king is that you can delegate unwanted tasks," said Belial, smiling to take the edge from his reprimand

"I suppose so. In any case, my point is this." The firelight flickered, lighting Annabelle's body, adding drama to her speech. "Believing nonsense like that helps those humans survive. Suddenly, they're not just a human, but a *chosen* human—a protected, significant human. They can walk the Earth with pride and put extra effort into the things they do because those things matter. Their belief adds a richness to their lives that they didn't have before."

"So you're saying it doesn't matter that our hypothetical human's belief in heavenly favor is nonsense," said Belial. "It just matters that they believe it because of the way their belief gives them strength."

"Exactly!" said Annabelle. "Just as, in the same vein…" She moved towards Belial, closing the last inches of space between them and putting one hand on his chest, stroking it with just the tips of her fingers. She lowered her voice to an inviting whisper, looking up at his poker face through her lashes. "It doesn't matter if your heir is really born from Avaira. It only matters that everyone believes he was."

Belial's eyes widened, but he said nothing.

"After all," Annabelle purred, "everyone knows I'm a hermit. No one but your front guard saw me come here as I teleported in. I might as well not be here, since no one will ever know.

"And of course, were General-Queen Avaira to disappear from the public eye suddenly, when she usually inspects your troops so publicly every day, you won't even have to openly announce her pregnancy. The court gossips will do it for you. Within a few days everyone who matters will know she's pregnant. By the time Her Highness emerges once again, baby in her arms, no one will be surprised."

"I see," said Belial. He took a strand of Annabelle's black hair and wound it around his fingers as though examining the texture. "And if 'Avaira' gives me a girl?"

"Then she'll get pregnant again, though we'll probably have to wait awhile for the sake of credibility."

Belial's hand balled into a fist, jerking Annabelle's head back to expose her neck. He didn't speak, but spent a long moment staring at her pulsing jugular. Annabelle felt prickles along the sensitive skin, as though a knife was being dragged across it and not just a pair of eyes.

Belial released her and Annabelle stumbled back, her wine glass dropping to the ground and shattering in a mess of crystal shards and blood-red liquid.

"And what would you get out of this, honorable Lady?" he said, voice still pleasant and mild.

"King Belial, you wound me," said Annabelle, smoothing out her hair and straightening, refusing to show any fear. "But if you insist, I can think of something you could do to show me your gratitude."

"Really," said Belial. "And what might that be?"

"I need a portal to Earth."

"Really," said Belial again. "A succubus, with the ability to get to Earth on her own, needs a portal. What sort of cargo are you bringing, that you can't just put in your pocket when you teleport?"

"I'm afraid one condition is that you ask no questions," said Annabelle, trying to look regretful. "And that, when I go through the portal, there can be no witnesses. Not even yourself."

Belial drew back and looked Annabelle up and down, perhaps searching for some clue about her thoughts in her body language. She did her best to show nothing, keeping her muscles relaxed, her face fixed in a pleasant smile, her mind shielded. But Belial intimidated her with his stare, and the shrewdness behind his icy eyes made her very nervous.

Then Belial smiled, a look so terrifyingly friendly that Annabelle felt her blood freeze in her veins.

"I will think about your proposition," said Belial. "Do you need an escort back to your house?"

Talk about learning a lesson. Annabelle had always taken for granted that her position as one of so few guaranteed fertile demonesses in Hell would protect her. Perhaps fate had sent her to Belial's castle to show her how wrong she was, for if she wasn't even safe in Hell, Earth, where no one knew or valued her, would kill her. To live above ground would be to court constant danger, as humans themselves did.

Annabelle's mind spun with fear that sapped her courage. She teleported right into her room to collapse in bed beside Harry, throwing one arm over her eyes to block out the dizzying light. She could still feel Belial's eyes on her neck, Avaira's breath at her back. Part of Annabelle, a huge part, yelled that she shouldn't go to Earth. Harry wasn't her responsibility. She should turn him out or at the most, keep him in her home. It wasn't her fault the captivity would destroy him.

Slowly raising her arm, Annabelle turned to look at Harry. He was huddled against the headboard as he had been from his very first day in her house, thumb sucked deep into his mouth, eyes vacant.

Just looking at him strengthened Annabelle's resolve. The feeling of purpose she'd gained since meeting him, the feeling of being needed, was precious. She wouldn't give it up, not to jealous, neurotic wives, and not to her own fear. Physical danger meant nothing compared to the pointless existence she'd battled for years.

The next day, Annabelle learned her time with Belial had been fruitful. When she sent her imps into Jigoku to buy new blankets—Harry had shredded the old ones in a panic-induced tantrum—they came back with information. The city gossips were abuzz with the news that General-Queen Avaira had not left her chambers all day. Was she sick, they wondered? Was she being punished for some transgression? Or, could she be...?

Annabelle walked up the stairs to her room and opened her closet, where Harry had hidden after destroying the blankets. He lay curled in one corner, buried under a small mountain of tattered silk and leather.

Only his blue eyes, so much darker and more substantial than Belial's, shone through.

"I wanna go home," he whispered, like a small child. "I wanna get out…"

"You will," said Annabelle, kneeling slowly down and easing herself beside him. "*We* will. Just hold on, just six months and—"

Harry wailed when she said "months," the keening cry of a man with a shattered soul.

"I know," said Annabelle gently, "I know! I feel it too; I feel so trapped. I didn't realize it until I met you, but now…shit, now I can barely keep from tearing my hair out. It's like the walls are closing on me. But Harry, we have to wait. I'm designed to pop out as many babies as possible, my gestation period is only a day, and I can't give birth before Avaira is supposed to, can I? We have to wait until it's believable, and she'd take nine months like any normal—"

But Harry was shaking his head over and over, beyond any explanation she could give. Annabelle slumped back into the wall, hanging her throbbing head in frustration, knowing she could do nothing for so many months.

"Just hang on, Harry," she said wearily. "Just wait. Just wait."

Seven months passed before a messenger came for Annabelle, the same winged demon whom she had first spoken to at Belial's castle. Instructing her imps to look after Harry for the twenty-four hours it would take her to deliver her baby, Annabelle teleported to Belial's castle. It was empty again; Annabelle's footsteps echoed like gunshots in her ears.

The winged gargoyle led her to Belial's bedroom suites, a huge chamber in various shades of blue that reminded Annabelle of the twilight sky on Earth. Belial waited with alcohol at the ready, considerate and polite as ever.

The sex was less violent than befit a demon lord, but active enough. Belial growled and hissed, scratched Annabelle's flesh and marked her with his fangs. Desperate not to show Belial how terribly bored she was, because it would be unspeakably stupid to insult him into breaking their bargain when she'd come so far, Annabelle made all the right noises and twitched her toes as she faked orgasms.

But her energy flagged quickly enough, and it became harder and harder to pretend. She tried to think of something, anything to arouse her, or at least amuse her enough to keep her from falling asleep. In the end, no thought she could conjure up did anything for her libido.

And then, from nowhere, hitting Annabelle with all the force of a rock bashing into her skull: *I'm going to be free.*

There! There was the excitement she needed. Annabelle rose up above Belial, smiling in the predatory way she knew men loved. Belial didn't have to know it wasn't he that made her feel so alive. He never needed to learn that a taste of freedom, and the idea that she'd found someone as trapped as she in Harry, gave her the energy to go on. Leaning down, Annabelle sunk her teeth into Belial's nipple and ground against him, laughing when he bucked underneath her.

I will leave here. In just days I will escape this place and be free.

Chapter

4

The pain began immediately.

Seconds after Belial's seed spilled into her, Annabelle's insides started groaning in protest. Sperm met her waiting egg and divided again, again, again. In an hour, she had a zygote several inches in size feeding from the sustenance of her womb.

Keeping her composure through Belial's farewell pontifications, Annabelle arrived home just in time to vomit into a basin her imps held at the ready. Her belly moaned and swelled. Her feet ached and her breasts felt so tender that lying on her front was agony. Every inch of her skin felt too tight.

Imps brought wet cloths to wipe the sweat pouring from her brow and removed her heeled boots and leather clothes. They replaced the constricting garments with a soft cotton robe and slippers to protect her from the cold floor and stretch as her feet swelled. Several of them helped her to her feet. It hurt to walk, but she had to. The imps were too small to support her, and teleporting could hurt the baby.

A wave of nausea made Annabelle squeeze her eyes shut. She tumbled forwards and flailed for the stairwell banister.

When hands grabbed her shoulders, Annabelle stiffened in panic. She turned and smacked Harry with ropes of sweaty hair even as she registered that he had saved her from falling. He stood beside her, supporting her, though he looked even more frightened than she.

Poor thing, of course he was scared. Already half-mad, and now to hear Annabelle, his protector, in pain herself? It must have made him feel even more vulnerable and trapped than he already did. That he found the compassion to reach out to her anyway touched Annabelle deeply, and she forced herself to smile.

"Just a day," she croaked. "Just a day, this has happened to me before, it'll all be over tomorrow. Can you make it until tomorrow?"

Harry nodded as though he had a choice. He moved closer, one arm sliding around Annabelle's shoulders, the other moving down to grab her legs. Annabelle frowned, not scared or offended, but confused until he picked her up.

"Oh!" she blurted. Then she shut her mouth to keep from throwing up.

Once the initial vertigo passed, being carried up the stairs was undeniably better than having to walk each step. Annabelle pressed her lips tight and squeezed her eyes shut until colors burst behind the lids, clenching her hands into fists to keep from making a sound as her growing child squashed her organs, stretched her belly, and consumed all the nutrients in her body.

The hours passed in misery. Annabelle ate constantly, wolfing down steak, omelets, tofu, nuts: things high in protein to keep her strength, though her baby stole it all. Harry kept a silent vigil beside her, switching cool washcloths on her forehead and twice lifting her so imps could change the sheets.

Some twenty-two hours later, the fully formed baby demon began fighting for freedom by kicking at its prison walls, rupturing Annabelle's insides in a dozen places. Annabelle spit up blood by the pint, a sight Harry couldn't take. He fell back to a corner of her room, wailing almost as loudly as she, holding his hands over his ears but unable to shut his eyes for shock.

"Get out!" Annabelle screamed at him. Her vagina had stretched to ten inches within seconds; blood and fluid spilled out in a wash of gore. "Get him out of here!"

Several imps rushed to obey, pushing and dragging Harry from the room. His eyes, etched with horror, stayed locked onto Annabelle until the door shut.

It took only two pushes and a moment of blinding agony where Annabelle felt her whole life slide from her before the sticky, red mess that was her baby sat between her legs. Imps cut the umbilical cord and cleaned it. Annabelle was grateful for their work, because she couldn't do it herself. She fainted as her son came out.

A succubus heals as quickly as she gives birth, however. Annabelle awoke ten minutes later, her organs already beginning to repair themselves, her womb sliding back into place in preparation for her next pregnancy. Exhaustion still clung to her like a sheen of sweat, and would continue to do so for a few hours, though more food and sleep would speed her healing.

A prick of pain in her left breast wormed its way into Annabelle's muddled consciousness. She looked down to see her son sucking hungrily at her nipple. Heedless of his mother's condition, he'd slogged over her bloody front, re-staining his pink flesh with sweat and gore, and ripped through her nightgown with his claws to get what he wanted.

"You are definitely Belial's son," Annabelle said to him. He didn't look up at the sound of her voice, nor did he pay attention to the imps gently wiping him clean.

With a groan, Annabelle turned to the imps not tending to her son; they stood by her bed, waiting for orders. "Get me a sponge bath, at least, and a new gown, and prepare one of the guestroom beds. I'm sure not sleeping here."

It had all been going so well.

But then fate intervened, as it did, intervened to mess everything up. And just when Annabelle thought that, for once, things might go her way.

Two days after she had given birth to a healthy baby boy, and one after she had delivered it to Belial, she was home trying to tend to Harry. He made this difficult by ripping her curtains down and trying to jump out her bedroom window, screaming that he had to escape.

Running across the room, Annabelle grabbed the back of his blue t-shirt and tossed him back inside, hearing a *thunk* as he impacted against the bedpost. Her momentum pushed her into the windowsill, smashing her face up against the glass into a caricature of its normal appearance. With her skin squashed high enough to partially obstruct her vision, Annabelle couldn't clearly see Samantha standing right outside the window, but glimpses of shiny blonde hair and the lingering sparkle of Tiffany diamonds told her who spied on her.

"Shit!" Annabelle yelled, teleporting outside before Samantha could escape. She landed in a clumsy skid of gravel, kicking up clouds of pebbles and dust only to find Samantha making no attempt to run away.

"Why, Annabelle!" she said, smiling so widely it looked as though her face would split in half. "You are home after all." She looked down at Annabelle past her upturned nose, superiority and smug satisfaction in every line of her posture. Over her shoulder, though miles away, lava boiled and humans screamed, the perfect background for the cruel amusement in Samantha's eyes.

"Oh, shit, Sam. Don't do this." A ball of ice formed in Annabelle's gut. She couldn't kill Samantha. The price for murdering one of Hell's few remaining succubi would be steep even for another succubus. Her mind raced, trying to think of some way to keep her friend quiet.

"Don't do what?" Samantha's eyes widened innocently, in the same way they widened every time she told a man, *No, I've never done anything even like that in bed before!*

"Give her souls," said Harry. Annabelle turned to see him crouched in her front doorway, peeking around the half-open door with wide eyes. Brilliant. The guy could barely make it from one room to another, but he'd found a way to walk safely down the stairs and out the door just in time to reveal himself to the wrong demoness. If Sam hadn't seen him upstairs in Annabelle's room, she knew he was there now. "Feed her souls."

Samantha laughed aloud, though her eyes stayed on Harry, who shrank under her scrutiny. "You think I want some puny human soul? Silly boy, what would I do with something that worthless?

"This one might as well be named Nutty McNutcase, 'Belle. I can't see why anyone would keep one of *these* unless they have a fetish for drooling monkeys."

Annabelle barely heard her; her mind was racing. Harry had suggested she bribe Samantha with what he'd assumed was a demon's greatest desire. Though he'd gotten the object wrong, the idea itself wasn't a bad one. What did Samantha want most?

The answer came to Annabelle in a burst of brilliant inspiration, so that she smiled like a woman seeing the sun for the first time.

Harry huddled even smaller in the doorway. Samantha stopped laughing and took one suspicious step back.

"Oh, Sam," Annabelle said, putting one hand on her hip and waving a finger scoldingly. "I never knew you thought so small."

"What?" Samantha said, confused and wary.

"Bringing this little breach of law to the authorities? Why, you'll get thanks from an earl at most; no one important is going to hear about such a small infraction. And here I thought you wanted to make the most of your life. Imagine selling me, your best contact to *real* nobility, down the river for no real advantage. I guess you're not as clever as I thought."

Samantha's eyes narrowed, then began shifting back and forth with indecision. Poor Samantha, with her low birth and her vulgar manners. Being a succubus was enough to buy her luxuries, safety, and the lust of men and demons, but not respect or true weight in the circles of Hell that mattered.

"Of course," Annabelle continued, crossing her arms and turning away as though Samantha was hardly worth her attention (but really to hide her own feelings and keep Samantha off-balance), "if you were to do me the favor of keeping your mouth shut, I might be able to introduce you to some more important people." She turned just slightly and smiled at the look on Samantha's face. It was exactly the look Annabelle had been hoping for.

Annabelle had spent over a century refusing to introduce Samantha to anyone, unwilling to sully her own reputation by treating Samantha as an equal. She'd been almost sure Samantha lied back at the New York Starbucks about kings coming to her with marriage proposals. No king would know her name or even think to propose marriage to a commoner.

Samantha put one shaking hand to her mouth, her gaze unfocused as she saw her dreams approach her on the proverbial silver platter. "This is…this is it, what I've been…now the kings are all so desperate for legitimate heirs…if I go with you, get a real audience with them, then maybe…"

Her gaze snapped back to reality and she rushed forward, grabbing Annabelle's shoulders and shaking her. "Who, Annabelle? Who will you show me to?"

Bingo. "I can show you to all of them, *darling*," said Annabelle, prying crimson nails from her flesh. "But I know one in particular who's desperate for marriage. If you really want to live at the top of the junk heap, Samantha, we'll go see King Bael."

Belial's portal to Earth gave off a spectacular light show. It reminded Annabelle of what she'd read humans saw during near-death experiences. *Walk into the light...*

She imagined Frankenstein's monster stumbling its way toward a light bulb and laughed.

After all she'd been through to get to this place, arriving made her euphoric. Bribing one king, misleading another by dangling her best friend in front of him as bait, giving birth... To escape from politics, she'd buried herself in a political minefield one last time. Now, literally approaching freedom step by step, Annabelle made a promise to herself: never again would she allow herself to be dragged into politics. Never again would she sleep with anyone, or have any baby, that she herself did not choose and want. Her actions would be her own, driven by her own desires. Living on Earth with Harry would be her new beginning and she would make it a beginning to be proud of. If life began to bore her again, Annabelle was determined to have the chance to ease her torment without having to fear her every gesture might bring the rage of powerful and malevolent demons down on her head.

Shuffling beside her, Harry made no sign that he'd heard Annabelle's laughter except for a tiny flinch. He stared at the portal as though transfixed. Annabelle wondered if the flashing spectrum of color had literally hypnotized him and hoped she wouldn't have to knock him out and drag him through to Earth.

It was late autumn, so Annabelle had dressed Harry warmly in a thick wool sweater and jacket. Right now he glistened with sweat from the thick clothes and boiling atmosphere (it might be autumn on Earth, but Belial had opened the portal in the driest, hottest stretch of desert Hell offered), but he'd appreciate them when he arrived on Earth. The colors suited both the season and Harry's chestnut hair; she'd spent hours picking out the perfect shades of brown. It was a particularly important decision because they were going to Earth with literally nothing but the clothes on their backs aside from a few papers in Annabelle's pockets. Annabelle wanted to keep nothing from her life in Hell, no reminders of any kind.

Annabelle's own clothes were simple darks, clean and pressed, and she'd made sure to clean up before leaving home. She'd had to scrub her nails particularly hard to get all the imp blood out from underneath them. A shame to kill such loyal slaves, but she couldn't risk them talking.

And arriving on Earth only to see servant blood on her hands first thing might ruin her good luck. So, one last scrub in the bathtub. It hardly mattered that no one remained to clean it now.

Harry still didn't like Annabelle touching him, but by choosing his clothes, she felt she'd left a mark on him nonetheless. When they were on Earth, he could recover the parts of his mind that had scattered. She enjoyed talking to him when he was together enough to be aware of her.

"You watch, Harry," she said, grinning fondly at him. "We'll go up there and you can go outside whenever you feel like it. We'll do whatever we want, and I won't do whatever I *don't* want. Heck, I might never get pregnant again. After the ten-thousand-thirty-sixth child, I lost interest."

Harry looked at her long enough to say "Ow" before returning his gaze to the portal.

Annabelle laughed. "You said it, Harry. Try passing a watermelon and you'll get the idea." She shivered and rubbed her arms. Despite the heat and her jacket, she was starting to feel cold, a surprise since they were still a quarter-mile from the portal and the autumn air on its other side. It wasn't just her, either. Beside her, Harry shivered so hard the sweat shook right off his collar. Annabelle's very bones felt like they froze under her skin, like frost formed upon them, spreading slowly out to her organs and tissues.

Beside her, Harry began to whimper. His eyes never left the portal, even as he collapsed to his knees and shrunk into himself, trying to pull into a non-existent shell.

And suddenly, everything around the portal grew dark. Impossible! This area was completely deserted. Rocks and dirt stretched for miles in every direction. Even though Belial had shown Annabelle where to go on a map, it took hours of walking and teleporting to find it, and they hadn't spotted a single demon or human soul in all that time. The sky, while overcast and blood-red, was nevertheless plenty bright enough to see by. Nightfall wouldn't come for hours.

Yet Annabelle turned to see shadows spreading toward her over ground and sky. They crept over the ground like a pitch-black tidal wave closing in on her and Harry, two tiny and insignificant grains of sand bobbing through an ocean of it.

Annabelle felt the darkness like a physical presence and knew what stalked her.

"*Choronzon,*" she whispered, though she couldn't hear herself. The word fell into the great shadow of Choronzon, the demon of darkness that haunted every shadow in Hell. He heard every conversation, saw every atrocious act, and allied himself with no one. He was the boogeyman demonesses told their children about at bedtime, for no one knew when and where he would strike, who he would help or act against. To ask for his help was dangerous, as he was as likely to suck the demon asking for his aid into his abyss as agree to assist him. Even Hell's kings feared him.

Annabelle knew who had been desperate and jealous enough to request Choronzon's assistance this time. *Avaira, you bitch!*

Harry wailed, and that sound too tumbled into Choronzon's pitch belly, leaving only Harry's despair and loss behind. Annabelle knew that touching Choronzon meant falling into him, and falling into him meant being lost in the dark forever, self and identity drifting away in his vast emptiness.

Choronzon advanced, spreading like water saturating paper so that he blocked out the sky and slid over the ground.

Annabelle felt herself speak as if through frostbitten lips and never knew what she'd said; the words fell into nothingness even as they left her vocal cords. She was lost in the cold, limbs losing sensation, feelings and thoughts being sucked away...

Then Harry touched her arm. She barely felt the contact and couldn't see a thing through the dimming air. But his fingers closed around her, tugging on her jacket and pulling her backwards, away from the gaping maw of Hell's boogeyman when he was barely inches away.

Blinking, Annabelle turned and saw Harry, the shape of him and those blue eyes she'd become so fond of staring up at her and begging for her help.

She couldn't fall apart. She didn't have the luxury of falling apart. She hadn't earned the right to relax yet.

She grabbed for Harry, but her frozen fingers couldn't grip anything. It angered her that she couldn't see signs of cold upon her body, no frost nor reddened flesh. She felt weak, being so helpless when she looked so normal.

Annabelle desperately stuck her whole arm down the back of Harry's jacket so she could drag him with her. Then she ran, ran harder than she ever had in six millennia of existence, too frightened to feel how frightened she really was.

The great abyss loomed behind her. Harry stumbled along, forced into an awkward sideways crouch by Annabelle's arm, his own arms wheeling and flapping with each clumsy step.

The toe of Annabelle's boot hit a rock and she fell, sending Harry sprawling to the ground so that her arm bent at a painful angle. Choronzon gained on her, creeping up until tendrils of shadow reached her legs. Annabelle locked her free elbow with Harry's, pulled up with the arm still in the back of his jacket, and leapt up, yanking him along behind her. The portal crackled before her, close, closer—

Annabelle hit the portal head-on. For a moment she was frozen in place, color and energy dancing around her. Then she fell through to Earth.

The feeling was nothing like teleporting or moving through solid soil. If anything, Annabelle felt like she sat in an electric chair, like bolts of lightning slid over her skin.

Oh please, she prayed, though she didn't know exactly who she prayed to, *please don't let Harry die. This hurts so much, and I don't know if he can stand it...*

With a booming crack, the portal spit Annabelle out. Harry followed with his jacket still half-tangled round her arm. Another crack and the portal closed behind them, leaving Choronzon behind.

Annabelle landed hard on her shoulder, the impact jarring her arm loose from Harry's jacket. She heard him hit the ground microseconds later with a small sound of pain and a squish that told her he'd probably landed on mud and grass.

Rain fell in a quiet, steady cadence. Annabelle felt the soft impact of each drop as it splashed on her face. She turned her head upwards towards the sky, the beautiful sky and all the possibilities it represented. She had seen it a million, a *hundred* million, times before but now it seemed new. Now that Annabelle knew she wasn't returning to Hell, now that she had someone with her to look after and a new challenge to live for, Earth's sky was beauty itself.

Harry cried out from beside her. Annabelle sat up, bruised shoulder already healing, to see Harry staring at the sky just like her. He rested on his knees and stretched up, arms thrown wide, head as far back as his neck would allow. His mouth hung wide open, letting him taste the rain and scream freedom at the same time, resulting in a ridiculous gurgling noise that made Annabelle laugh hard and long. It was a moment of joy, pure and untainted, and she would remember it for the rest of her endless life.

Harry turned to her, closing his mouth but unable to suppress his smile. Then he opened his arms, and the next thing Annabelle knew he'd wrapped her in a hug.

She hugged Harry, dear Harry, back. She laughed again, laughed and yelled at that wide-open sky, challenging it to show her all it had to offer.

Chapter

5

Two months later, Annabelle scraped spitballs from the edge of a window as tall as she and reflected that this wasn't quite what she'd expected "freedom" to look like.

When she'd arrived for work at the usual time that day, her boss Douglas had greeted her with, "I think it's best we take you out from behind the register" before she'd even pulled her jacket off.

Annabelle sighed. Friggin' preposterous to be penalized for telling the truth. She knew why the register was suddenly too good for her. Yesterday, Clarice, the bimbo who ran the drive-thru window, came running through the kitchen looking like she'd just seen someone set her car on fire.

"Oh, what do I *do*?" she squealed, ignoring the long line of customers Annabelle was trying to help. "Someone *threatened* me!"

Wuss. They worked in a fast-food restaurant. Did Clarice expect classy people in top hats and tailcoats? All the staff got cussed out by loopy people yelling things like, "You young people would never make it in the army today!" on an hourly basis. Clarice had worked here for months longer than Annabelle, yet still made a big production out of every little bomb scare.

Annabelle made a polite "just a minute" gesture to her customers. "What now, Clarice?"

Flittering around like a moth in a glass jar, Clarice wrung her lily-white hands and sniffled a little before getting out, "Some boys at the window...they drove up and...and...and *rapped their order!*"

Annabelle blinked. Half a dozen cooks flipped burger and fish patties behind them, sending steam and the smell of burning meat to fill her senses. A huge mess of cola and ice cubes lay drying on the floor; two people had almost tripped in the last ten minutes. At the register, the line grew to at least a dozen people, and a quick glance at the drive-thru window showed five cars or more waiting in that line, too. Clarice couldn't be bothering her now with all that going on, couldn't be saying what Annabelle thought she'd just said.

(How odd that she felt so incredulous when, just like every other human experience, Annabelle had dealt with stupid, histrionic people before, both in and out of work settings. But somehow, perhaps because now Annabelle had to keep her job to support herself and Harry, living with the Clarices of the world frustrated her more than it ever had. There was no walking away from a job and back to her life of luxury in Hell should she grow too annoyed.)

"They…you mean they spoke their order in rhyme?"

"No, not in a rhyme," said Clarice, shaking her head solemnly, eyes wide. "In a *rap*. Like *rap lyrics*."

Annabelle found herself at a loss for words.

"C'mon!" yelled a purple-faced customer from the register. "You gonna take my order or what?"

Making another "one minute" gesture without looking away from Clarice, Annabelle said, "And in this rap they, what, threatened to rape you? Said they'd bust a cap in your white ass?"

Clarice jerked back, looking offended. "I don't think there's any need for that sort of language…"

"So that's a 'no,' then."

Clarice crossed her arms and tossed her head back. "Don't be *rude*. They just gave me their order but did it by *rapping*. It was *threatening*. It *threatened* me."

"An amazing feat," Annabelle said, turning back to the register, "since it doesn't sound like anything other than your extraordinarily limited intelligence was threatened in any way."

It took Clarice a minute to realize she'd been insulted. For a few seconds she stood with her arms crossed, scowling, angry that Annabelle didn't take her seriously. Then a light bulb went off and she squeaked with indignation. Clarice pushed right up to her, hands on her hips, and cried, "You're so *mean*! It's women like *you* who don't take assault *seriously* that hold *all* women back!"

"Look, I'll donate my life's savings to N.O.W. if I can just get my burger, please," the front customer snapped. Clarice took a moment to sniffle loudly as though holding back tears before making her dramatic exit past the stoves.

Today dawned bright and early, and Annabelle got to watch the sun rise over the shoulder of her boss, who had a face that looked like the genetic cross-mixing of a bulldog and a toad and held up a squeegee for her to admire.

"Now," said Douglas. "You and Mr. Squeegee here will be good friends. What is Mr. Squeegee good for?"

Annabelle calmed herself enough to speak by imagining half-a-dozen ways to kill him with the thing. "Washing windows," she said sullenly.

"Very good!" said Douglas as though complimenting a child who had successfully colored a picture within the lines. "However, your tone worries me. We want a happy, smiling Annabelle to introduce to Mr. Squeegee. The windows won't sparkle until you approach your work with a freshly-squeegeed heart."

Annabelle decided she didn't want some new experiences as badly as she'd thought.

Other new experiences were fantastic. She loved letting the air out of Clarice's tires later that evening, for example. Cackling while teleporting into a tree so she could see Clarice's face when the other woman left work, Annabelle added a checkmark to her mental list of Fun Things About Blue-Collar Living on Earth.

About a week later, Annabelle added another checkmark. She'd purchased illegal identification papers for herself and Harry before leaving Hell and now had proof of a steady income with her first paycheck. It was time to stop breaking into the houses of vacationing people and buy her own.

"You're not supposed to be this excited," said Harry, cocooned in blankets on his latest bed, a floral nightmare inside a small Des Moines apartment. Annabelle smiled, pleased by his lucidity.

Judging Harry a relatively modern man by his haircut, Annabelle assumed watching an action movie would make for a nice evening and turned on *Rambo*. But every gunshot made Harry jump, every injury to any character made him cringe. Ten minutes into the first shootout he was gasping like a fish on land and so confused he walked right into a table when he started pacing to calm himself.

(Actually, Annabelle hadn't seen him hit the table, but he walked by it and it shook, so she supposed he must have.)

Worried, Annabelle wrapped Harry securely in blankets, imitating the way he'd felt most comfortable in her old home, and flipped to the Disney Channel. To her relief he calmed quickly. Though he spoke in a quiet, timid way after that, as though using a normal voice would call horrible punishment down on him, he whispered coherently and without fear of her.

Unfortunately, the apartment's owner returned just when Harry seemed recovered, forcing Annabelle to knock him unconscious and stick him, bound hand and foot, into his hall closet ("He's fine," Annabelle reassured Harry as she dragged the man over hardwood floors by his hair. "Just keep watching and tell me when Fairy Godmother shows up. I love that woman.") Annabelle planned to let him go when she and Harry left in a minute, as he hadn't seen either of their faces. She congratulated herself on her kindness before answering.

"Humans aren't excited to get their first homes?" Annabelle asked. A rhetorical question; she knew the answer from many, many experiences with humans on the cusp of adulthood.

"It's not your first home."

"Of course it is." Annabelle turned from a dressing table mirror she'd been using to put her hair into a ponytail and smiled at Harry, hoping to communicate her giddy feelings. "This isn't a house I'm getting because I'm a noblewoman or for sleeping with somebody rich. This is money I'm making on my own. I'm buying a house for myself with money I've made scrubbing floors and smiling when people insult me. I've never done that in my life."

"Thought you said you'd done labor-type jobs before," said Harry, not petulant, just curious.

"Sure, but it was like a game. I never needed money. Now if I don't pay rent I'll be evicted," said Annabelle as though this was the best thing ever to happen to anyone. "It feels totally different!" Unable to contain herself, she squealed and clapped her hands. Harry tried not to show how crazy he thought she was, which amused her further.

"Are you sure you need my help?" he asked a moment later as Annabelle dragged him out the door and into an overcast day (leaving the unconscious apartment owner unbound and in bed). Everything looked dreary, like the heavy, gray clouds in the sky had seeped into buildings and sidewalks until Des Moines became one long, uniform stretch of depressing colorlessness.

This did nothing to dampen Annabelle's enthusiasm. She marched down the sidewalk with her head high and purpose in every step, not noticing the way Harry shrank into himself and whipped his head around, starting at every sound and rustling blade of grass. "I've never bought a house before. I know I'm supposed to talk to a realtor, but that's as far as I go. I need your experience."

"Can't you just pick the information from someone's head?"

Annabelle laughed as she slid through the door of someone's blue Sedan parked on the nearest corner. She unlocked the passenger door for Harry and hotwired the dash as he sat down. "Human minds aren't like books, where I can turn a page to look up the information I need. I see whatever they're feeling right on the surface, that's all."

Before Harry could shut his door, Annabelle peeled off in a cloud of smoke raised by burning rubber. She whooped, careening towards the realty office she'd set her appointment with, not looking to see Harry go pale and grip onto his safety handle, his eyes wide and terrified as the Sedan barreled down the street.

Though only twenty minutes from their appropriated apartment, arriving at the realty office was like crossing into another world. The gray sky cleared to bright blue and the dull, cookie-cutter buildings made way for more varied architecture, decorated by trees dressed in fall colors. Harry gaped at the sight, pressing his nose up against the window glass to get the best possible glimpse at everything.

"Beautiful," he whispered. Annabelle felt happy. Seeing autumn through his eyes, it stopped being dull and became pretty to her again.

The sight of the realtors office excited her more, so she cut across two lanes and almost ran over an old lady to grab a parking spot. REDLAND REALTORS blazed from the huge sign above the door, which was strange, because Annabelle thought they'd been called Realty 21. She thought she'd found the right place, though; she couldn't see an address written on it or the buildings beside it, but the last address she'd seen on the previous block had been only twenty numbers away.

Leaving Harry staring at passing traffic like a man tripping on LSD, Annabelle almost danced into the office, ready to bounce off the white-plaster walls with the thrill. Inside, a heavyset man in a nice suit sat behind a desk cluttered with papers and files. Pictures of large, expensive-looking houses and certificates of awards and laureates hung neatly on the walls.

Looking at those, Annabelle decided she wouldn't give this realtor a chance to sweet-talk her into anything she couldn't afford. Squaring her shoulders and hiding her excitement, Annabelle marched forward before the man could do more than look up and smile. She pulled the computer printout of her chosen house from her pocket and slapped it down on his desk, scattering several loose papers.

"I'm your 10 o'clock appointment, and I don't need anything but a look at this," she said, pointing to the small, one-story house on the printout. "No fancy extras, nothing more expensive, just this one. Got it?"

"Um, yes," said the man, leaning over and peering at the picture. "Except, I believe this house is for sale through Realty 21 across the street."

Turning to follow where he pointed, Annabelle saw another building with REALTY 21 on the sign above the door and the correct address printed below it.

Damn.

"Well hell," Annabelle blustered, snatching the printout back, "why am I wasting time with you, then?" Turning on her heel, she walked out the door as quickly as possible without actually running. Passing by the sedan, she did not notice that Harry now huddled in his seat, wincing at the loud noises cars made as they passed him.

Realty 21's office was much smaller and dirtier than Redland's, with far fewer credentials and nice houses pasted on its brown walls. The man behind the plastic table wore jeans and sported something between two-o'clock shadow and a bristle board on his chin. The sexual imagery that flew into his mind when he got a look at Annabelle—who had comically huge breasts, sex-doll lips, and 80s-style big hair for him—involved rape and humiliation. Though Annabelle had thought she'd let him speak to avoid embarrassing herself this time, she changed her mind and just slapped her printout down before him as she had across the street when she saw those.

An hour later, she and Harry stood on the sidewalk of Renaissance Drive in front of the real house. Smaller than many apartments with one bedroom, one bathroom, and a kitchen/dining area a person could enter directly from the front door, nobody would mistake the house for middleclass, even if the locks and taps hadn't been rusting or garbage hadn't lined the street.

Annabelle loved it. She loved the dandelions, turned now to mostly-scattered puffballs growing freely in the unkempt yard. She loved the numerous trees lining Renaissance Drive and the explosions of color they added when she pushed aside the kitchen's yellowing lace curtains. She loved the tiny backyard with its old-fashioned chain-link fence, which she'd rarely seen in real life, and had never owned. She loved the peeling purple wallpaper and ugly furniture that released clouds of dust when she leapt onto some of it, giggling like a little girl.

The sound of a horrible squeal alerted Annabelle to the back door opening. Ducking out of the bedroom she saw Harry step out into the miniscule backyard, his head tilted up towards the sun. His thoughts were chaotic, with one idea running into the next, but Annabelle felt enormous gratitude and joy. Almost like the night they'd arrived on Earth.

Following him, she winced when the sun hit her eyes. She waited a few seconds for Harry to speak but didn't have the patience to wait for long.

"So, you like it?" She knew the answer but wanted to hear him say it out loud.

Face turned towards the sun, eyes shut, lips curled into a smile, Harry looked like a man communicating with the divine. "Oh yes," he whispered. "There's no more perfect angle anywhere on Earth."

To see the sun from, Annabelle assumed. She shrugged. If staring at the sky all day kept him happy, great. She went back inside to fill out paperwork, already thinking of where she'd drop off the stolen sedan. She enjoyed driving. Maybe she'd drive the sedan until it ran out of gas, leave it wherever it sputtered to a stop, then just teleport back to her new home.

Home. Annabelle shivered with joy.

Chapter

6

A month later, Annabelle sat on a padded chair inside a sparsely decorated little house, not her own, that protected her from the Des Moines winter outside. The lights were off; she waited in the dark.

She couldn't see the young man walking down the wide, suburban streets outside, but heard his thoughts and knew he headed towards her. His American name was Jimmy, and he was a dead ringer for the actor Aidan Turner, or would have been were he not so skinny and haggard looking. (Turner was Irish and Jimmy was Afghan, but humans mostly looked the same to Annabelle.) He walked hunched over, face half-concealed by the high collar of his blue coat, strands of coarse black hair he'd been too busy to cut bouncing free against the nylon collar with each step. The furrows round his eyes ran so deep that it was easy to imagine the frown he had to be making. Everyone he passed gave him a wide berth.

Fortunately, Jimmy did not encounter many people, for it was nearly midnight and most of the people in the small Iowa suburb he called home were asleep. He liked it that way. If someone made him lose his temper and he wound up yelling, he knew he'd feel guilty later on. Given how terrible his mood was already, that would be an extra burden he didn't need.

Stupid Father. What right did the old man have to tell Jimmy what to do? Heck, Jimmy was going to be twenty-nine in a month, old age as far as most children were concerned. But did his father accept that? Of course not.

Nothing Jimmy did was good enough, not for the great Holy Man of Albuquerque. No, Jimmy was pursuing a wasteful, sinful profession in psychology. What was psychology, the old man had sniffed, but an excuse for lazy people? Telling husbands too weak to provide for their families that it wasn't their fault, they were just "depressed," telling wives and children who didn't properly take care of each other that they shouldn't have to do anything that encroached on their "independence." Selfishness!

Furious at the memory, Jimmy kicked a rock that did not make way for his anger, leaving him hopping down the sidewalk on one green Converse sneaker, rubbing the other now-throbbing foot with his fingers and cursing with language his father would probably have shot him just for knowing. The thought of offending his father that way pleased Jimmy, so he began to curse under his breath in every language he knew (English, Farsi, Dari, Spanish...) He wished he could shake one fist in the air without looking like a moron but worried too much about his appearance to dare. He could almost see horrified people staring out at him from their windows, clutching their children close and planning to call their neighbors with warnings about "that crazy shrink." Embarrassed, Jimmy put his foot down and started walking normally (and silently) again.

To his left, an offended-looking stray cat that looked somewhat like his father turned and stalked away, tail high in the air. Jimmy scowled after it.

If it was just the psychology that Jimmy's father had a problem with that would be one thing. After all, Jimmy had been trained to understand that everyone had their prejudices. But no. At this point, Jimmy knew full well that what his father had a problem with was anything Jimmy did. The soccer team in elementary school? Too aggressive, teaching physical violence when Jimmy should be learning passion for God. Writing classes in middle school? Wasteful, for Jimmy was writing stories about UFOs and superheroes when he should have been writing about God. Dreams of becoming an astronaut in high school? Arrogant, for if God had planned for man to travel to the stars, He would have given man wings.

When Jimmy had pointed out that wings alone wouldn't take any creature into space, his father had given him a look of such contempt that Jimmy had felt his testicles shrivel up and crawl into his body. Good-bye, dignity.

Sometimes Jimmy wondered if he hadn't chosen psychology out of desperation, hoping to study just what his father was thinking. So much for that. After twenty-eight years knowing him, Jimmy was coming to think that the old man was just a jerk, and that was all there was to it. Nothing would make him happy, except maybe Jimmy crawling into a cave and devoting his every breath to prayer. No, even then he would probably find something wrong. Jimmy would be selfish for not saving the world single-handedly or not keeping his cave tidy enough or something.

A chill wind blew past Jimmy's skinny body and he shivered, trying to pull his coat tighter. His father had probably called the stupid winter weather down on him too, to punish Jimmy for not following his every command. Jerk.

Turning on Runner Street Jimmy saw his house, small and one story with a blue door. He jogged gratefully toward it, eager to get out of the cold and dark. Being outside so late at night, even in his very safe Des Moines suburb where nothing ever happened, made him nervous.

His numb hands fumbled with his keys before finally getting a sufficiently firm grip. The silver metal glinted under his porch light. Jimmy grew tenser and tenser with each second that passed, as a feeling of being watched crept up his neck.

It's just paranoia, a voice that sounded very much like his father's whispered into the back of Jimmy's head. *Who'd follow you, you nobody?*

The key jammed home into the lock with a click. Jimmy pushed his way inside; before he could close the door, the wind blew it shut.

His father probably never had doors pulled out of his control. No, the old relic would have held on until the door slammed shut on his fingers or the wind blew him away. Chuckling at the thought of his father being blown through the air like a hirsute balloon with a blue door in his hands ("You can never make me let go!" he'd shriek at rescue workers trying to pry it from his grip), Jimmy found the light switch and flicked it on.

He saw Annabelle waiting for him, sitting in his armchair and sipping from a can of soda from his refrigerator.

"*Aaaah!*" screamed Jimmy.

"Hello, Dr. Hamid," said Annabelle. "Do you always work such late hours? Because you're not going to be able to do that for a while."

"Holy crap! Who are you? What are you doing in my house?" Jimmy looked wildly around, eyes wide as white frying pans as he twisted to one side and then the next, trying to see if anyone else invaded his sanctuary. Annabelle rolled her eyes. He wouldn't have been able to see anyone even if they were standing right next to him, whipping around that quickly.

"I'm a client," she said, then added, "I wouldn't do that if I were you," as Jimmy reached into his pocket for his plastic green cell phone.

"Why not?" Jimmy snapped, his voice several octaves higher than his dignity preferred. "What're you gonna do, kill me?"

"No," said Annabelle, "I need your help. I'll kill anyone who interrupts us, though. I'm trying to keep a low profile."

Jimmy froze, as Annabelle knew he would. Slowly raising his head, Jimmy tried to calm himself, to process his emotions. Annabelle empathized, as she had been going through the same thing for so many years now. It was a terrible thing not to know your own heart. Were you scared or angry? If scared, who were you scared for, yourself or potential victims affected by what you did? If angry, were you angry at yourself for being weak or at those who were showing you your weakness? The confusion made her want to go to sleep and never wake up sometimes, just to end the conflict.

Apparently deciding he at least needed to say something, Jimmy managed, "Um. So, you need my help?"

"Yes. You are a psychologist who has experience with hypnosis and trauma victims. Your reputation is impeccable, your personal leanings towards compassion over money. Which is good, because I need a therapist right now but I'm not sure how regularly I can pay you. I'm trying to keep a low profile, see, and murdering too many people for their money would probably be ostentatious."

"What?" Jimmy blurted, immediately followed by, "don't answer that."

Annabelle accedingly nodded and gave Jimmy a moment to pace back and forth through the living room. It was a lovely space with hardwood floors and several windows placed high up, giving the room both ample light and privacy. A shame Jimmy put so little in it; a few paintings would have made the place as cozy as a Martha Stuart project.

"You're..." Jimmy spoke suddenly, jerking to a halt and looking thoroughly befuddled. "You broke into my home at midnight on a Wednesday to ask me to give someone pro-bono therapy sessions?"

Annabelle considered pointing out that she wasn't "asking" for anything but decided to let that go. Humans tended to react more positively when they believed they had a choice in things. "That is what I said. Are you very slow, or did I miss something?"

"I think you're missing a lot of things," said Jimmy. "Why didn't you just call my office?"

"Did I or did I not say that I'm trying to keep a low profile twice now? Really, I don't know how you're of any use to all the trauma victims you see if you can't even keep up with stuff people state directly."

"You can keep your low profile. My office records are confidential." Annabelle saw that, in Jimmy's mind, their conversation had taken on the surreal characteristics of a dream. A part of him screamed at him to run or call the police, but the situation struck him as so strange he had trouble deciding on any course of action.

"That's not what I mean by 'low profile.' I mean that there will be no records. No paperwork, no tapes, no videos, no psychology journals. There will be you and Harry—that's the patient—talking together a few nights a week, for which I'll pay you what I can, when I can. And you will never mention him or me to anyone. Not your family or friends, not your professional colleagues, not even your sister, however well she keeps secrets."

Jimmy's head jerked up. "Have you been studying me?"

"Of course. I'm not leaving Harry's care in the hands of just any moron with a degree. You are not only the best and most compassionate doctor I could find locally with experience in trauma patients, you're the best doctor in all of Iowa, with one of the purest souls I've encountered anywhere on Earth."

"Don't flatter me," Jimmy snapped. "It's cheap."

"I'm not flattering you. I'm insulting you. Where I come from, a pure soul is a burden and an irritant. A person with a heart and personality like yours is a sucker, someone who can be taken advantage of because you can't not 'do good' when you have the opportunity. Look, if you weren't that sort of guy, you wouldn't have gotten sick of the bullshit politics of religion and come here."

Annabelle felt Jimmy grow confused at the same rate he grew offended. Her words had insulted him, but as he'd often had negative thoughts of his own about religion, he wasn't sure why. "What do you know about it? People serve God out of righteousness and love."

"They say they do," said Annabelle, "and some of them even mean it in the beginning. But once they gain any actual power, they start to serve God out of a desire to retain power. You know this. It disgusted you when you saw it."

Jimmy snorted, the rudest thing he could think to do aside from outright spitting at Annabelle's feet. "Look, I don't know what fantasy world you come from, but I make quite a good living working for money."

"Harry," said Annabelle, who decided to let Jimmy avoid the subject of his own beliefs, because she knew Jimmy knew she'd spoken the truth and didn't want to admit it, "has been erased from reality. If you look him up in any database, he will be listed as deceased. He was taken and tortured for years, and now has very little mind left to him. I call him Harry, but that's not his name. He can't remember his name or even how to talk some of the time. I keep him safe now, but his behavior is still erratic. He can't even leave our house, let alone work or socialize. He's haunted by hallucinations and flashbacks, and at times, doesn't recognize me at all.

"If it'll help you treat him, I can tell you specifics about the torture. For now, I'll just say that the nicest of it was water boarding and electrocution. Every day. For years."

Jimmy had stopped moving and stood solemn before her. He didn't look surprised, but a sadness fell over him.

"Wow," he said, turning away and rubbing the back of his neck. "It sounds like what you need is an institution."

"Institutions are made up of many people, and while some might be kind and experienced, others will be stupid and mean. I wouldn't put Harry near assholes like that even if I could keep myself secret from all of them."

Annabelle knew Jimmy had to admit she had a fair point. He had interned at a few different institutions while in graduate school. It had taken only weeks for him to grow so fed up with the bureaucracy and dysfunction that he'd sworn never to go near one again.

"Who're you, then?" he asked, dodging that line of discussion and rounding on Annabelle. She thought it was adorable, the way he crossed his skinny arms and tried to look tough. "Harry's loving sister?"

Actually, the fake legal documents Annabelle had procured for herself and Harry listed them as husband as wife, but she supposed "sister" worked as well as any title as far as Jimmy was concerned. It wasn't like her private life was any of Jimmy's business (though she had spent weeks making his business her own).

"Sure," she said. Jimmy waited for several seconds, expecting her to give him more information, then scowled when she said nothing else.

"I can't help if I don't know what happened," he grumbled.

"Since I had nothing to do with what happened, I don't see how it matters," Annabelle said, sitting back in the armchair and stretching as though she couldn't be bothered to take Jimmy's concerns seriously. "My name is Annabelle, I found Harry, saved him from that awful place, and brought him here. He and I have known each other for less than a year. Nothing I do is helping him recover, so I started researching psychologists."

Jimmy frowned. "You 'found' him? And…you're so determined to help him?"

"So are you, just after hearing his story." Annabelle didn't have to pry into Jimmy's mind to know that.

"But I'm a wildly compassionate loser with a jones to save the world, apparently," he said. "You break into people's houses and talk casually about murder."

Annabelle grinned, enjoying the way Jimmy jerked back with disgust and fear. "Maybe I'm one of those action heroes who kills lots of people and then saves kittens and little girls at the end of the movie."

"That would only work if we were in a movie," said Jimmy. Annabelle could sense his dislike for her. It bordered on outright revulsion. Though she was physically the perfect woman for him (a voluptuous, classy sort of lady with shoulder-length hair) as she was for all men, Jimmy could see, could sense, perhaps, Annabelle's true nature. It had been centuries since anyone had been able to recognize her so clearly at first sight.

Again, Jimmy rubbed the back of his head. It was a gesture Annabelle had become familiar with over the past weeks of surveillance, a sign of agitation.

"Well," he finally said, "I'll have to meet the guy before I decide anything."

Annabelle sighed. Foolish boy, he'd already made his choice. It wasn't like he had anything else to do after work besides watch TV and brood over his family. Was it pride that refused to let him give in too readily? "I'll bring Harry by tomorrow evening around this time."

"Oh, jeez. Let's try eight so I can be asleep like a normal human being by midnight. But listen," Jimmy added when Annabelle nodded, "if I decide it's in his best interest to be turned in to the authorities, I will call them."

"That would be stupid of you. They'd have to die, and it would be your fault." Annabelle stood, hiding her amusement at the way Jimmy tensed.

"I hope you don't think you can intimidate me into helping," Jimmy snapped, thoroughly intimidated as he stepped back to give Annabelle a wide berth to walk towards the door. "If you kill people that easily, then you'll probably kill me, too, so I don't have any reason to help you."

Annabelle turned the doorknob and threw a last, affronted look at Jimmy.

"Kill you? What a rude thing to say. You're doing me a big favor, after all. What kind of lady do you think I am?"

Sniffing and tossing her hair huffily over one shoulder, Annabelle stepped outside and shut the door behind her.

Chapter

7

A heartbeat and teleportation-aided step outside Jimmy's door, Annabelle appeared in a Baltimore neighborhood so filthy, few but the homeless lived there. Streetlights along the entire block had either been knocked out by vandals or left unattended until they no longer worked, leaving the street lit only by the moon (barely a sliver) and stars (mostly hidden by clouds and smog). The smell of rotten eggs and nastier things wafted through the air on a light, cold breeze.

Annabelle was not happy. She'd planned her trip to Earth around the idea of doing things for herself, yet had quickly learned she couldn't take care of her own human. With Jimmy out of sight, Annabelle let her smirking façade drop and scowled honestly into the dark. Why wasn't she enough for Harry? Her hard work, her attention; she couldn't understand why they weren't enough. Why did he have to need more?

But he did need more, and Annabelle couldn't deny it any longer. She couldn't stand any more nights listening to him whimper from under their bed or days watching him staring dully at a blank wall as if he just wanted to disappear.

Well, if her trip to find a psychiatrist had been unpleasant—minus watching Jimmy squirm, which had been very pleasant indeed—this next errand would boost her spirits. Annabelle planned to take advantage of everything life on Earth had to offer her, including its unique methods of protection against humans and demons that might come looking for her.

They'd done well for themselves in learning to destroy despite their flimsy bodies humans had. Annabelle knew about human weapons as she knew about most of human life, having studied them when bored. However, wielding human armaments in her own defense had to be different from watching humans kill each other from a distance...and Annabelle wanted to find out how.

Annabelle had to walk about half a block to find the spot Topher had specified to her, a building so derelict even the homeless hesitated to squat in it with a rusty, overgrown playground next door. Once, children had played there. Now only metal skeletons and a single swing, hanging in rubber strips as though someone had sliced it up with a switchblade, remained.

Annabelle had rediscovered her kinship with the night the moment she started living on Earth. She had been born in the dark and still knew how to wrap it around her like a lover's shirt. Its scent soothed her; its sounds were a comfort. Rats squeaking by made her smile fondly and roaches mating next to her beat-up combat boots aroused her in a wonderful, energizing way.

Despite little need for sleep, it took great exertion to acclimate herself to a diurnal schedule. Annabelle worked hard adjusting to her new home, trying to make herself as normal as possible, but she was a creature of the night born and bred. However well she learned to fit in during the day, it would always be an act.

Granted, no one who got off on the way cockroaches mated was ever going to fit in well with humans whatever she did, but Annabelle liked to think the effort counted for something. Snickering, she leaned against the building and waited.

The three men who appeared from beyond the park did not attempt to hide their footsteps as they approached. They, too, were creatures of the night, the biggest, baddest kids on the playground with nothing to fear from kids or teachers. Certainly not from a woman.

Annabelle smiled.

"You Samantha?" the man in front asked. His name was Topher, or at least, he'd given that name on the phone. His voice sounded like tires on gravel from too many joints and cigarettes, and his attitude told Annabelle he expected her to fear him, as most people feared him. A peek into his mind showed her how she confused him. Who was this woman, he wondered, stuffing her beauty in such a raggedy-ass getup? No makeup, no jewelry, hair pulled back in an old-lady bun as if she couldn't be bothered with it. What woman spent the time working to get their body in such perfect shape, made their hair so shiny, kept their skin so smooth, only to dress up in rags and walk around drug corners in Baltimore?

Annabelle was pleased by how well she'd dimmed her natural appeal to men. Skip a few weeks of showers, put a few tangles in her hair, wear baggy, ill-fitting clothing, and voila! No longer did men throw themselves out of car windows to catch a glimpse of her.

"That's me." Annabelle glanced down at the suitcase held by one of the men behind Topher. Poor little nobody. Poor little follower. Annabelle read his thoughts and found his name was Jackie and that he'd always been a follower. As long as he lived, he would always be a follower. Annabelle could well understand that and felt his pain, the pain of having no life or thoughts of one's own. "Those are the goods, I presume?"

"You *presume*," said the third man, and all three laughed. It was a sinister sound, designed to provoke nervousness or worse. Annabelle couldn't help but roll her eyes at them, at pitiful little boys who thought they knew how to be frightening. Thankfully, they couldn't see it in the dark. She didn't want to deal with their tantrums.

"Well then," said Topher, "I *presume* you'll be impressed by these." He grabbed the suitcase from Henchman Number One, a.k.a. Jackie, and flicked it open with a flourish, revealing two compact, semi-automatic pistols.

They impressed Annabelle very much. She liked the way the black one disappeared into the dark, while the silver one found a way to gleam in even the tiniest bit of light.

"They're *beautiful*," she whispered, enjoying the way the men shifted uncomfortably. They hid it well. A lifetime of practice had taught them how to be tough on the outside, whatever their feelings. Annabelle however, recognized the intoxicating smell of fear just like she knew the smell of pure darkness. "Untraceable?"

"A hundred percent," Topher confirmed.

"Good."

Topher flinched when Annabelle reached for the guns, but she moved so much faster than him that she'd taken them from the suitcase before he could pull away.

Annabelle frowned, examining the silver semi-automatic's chamber as Topher and his sidekicks spluttered. "The ammo. Where is it? Give it to me."

"Wh—" Topher and his cronies gaped into the empty suitcase. Topher pulled it up to his nose, shook it, and turned it upside-down as though she'd just hidden his precious guns in a secret compartment. "You...bitch! You don't just take those!" All three men advanced, stomping hard on the ground and flexing their muscles threateningly, only to pause when Annabelle didn't bother to look up.

Thoughts spun confusedly in Topher's head. A strange-looking woman, unafraid of him, faster than him, and trying to order him around. None of it computed in his limited reckoning on How the World Worked.

The fact that Annabelle moved faster than any human could was so far outside that limited reckoning, Topher refused to believe it had happened at all.

"If you don't give me the ammunition," said Annabelle, "I'll have to take it from you." She smiled and licked her lips, liking that idea almost as much as the look of her new weapons. The sympathy she'd felt for Jackie a moment ago was gone, burned away in the fire roaring in her belly.

...No, she would not kill them. Much as the thought of letting these pieces of walking garbage live galled and disappointed her, it was one of the prices she had to pay for living as a human. Human beings didn't simply haul off and bash each other's heads in over simple business transactions. It wasn't done. So as Topher, Jackie, and Henchman Number Two pulled guns and knives on her, she sighed and pretended to back down in fear.

"Oh, all right. Just don't hurt me," said Annabelle, failing miserably at trying to sound scared. She reached into her pocket, pulled out the fee Topher had demanded over the phone, and tossed it to him.

But now Topher was mad. "Samantha" had confused and frightened him, and nobody made Topher Watts feel weak, nobody!

Henchman Number Two, too stupid to feel afraid—his mind was so empty Annabelle couldn't even pick out his name—loved the idea of hurting Annabelle. He loved the thought of scaring her, of causing her pain; it was better than drugs, better than food, better than sex. His hand tightened around the blade in his pocket. And Jackie, poor Jackie the mook, who had probably never taken an independent step in his life...he'd kill her because Topher told him to.

Well heck, if they weren't going to let Annabelle leave, she had no choice but to kill them!

The idea sent a thrill through Annabelle's body. She could no longer deny she'd planned this meeting with murder somewhere in the back of her mind. She'd set the circumstances to be perfect for it. No one was going to connect a young woman living in a suburb of Des Moines to a couple of gang killings in Baltimore. These men would be lucky if anyone, human or otherwise, investigated their deaths at all.

Annabelle had left Hell to find a new way to live. Yet still Hell remained a part of her, imprinted on each of her cells. Annabelle could hear her true home whisper to her, telling her to follow her instincts.

How strange, to have been so sick of everything to do with Hell just months ago, but now that she lived away from it...

She licked her lips.

"Yeah, you just try it, bitch," sneered Henchman Number Two. He pulled a clip from his jacket pocket and dangled it from his fingertips while his friends laughed. "You got more cash, you get the bullets. After that bullshit, you owe us a lot more."

"Cash," said Annabelle. She smiled and walked closer to them, pulling the tie from her hair so that soft black surrounded her face and shoulders, and then looked up at the sky as though contemplating the nature of life, or whatever it was humans did when they looked so thoughtful. "Little green slips of paper passing from hand to hand. You want paper, sweetheart? You just want paper in return for these beautiful pistols?"

More snickering. They thought Annabelle was offering them sex, probably the only thing most women without money could offer them. The thing terrified women usually tried to offer in exchange for their lives. Annabelle twisted a lock of hair around the barrel of the black gun, tying it up to free her hands.

"Bitch, you think we'd risk the diseases?" Topher said, though seeing Annabelle up close made him want her. He just wanted to humiliate her first.

"Diseases?" said Annabelle. She slowly tied the silver gun into her hair, loving the way the weight pulled at her scalp and hit her back. "Oh you little, little boys. You know nothing about the diseases I can give you." She drew out the s-sounds in her speech, lowering her voice into a low hiss.

Annabelle pulled a different side of herself to the surface, a part of her that had existed long before humans had learned to see her as they wanted her to look. She did not shape shift; rather she performed a mirror trick without a mirror, forcing her victims to view her from a different angle. Her limbs lengthened in the boys' eyes, thinning and stretching until she dropped forwards and walked on all fours like a grotesque, giant insect. Her face stretched and her mouth widened into a slash across her face, teeth growing until they ran over her lips. Her eyes grew and lightened into pure-white orbs that shone like the silver pistol now tangled in her hair.

"Come and see," Annabelle purred, her tongue dangling obscenely from her mouth. She skittered forward, slow enough that the trio saw her coming, fast enough that they couldn't do a thing to stop her. The guns bounced against her back with each step.

I am the thing in the night that you fear, the monster that you hide under your covers to escape. But there is no escape from me.

Annabelle always tried to return to her new house on Renaissance Drive, a little under two hours by car from Jimmy's place on Runner Street, before dark due to the neighborhood's less-than-upstanding reputation. Though Annabelle didn't have to worry about muggers herself (she nudged her back teeth to dislodge one last stubborn bit of Topher's bone marrow), she locked Harry tightly away upon leaving for work each morning. She didn't know how tough his non-body was and didn't want to find out by letting him stumble across a mugger and be stabbed.

Just thinking of leaving Harry alone in his room with his eyes bloodshot and his body trembling made Annabelle's heart ache, ruining her earlier high. She couldn't think of what else to do, though, at least until he started seeing Jimmy. Harry had been thrilled to arrive on Earth, but after so many years in Hell, even little noises overwhelmed him. He ran screaming from cars, gaped at people passing by until they thought he was some kind of stalker, whimpered when someone nearby played music too loudly...

The fact was, Harry remained a danger to himself. Annabelle felt crushed under the weight of her own disappointment, but she couldn't think of anything to do for him. She could only be with him for just so long each day, her paycheck being a sad necessity, so she brought home cheap, used paperback books by the armload to keep him occupied and padded his room with anything she could find: thick rugs, air mattresses, pillows. Still, leaving him in there with nothing to do but read for hours at a time couldn't be good for his mental health. And looking after him was making Annabelle, who did not often need to sleep, exhausted enough to find herself nodding off sometimes. Thinking of how angry she'd been leaving Jimmy's, she worried she might lose her temper and hit him. She'd had to bite back harsh words more than once already, and patience got more difficult with each passing day. The few times she had lost her temper, Harry shrank back from her as though fearing for his safety. Annabelle had been left feeling like the biggest bitch on Earth since Empress Cixi built a marble boat while her people starved in the streets.

Much as it galled and humiliated her, Annabelle had to accept that she needed help. She thought of Jimmy again and sighed.

After leaving three gory smears on Baltimore concrete, Annabelle walked down the street and turned a corner before vanishing, appearing seconds later in front of her own house. It was graying around the edges with several roof tiles missing, but it was her house, paid for with money she'd made herself. Annabelle was amazed how proud it had made her to sign the contract, to have earned the *right* to sign the contract without having slept with any of the businessmen involved.

Pulling out a cheap plastic key ring with a dozen keys on it, Annabelle unlocked the half-dozen locks she'd installed on the front door and went in. Flicking on the light, a single bulb swinging from an exposed wire in the ceiling, she took a quick look around with her eyes and mind to make sure everything was where it should be in the front kitchen/dining room.

Everything looked normal, and no one waited inside save Harry, whose thoughts felt peaceful enough. Annabelle moved deeper into the house, past the bathroom to reach her and Harry's room. Concentrating on her key ring, trying to find one of three keys needed to unlock the many bolts she'd attached to the door, Annabelle had almost reached the room before she realized the door hung halfway off its hinges.

"Harry?" Annabelle yanked the remains of the door open. The room was empty. She'd known it would be, but the knowledge didn't make her stomach drop down to her toes any slower. The bedroom window wasn't broken, so how had someone gotten through the door? It was thick oak wood, and the locks were all heavy-duty. "Harry!"

Annabelle ran back into the hall, pushing her way into the bathroom, the hall closet, then out the back door, which swung open and shut on rusty hinges in the winter wind.

Nearly throwing herself into the backyard, heart slamming in her chest and limbs shaky with panic, Annabelle found the object of her search sitting on the tiny, weed-ridden lawn.

Her panic turned immediately to anger. "Harry! What the hell!"

Harry did not answer at once. He stared at the sky, wearing only the raggedy jeans and undershirt he'd had on underneath the sweater and jacket Annabelle had left him with that morning. He didn't seem to notice the cold but focused completely on the sky.

Which, Annabelle realized when she looked up, was quite something. Their view of the stars was so much clearer than it had been when she and Harry first arrived on Earth some three months ago. The stars looked like fireworks suspended in the sky, points of light merrily reminding humans that there was so much more to the universe than their limited brains could grasp, daring them to dream and wonder. Annabelle could not help but smile and felt herself relax.

This time when she said, "Harry?" it was a gentle question. Harry turned his head just slightly, and Annabelle saw tears in his eyes.

"Beautiful," he whispered, turning back to the stars. "Annabelle, they're *beautiful*."

"I know, sweetie," said Annabelle. She sat down beside him and Harry put his head on her shoulder. They wrapped their arms around each other and leaned back against their house, looking up silently.

Still, Annabelle couldn't stop thinking about the door to Harry's room. A demon couldn't have found them, because Harry was still as alive as a dead man ever got. She hadn't seen any sign of forced entry, so a human hadn't gotten in either. Had Harry forced open the door himself?

For the first time, Annabelle realized how little she knew about damned souls. Though she'd heard of the occasional soul finding its way back to Earth, that was only in myths, and she didn't know anything about what happened once they'd arrived. Earth was Harry's home, but the prison that had been his body now rotted under the ground somewhere. Were souls stronger than the bodies they came from? Did they have abilities beyond when they'd been encased in flesh and ruled by firing synapses and raging hormones?

It was just another mystery. No point obsessing about it now. Annabelle sighed and stroked her fingers through Harry's hair, looking up at the stars and trying to take strength from their splendor. She'd put Harry under Jimmy's care for at least a few hours a week and use the time to investigate.

At eight p.m. the next evening, Annabelle materialized in Jimmy's kitchen to the sight of his blue-jean-clad rear. Having apparently just dropped something, he was bending over in front of his kitchen table, leaving his plaid shirt to fall into his armpits.

"Nice," she said. "Bony, but—"

Jimmy jumped high into the air with a girly shriek that sounded something like, "HolyAUGHaaYAHSHIT!" He spun in midair, legs tangling together so that he fell back upon landing again, and caught the table for balance. His free hand thrust outwards, shoving a cross, a Wiccan pentagram, Buddhist beads, a copy of the Koran, and a Star of David into Annabelle's face.

Neither of them moved for a long moment as Jimmy tried to catch his breath and balance, and Annabelle tried to figure out what he was trying to do.

"What," said Annabelle, blinking at the religious symbols, "were you trying to be politically correct?"

Jimmy had the grace to look embarrassed. "No," he said. "Just inclusive." Straightening up, he pushed his newly-freed hand into the pocket of his jeans and whipped out a tiny bottle full of clear liquid that Annabelle assumed was either mace or holy water.

Sighing, Annabelle reached forward and touched each of the religious symbols in turn, proving that they didn't hurt her. Jimmy looked first crestfallen, then annoyed.

"Faulty methods aside," said Annabelle, "how did you figure out what I am?"

Backing up until he was pinned against his kitchen table, Jimmy kept a wary eye on Annabelle as though expecting her to attack at any moment.

"First of all, you broke into my home without ever opening any of the doors or windows," he said. "And..." he hesitated, squinting in concentration. "You feel wrong."

Annabelle remembered how queasy and cautious Jimmy had acted the evening before. Was he psychic, or was this something all people with souls as unusually warm as his could do? She had always made such a point of avoiding pure-hearted people like him (not difficult, as very few existed) that she couldn't tell.

"Look," Jimmy said, "I don't know what you are, exactly. But I'm pretty sure you're nothing I can trust."

"Maybe not," Annabelle said, cutting him off before he could try to throw her out. "But Harry is a different story. You'll see."

Hurrying out the kitchen and through the living room, Annabelle spotted the front door and nearly launched herself onto it. By the time Jimmy recovered himself and left the kitchen, she'd pulled Harry inside and shoved him in front of her, right into Jimmy's line of sight.

Though Annabelle couldn't see Harry's expression, standing behind him as she was, it stopped Jimmy in his tracks. He stared at Harry as though hypnotized.

Slowly, completely ignoring Annabelle, Jimmy stepped forward, his face moving from angry to solemn, contemplative. The look reminded Annabelle of Harry gazing up at the stars; her hope that she'd found the right doctor grew stronger.

"Hello," Jimmy said.

Harry looked at the floor and tried to hide behind his brown bangs and baggy clothes. Jimmy waited patiently, his body language open and friendly. Annabelle could sense fear pouring off Harry in waves, and despite Jimmy's thoughtful look, she felt almost as nervous. What if this didn't work? What if she'd chosen wrong and Jimmy turned out to be useless? What if Harry decided Jimmy scared him? She was suddenly sure that Harry would be lost to her forever, that he'd never be able to enjoy the world without fear. She put one hand over her heart as it broke into jagged pieces that cut her from the inside. She closed her eyes and concentrated to keep from bursting into tears of frustration and fear and thus missed the glance Jimmy threw her way.

"Hello," Harry said, so quietly Annabelle barely heard him. Her eyes flew open and she gasped in spite of herself, one hand flying to her mouth.

This time she saw the measuring look Jimmy gave her but felt too overwhelmed to think much of it.

Jimmy turned back to Harry and smiled. When he spoke, his voice was low and soothing, a tone used to calm and prevent panic.

"I'm glad to meet you, Harry," said Jimmy. "I'm going to be seeing you a couple times a week from now on, if that's all right with you."

Another long silence as Harry fiddled with the edge of his sweatshirt, blinked rapidly, and shook his head several times as though trying to dislodge a fly. Annabelle fought the urge to grab his shoulders and force some sort of answer from him. *He'll answer when he's ready,* she reminded herself, digging her nails into her thighs until her jeans nearly ripped, *panicking him won't help…*

And indeed, after a full minute of twisting the edge of his shirt, Harry said, "I guess…okay?"

Annabelle let out a breath she hadn't realized she'd been holding and sagged forward, her head landing against Harry's back. Turning to tangle one hand in her hair, Harry whispered, "Sorry…"

Leaning back and crossing his arms, Jimmy scrutinized the pair of them. His sharp eyes didn't miss a thing.

"It's fine, Harry," said Annabelle, forcing herself to ignore him. "Everything'll be fine, now."

Chapter

8

Winter fell on Des Moines and its suburbs with ferocious winds and freezing cold that made anyone unlucky enough to be outside feel like knives sliced at their flesh. During the worst days, no amount of clothing could protect Annabelle and Harry; they might as well have been naked and buried in snow every time they opened their front door.

Fortunately, sensitivity to cold was one of their only weaknesses. Without the need for food or medicine, even the salary Annabelle made working at a fast food restaurant afforded them a good heating system.

Even better, it let Annabelle pay Jimmy most of the time. He deserved every cent.

A few days after replacing the oak door on her and Harry's room, Annabelle returned home to find it destroyed beyond any hope of rescue. Splinters scattered up and down the tiny house, some embedded into the walls like oak projectiles. Inside she found Harry sitting, looking like a naughty child hoping to avoid a scolding. The books she brought home for him, that he always stacked in such neat piles by size and color, now looked like confetti floating through the air.

"Sorry."

"You mean *you* did this?" Annabelle turned a full circle, gawping at the mess. Metal clinked; looking down she saw one of the locks, the metal melted out of shape.

Harry ducked his head. "Sorry."

He'd never done anything supernatural in Hell. But the longer Harry stayed on Earth, the more strange things happened around him. When something frightened him, glasses trembled in the cupboards and furniture slid over the floor. When he laughed, little objects like pens and coins danced around his head.

Perhaps, Annabelle reasoned, the unnatural phenomenon came from Harry's unnaturalness. He belonged in Hell with other damned souls, and Annabelle had never heard of a damned soul returning to Earth.

Well...she'd heard human ghost stories, which she now felt inclined to take much more seriously. Harry perfectly fit the definition of a poltergeist, when she thought about it. Did that make him a poltergeist? In so many tens of thousands of years of human history, Harry couldn't have been the first soul to escape Hell somehow. Maybe those ghost stories had been the stories of other escaped souls.

Whatever gave Harry his new powers, he gained more and more control over them as he wrested control over himself. Jimmy's sessions helped give him a clearer head, and if Annabelle felt jealous that he'd found something with a shrink that she hadn't been able to give him, her gratitude at both Harry's increasing lucidity and the control it gave him over his telekinesis balanced that out. Books, doors, and locks weren't free, after all.

During an unusually warm day in January (still nearly zero degrees, but thankfully lacking in wind), Annabelle drove Harry to his session with Jimmy, as she always did, in the not-so-new clunker she'd bought for about a thousand dollars from a junk yard. A few illegal maneuvers and several ignored red lights later, they arrived almost an hour early.

Remy and Anna Marie's Kitchen was a small restaurant a few blocks from Harry's house with the best Cajun food in Iowa. Though Annabelle didn't need to eat, and Harry couldn't eat, they enjoyed the lively, playful ambiance that made the place seem more like an unusually family-friendly bar than a restaurant. She and Harry would order hot drinks, usually tea, and watch Remy and his wife Anna Marie cook and clown around in the open kitchen. Their obvious affection for one another warmed Annabelle as much as the tea in her hands. What a sentimentalist she'd become!

Most of all, she enjoyed it when Harry enjoyed himself. He loved to observe people dancing between the tables, cooking in the kitchen, laughing in groups. Annabelle thought he was re-learning how to be a human being. He didn't have the stability to forge relationships of his own yet, but now that every little sound didn't terrify him, he could study how other people did it, absorbing basic rules of socialization long tortured out of him.

She didn't know how she felt about that. Annabelle wanted him to be happy and loved that he didn't cling to her as he had before. Yet a large part of her enjoyed the way he depended on her and felt jealous of future people who would capture some of Harry's attention and affection.

"It's all so jumbled," said Harry suddenly, jerking Annabelle out of her thoughts. She looked up from the dark, rapidly cooling liquid in her cup to see him gazing around the room, looking contemplative.

"Hmm?"

"Human relations. Hell, human beings. They're all jumbled and chaotic and unpredictable. Look at Remy and Anna Marie. They love each other. They do the same job every day. But every time we come here things are different between them. Last time they were fighting and stood at the opposite ends of the kitchen all evening. And now…" He pointed to the open kitchen, separated from the restaurant by only a counter. Behind it, Remy, a swarthy man with a ponytail, had his arm around Anna Marie, a tall woman with striking green eyes. He smiled down at her and said something that made her laugh as she absentmindedly stirred a boiling pot behind him.

"We're always changing," Harry continued, "always flowing from one face to the next, finding parts of ourselves even we didn't know were inside of us." The smell of spices filled the air, drifting from the kitchen and plates dotting dozens of tables big and small around the restaurant. Harry closed his eyes and inhaled.

"That would be a beautiful thing to say if you didn't sound so melancholy," said Annabelle. "You okay?"

"Are you kidding?" He lifted his cup as if to toast her and grinned. "I'm better than I've been in god only knows how long. I know my name was Steve Silver when I was human and if I had any need to use the toilet any longer, I'd be able to go on my own at this point without having to hold your hand.

"But you know, part of Dr. Hamid's treatment involves me sorting through memories I'd rather leave buried." Harry sighed and looked at the table for a long moment before looking up at Annabelle again. "I'm thinking a lot about how confused I was before I died, I think. No, I'm sure. I was a confused person, 'Belle, and there are some things I'm seeing that don't make sense even now. Nothing made sense while I lived. Everything was wrong, and I think...I think I handled my uncertainty badly."

Harry's eyes widened, and Annabelle knew he wanted her to understand, begged her to do so. But when he was so unsure of what he saw inside himself that he had to say "I think" in each sentence, how *could* she understand?

"If you mean that you didn't know why you were alive, what your purpose on Earth was, most people have trouble with that."

Harry started shaking his head before Annabelle finished her sentence. "That was part of it, but not all. It's more like, I didn't want to be alive and couldn't understand why I had to live in the world when it made so little sense. Which pissed me off." He paused and looked down into his tea. "Really pissed me off."

"You felt trapped," said Annabelle, very much understanding that.

"Yeah." Harry shook his head again, this time reminding Annabelle of a horse dislodging an annoying, unwanted fly from its head. "And I'm wondering, 'Belle. I seem to have a second chance, at least for the moment, and you know I'm grateful. But hell. Do I deserve it?"

Annabelle smiled and scooted her chair around their little table until she sat beside him. She comforted him with an arm around his shoulder, since she didn't actually expect the cosmos to give him an answer. The world just didn't work that way; answers didn't fall into one's lap, so there was no point asking questions like that. They'd drive him crazy.

But sharing warmth while surrounded by happy people and good spices was its own answer and no small comfort. Harry smiled back and put his arm around her waist, relaxing and watching the restaurant patrons once again.

As she turned on Runner Street and approached Jimmy's blue door in her car ten minutes later, a knot formed in Annabelle's belly. She didn't know what was wrong, but something was, wrong enough to make her feel ill. Annabelle had no powers of premonition, and she'd closed her mind to the thoughts of others for the moment. Whatever turned her insides to ice had nothing to do with supernatural powers, just simple intuition.

Though she hoped she just felt unsettled after her talk with Harry, Annabelle decided to check on Jimmy before letting Harry see him. The knot in her gut grew so tight, she knew before she parked that Jimmy was hurt or dead, somehow beyond where he could help Harry any longer.

She was wrong. Jimmy lived. Annabelle opened her mind as she pulled the parking brake and sensed him, energetic and active as always, pacing back and forth in his living room. In her relief, she disregarded the anger simmering inside him. He was a professional, able to push past his personal feelings to do his job. Something had made him spitting mad, but he didn't take that sort of thing out on his patients.

Annabelle would have pried anyway if Jimmy interested her, but as she found him dull and didn't care if he was happy or not, she broke the mental connection and grabbed Harry's gloved hand to pull him from the car.

When Annabelle knocked on the front door, Jimmy opened it with startling speed. He looked terrible, with dark circles around his eyes and hair that stuck in every direction. He wore wrinkled, stinky sweats, making Annabelle cringe.

"Come in, both of you," said Jimmy. "We need to talk."

Annabelle exchanged a surprised look with Harry before the two of them stepped inside, too startled to disobey. Jimmy slammed the door behind them.

The state of Jimmy's house shocked Annabelle once again. Though she hadn't been inside the place for a few months, she had trouble believing such a smothering, stale atmosphere could have permeated it so completely since her last visit. Jimmy might as well have boarded the windows and doors over and left the air inside to ferment. The lack of dust showed that Jimmy couldn't have been shut away for too long, so she couldn't imagine what made the little house feel so inhospitable in so short a time. Annabelle could almost smell an undertone of despair saturating the air.

Jimmy walked over to the sofa by the left wall and picked up a folder.

"You know," he said, glaring at the folder like it had done him a great wrong, "I'm about to break doctor-patient confidentiality for the first time in my professional life. Which, admittedly, hasn't been very long, but. Still. It's a fucking abominable thing, a total violation of the rules, both legal and moral."

Harry started when Jimmy swore. Just a week ago he had laughed with Annabelle at how clean Jimmy's language was, how he blushed at certain vulgar euphemisms for human genitalia.

"But I'm doing it anyway, because this is a situation the board of ethics never even considered, let alone made a loophole for me to exploit. Are you even a patient, since there are no records? Do you even count as human? What are my obligations to a dead man?" Jimmy laughed, a sound with no humor, and gripped the files hard enough to bend the entire folder.

"Jimmy—" Annabelle began, growing angry as Harry started trembling. In the back of her mind, she registered that Jimmy had called Harry a dead man. He knew.

Jimmy ignored her. "See, last week, Steve and I were going over a scene from his past, the first we'd managed to get to, involving his teen years. From earlier sessions I knew he'd been in jail." Jimmy laughed in that grating, bitter way again and collapsed onto the couch. "And oh, the stories he had about that! But that's not the issue, now."

Completely bewildered by this point, Annabelle couldn't gather her wits enough to ask him to spit out what he wanted, or to stop calling Harry "Steve." He hated being called that.

Opening the file folder, Jimmy reached in and took out a glossy, 4x6-sized photo, which he tossed across the living room. It flew out and hit the floor, where it slid to Harry's feet.

Glancing down, Annabelle saw a young black man, handsome and smiling.

"Recognize him, Steve?" Jimmy asked.

It seemed Harry did, for he turned deathly pale and his eyes widened.

"N-n-no..." he whispered. He was not denying knowledge of the man in the photograph, but instead expressing distress.

Annabelle frowned. "Did he hurt you somehow?"

Jimmy suddenly began laughing so hard that he nearly fell from the couch. "Did *he* hurt *Steve*?" he gasped. Jimmy found his own words even funnier than Annabelle's, enough so that he went from laughter to outright hysterics.

Beside Annabelle, Harry began hyperventilating. He shut his eyes tight to block out the photograph and almost collapsed to the floor, gripping the wall to stay upright.

Fury gave Annabelle her voice. She knelt down and snatched up the photograph, crumpling it in her fist. "What the hell is wrong with you?" she snapped at Jimmy. "Do you make a habit of bullying your patients?"

Jimmy's laughter stopped as abruptly as it started. "Is he crying?" Jimmy asked her, nodding his head at Harry. "Does he have any water in his body that he can cry with? He's hyperventilating, but does he breathe?"

Annabelle froze, trying to think of what to say. He'd obviously realized that Harry wasn't any more human than Annabelle, but he might be pretending he knew more than he really did to try and trick information out of them. His rage made a haze that clouded his thoughts, one Annabelle was too confused and nervous to penetrate.

"Even if he can," Jimmy continued when Annabelle said nothing, "true ASPDs don't feel deeply enough for other people to emote like that at the suffering of another. He's faking."

"ASPDs?" Annabelle asked.

Again Jimmy opened the plain, manila folder. Such a simple, boring object to hold so much terror.

This time he tossed a printed newspaper article, dated eleven years and seven months before, at Annabelle. She read: RACIAL MOTIVATION SUSPECTED IN BRUTAL COLLEGE SLAYING. Below the headline were two pictures, one of Harry, the other of the handsome black man from the first photograph. Harry looked younger than now, with acne dotting the lower half of his face. His head was shaved and Annabelle could see the edge of a tattoo creeping over the collar of his white t-shirt.

"So last week, Steve and I were talking, and he remembered the name 'Ramón Baker,' though he didn't know where he remembered it from. Which sounded kinda familiar to me, so I looked it up, and it turns out I was thinking of the rather famous event that article is reporting on. There're murders on TV all the time, but man, this one scared me. No…no, it terrified me."

Looking back at the article, Annabelle scanned the text, picking up the most important bits. "Baker was an exceptionally gifted student and an outspoken, up-and-coming scholar focusing on race relations in America..." "Suspected to be the next Cornell West..." "Had received no less than a dozen death threats from the local branch of White Pride Chicago, which, far from silencing Baker, gave him new subjects for his speeches and articles..." "Baker's arm was found in Lincoln Park at six a.m. by a pair of joggers. A stray dog discovered one of his legs in a nearby fountain half an hour later..."

"Steve didn't just kill that boy," said Jimmy. His shoulders were so tense it hurt Annabelle to look at them. "Did you Steve? That's not enough punishment for those of us who pollute your lily-white blood or question your superiority. No, we have to suffer!"

Then Jimmy was on his feet, stomping forward, spitting with rage. "You tortured him. Tore him to bits! Stabbed him twenty-three times! Castrated him while he was still alive and conscious! Stuffed things under his nails! Broke—"

Harry began to wail, a high, keening sound that cut straight through Annabelle's heart. "Stop it!" she yelled, putting herself between the two men. "Leave him alone!"

"Why should I?" Jimmy hissed, his forwardness surprising Annabelle once again. "Don't you get it? He's a Nazi, a Neo-Nazi! You're Asian, why would you stand up for him?"

"I do tend to be Asian for most humans. But as you've obviously put together, I'm no more from Asia than I am from Mars."

"Looks alone would have been enough to make Steve kill you," Jimmy snapped. "And what he did to that boy was enough for the government to kill him!"

Opening the folder one last time, Jimmy grabbed a sheet of paper and shoved it into Annabelle's face. On it was Harry's—Steve Silver's—obituary.

"Steve was executed over six years ago. You made it sound like his death had been faked by the mafia or something. But he really did die, a death he earned all by himself. The torture you talked about, it's the torture of Hell, isn't it? He's no trauma victim. He's a fucking psycho-killer, a Nazi racist who deserved every second of what he got!"

Annabelle slapped Jimmy, hard, barely able to control herself enough to keep from taking his head off. He fell to the ground, a crack echoing through the room as his elbow hit hard wood. The folder skidded across the floor.

"Listen to yourself! You're letting your own issues get in the way of helping your patient. You should be ashamed." Annabelle didn't care about the professional ethics of psychologists or whatever psychological pain Jimmy carried that made him act so viciously out of character. To get Harry his treatment, Annabelle didn't mind manipulating Jimmy, or anyone.

However, Jimmy did not shrink with guilt as she'd expected. Though Annabelle had given up trying to read his mind, the image of Jimmy's father formed so powerfully in his thoughts that she couldn't help but see it.

Bossing me around, he thought, and Annabelle knew he was "talking" to his dad now, not her. *You always think you can boss me around!*

"Don't you dare put this on me," Jimmy growled aloud, scrambling to his feet and sticking his face up into hers. "You brought that *thing*," Jimmy pointed at Harry, still shuddering and gasping against the wall, "into my home, and I let you do it. I let a child of Satan in because I thought there was a real human out there who needed me."

"So?" said Annabelle, lifting her chin. "You knew from the beginning what I was, or at least you had your suspicions, and you've always known what a pathetic sucker you are. How does this change things? Harry is still a brutalized, damaged person who you can help."

"Nazis aren't people," said Jimmy with brutal finality. "Especially not this one. Steve. He's Steve, not Harry. You've turned him into a doll for your comfort, and he lets you do it because you protect him from his rightful fate in Hell. You may have suckered me, but he suckered you, and he's still doing it."

"Nooo," Harry whimpered, shaking his head and slapping his hands to his ears.

"Shut up," Jimmy said, voice lowering to a growl once again. "You don't get to have an opinion. Only humans have that right."

Jimmy's sofa began shaking, like an invisible man rattled it back and forth. The lamp on Jimmy's work desk fell onto the floor.

Jimmy gasped and took a step back.

Hissing with glee at his fear, Annabelle raised her right arm, ready to strike with all her strength this time. If Jimmy wouldn't be useful to her, then he might as well be dead. She couldn't leave him behind for

Hell's kings to find and get information out of. Besides, for the level of disrespect he'd shown her, and the amount of distress he'd caused Harry, he deserved to die!

But to Annabelle's disbelief, Harry stepped between her and Jimmy. Though he did not raise his head or say a single word—indeed, he barely opened his eyes, and tears continued flowing their way down his face—he blocked every attempt Annabelle made to duck around him.

The sofa shook so violently it toppled over, though no one touched it. Sweat beaded on Jimmy's forehead as he glanced from it to Harry and back again and again.

"Move, damn it!" Annabelle finally snapped. "He deserves it!"

"No," whispered Harry yet again. "*I* do."

Behind him Jimmy looked, not just surprised, but actively astonished. Annabelle hoped he'd decided he was wrong, but anger almost immediately drove the shock from his face.

"Liar!" Jimmy spit. "You're just pretending to be sorry, trying to fool me again. Get out, both of you. I don't ever want to see you again. I don't know what kind of monsters you are, and I know I haven't been as devout in my religion as I could be, but I see you for the filth you are now."

Harry grabbed Annabelle's shoulders before she could attack again and turned her toward the door.

"Please," he whispered in her ear as Jimmy yelled again for them to leave. "Please, let's just go, we need to go, I have to get out of here, *please!*"

Annabelle threw one last glare at Jimmy and then stomped to the door, fists clenched all the way. She'd leave now for Harry's sake, but she'd be back. Nobody insulted a Lady of Hell, nor those under her protection, and got away with it.

And if, in the back of her mind, a little voice whispered that Annabelle had worked so hard to get away from being a Lady of Hell, her anger allowed her to ignore it.

Chapter

9

The next day Annabelle left Harry huddled in a corner of his room. Seeing him curled up in a ball, eyes wide yet unseeing, infuriated Annabelle anew. Soon the air in their room would be stale and lined with misery, just as the air in Jimmy's house had been. That would thrill Jimmy, she thought bitterly, knowing he had spread his own misery around.

Well, Harry had already made incredible progress in therapy. There were a few other good therapists in the Des Moines area, and though Jimmy had been the best, Harry had sufficiently healed for one of them to take over his case.

(A million problems erupted as soon as the idea popped into her head. How would she pay for a psychologist that didn't have Jimmy's weakness for the downtrodden or his sense of honor? Who would get Harry to the sessions if they took place during normal business hours? Could the therapists or psychologists coax memories from Harry's psyche without hypnosis?)

Annabelle kissed Harry's forehead and left for work, refusing to think about anything she couldn't deal with yet.

The morning flew by. Annabelle dropped hamburger patties on the floor, rung up half a dozen customers incorrectly and almost knocked a baby from his plastic high chair while mopping around one small, plastic table.

Usually only half a brain was enough to get her work done, but today, her whole mind focused on revenge and how she would get it.

There were so many satisfying ways she could kill Jimmy. Humans had a brilliant talent for murder, and it would be best to use their methods; if she used any of her paranormal abilities so close to her house, Hell might well track her down.

But human methods would do just fine. Humans used broken glass bottles and switchblades, short revolvers and long shotguns. Pens could stab right through an eye when pushed with enough force, and skulls collapsed under a heavy enough object.

Annabelle sighed with satisfaction every time she imagined Jimmy's death, earning her nervous glances from customers. She considered using one of the guns in her closet, but a bullet to the head wasn't painful enough to satisfy her bloodlust. Besides, if Topher and his friends were wrong about how traceable their merchandise was, she might wind up having to kill policemen, which would attract far more attention than she wanted from Earth's law enforcement. Much better would be burning Jimmy alive. Imagining the desperate look on his face as he tried to escape from his flaming house comforted Annabelle as she washed windows larger than she was tall, dirtied with straw wrappers and grease. Her lunch break couldn't come soon enough.

But finally it did, and Annabelle took only a second to drop her purple uniform visor into her locker before teleporting to the front of Jimmy's house. Runner Street came into focus, the perfectly trimmed (and now browning) lawns with their cutesy lawn sculptures and square hedges; the square houses with concrete front walks leading up to them, plus gates adorning the side if the occupants had a dog to worry about; the gray winter sky just beginning to threaten Des Moines with snow.

Annabelle had almost fully formed on Jimmy's front walk when she realized that Harry sat not two feet away from her on the steps.

Gasping, Annabelle fell back and managed to teleport herself behind the trunk of a once-green and now skeletal tree, one of many that lined Runner Street, before becoming visible. She fit behind the trunk as long as she stayed ramrod straight.

Jimmy's car rested in his driveway, but Annabelle would have bet her house and job that he hadn't driven Harry to his house. That meant Harry had been so desperate to see his doctor that he'd read a map (which Annabelle had never seen him do—she didn't even have one in the house), taken several buses (in crowds that must have terrified him), and now braved the open air, possible snow, rejection, abuse, and humiliation.

Looking at him, Annabelle grew so jealous that the fury she'd felt all morning seemed like mild irritation in comparison. What had Jimmy been doing in those goddamn sessions with her Harry? Had he been seducing Harry all along, turning him against her? Bastard!

Jimmy's blue door opened just a crack with the chain still drawn over the inside. The look of naked hope on Harry's face, the way he jumped up and spun around like a puppy begging for scraps, pained Annabelle.

"I swear to god, Steve," said Jimmy, just the slightest sliver of his angry face visible in the doorway, "I will call the police."

"If you feel you have to," said Harry. "I've been to prison. It was nothing—*nothing*—compared to Hell, and the mush Hell made of my brain."

"Don't try to make me feel sorry for you," Jimmy snapped. "Mighty white man, beating up on all of us who pollute your pure gene pool, like we'd want to be part of it! You'll never even understand what you did."

"But that's just it!" Harry cried. "I do understand. It was the worst punishment Hell put me through, Dr. Hamid, worse than the drownings and beatings and burns. I saw what they saw. I *was* them. I was all the people I'd hurt. I became every black man I'd ever called a nigger, every brown lady I'd ever…ever made to do something she didn't want to. I felt everything they felt, their humiliation, their fury, their…their…I don't know if there's a word for what they felt. It felt like nothing would ever feel safe again, like we'd be afraid of everything forever and pain would infect the rest of our lives and we'd just have to get used to it. The world was painted in this wash of wrongness that colored everything we saw.

"I know exactly what I did, Doctor. I relive the pain I caused every minute of my miserable existence."

A chill wind blew by, forcing Annabelle to duck back behind the trunk and grab her hair before it flew to the side and gave her away. She strained her ears but heard nothing, gritted her teeth to keep them from chattering. Did Jimmy have nothing to say?

Then, a light clattering noise. As soon as the wind died down Annabelle peeked from behind the tree and found Jimmy had opened his door and stepped outside. He stared warily at Harry, kept him at a distance and just looked at him like a puzzle he couldn't solve.

"You deserved it, you know," said Jimmy, voice so low that human ears would never have heard him from Annabelle's distance. "The punishment you got, you deserved every minute of it."

No hesitation: "I know."

Another pause.

"What, that's it?" said Jimmy. "No insistence that you've suffered enough? No defense about how your sad childhood made you do it?"

"I..." Harry hesitated. "I don't know what 'enough' suffering is. Sometimes Annabelle tries to hug me, and I move away, because it feels so good to be loved like that and I know I don't deserve to feel that good."

Behind the tree, Annabelle bit her lip and looked at the ground.

"But Dr. Hamid, I figured out I'm never gonna know when I've really paid enough. Was six years of torture and having my mind turned to jelly appropriate punishment for Raymond Baker's death? What about the suffering I've caused his parents, or the people I hurt before the law caught up with me? I know the rest of my life will be affected by what I did, and that guilt and shame will color the world for me forever, like that feeling of wrongness that colored the world for my...my victims. Is that enough suffering to balance the cosmic scales?

"Maybe no suffering'll ever be enough. Or maybe it would be better if I just stayed nuts; maybe that would make things more equal. I can't figure it out."

Annabelle dared to peek out from behind the tree again and saw the back of Harry's head, and Jimmy's angry, puzzled face.

"I do know that before I began working with you, I was so messed up I could barely string a sentence together. And as miserable as I am now, at least know why I feel so crappy. I got so lost I didn't even know why I was suffering anymore. I won't lie and say I want to continue hurting like this, but I can tell you I won't ever recover, not really, not totally. You're the only one who helped alleviate the pain at all, and even though I know it's selfish, even though I know I don't deserve the relief, the sessions with you are all I have to cling to. They're my only hope. It's only 'cause of you that I can think straight, and god, I'm so scared of falling back into the dark."

Harry grabbed fistfuls of his hair and shook his head violently back and forth, frustration eating at him.

"I'm not making any sense!" he wailed, looking on the verge of a complete meltdown even from the back.

"Yes you are," said Jimmy. He sounded resigned and exhausted; he buried his face in one hand, keeping the other on the doorknob. "You're making perfect sense." Peeking into his mind showed Annabelle a whirl of chaotic thoughts and warring emotions.

Harry collapsed back onto the stairs and squeezed his eyes shut. Jimmy glared down at him, though Annabelle couldn't tell if the glare came from the anger still burning in him or the confused thoughts rushing through his brain. He spun away from Harry for a moment, shoulders so tight Annabelle thought the shoulder blades might pop right out from under his skin. He looked like he'd just swallowed something disgusting, and sweat beaded his upper lip despite the cold.

"I don't want to hear about them," he said, even more quietly than before. "Those Nazi bastards, I swear, unfair or not, unprofessional or not, if I hear a positive word out of you about them—if I get any indication that you have any sympathy left for them at all—that's it, our sessions are over. *And goddamn you for making me say something that disgustingly childish.*"

Far from looking put off, Harry looked overjoyed. When Jimmy turned and saw Harry's grateful expression, he looked away. Shame and embarrassment washed over him, them and so many other negative emotions Annabelle was amazed he didn't collapse under the weight of them. She thought it might feel worse for Jimmy than for her seeing Harry's expression, and for her it was nightmarishly awful. Seeing Harry look so openly adoring of another person made Annabelle hate Jimmy all the more. Rationally she knew he wasn't trying to steal Harry's attention from her, but in her heart, she couldn't help but feel threatened.

Couldn't stop her hatred from burning a hole through her chest, making a fiery path through her veins. The winter cold didn't touch her now.

The latter half of Annabelle's workday seemed twice as long as usual. This time her "mistakes" were deliberate and malicious: an extra squirt of hot sauce onto the hamburger of a customer with sensitive taste buds, spitting into a soda cup, dropping food onto the floor before serving it. Annabelle suffered, and so she would make the world suffer with her.

She didn't know how she'd react seeing Harry again. The love she felt for him remained, but deep anger mixed with that affection now. Even worse, she felt disappointed. Annabelle had never believed that Harry would disappoint her, hadn't even thought it possible that he could. He was her Harry, and Annabelle had been positive he would always be her Harry. After all she'd been through on his behalf, what right did he think he had to go and change?

When Annabelle arrived home, the darkness there felt unwelcoming. Annabelle scowled at that darkness, something she was usually so fond of, and decided she should never have stopped locking Harry in their room.

She was halfway up the front steps when she saw a scrap of yellow fabric—the edge of a t-shirt—disappearing round the side of her house.

Déjà vu rose so strongly in Annabelle that she was suddenly sure that it wasn't yellow fabric she'd seen, but yellow hair. If she went round the corner of the house, she was certain she'd see Samantha, smirking and demanding something in return for not telling Emperor Lucifer all her secrets.

It wasn't Samantha waiting around the side of her house, but Douglas Crane, a Satanist Annabelle knew only by hearsay and had hoped never to meet. His beer gut and thinning hair combined with baggy jeans, a backwards baseball cap, and that bright yellow t-shirt with a pair of huge breasts drawn on the front made him look like a man having a midlife crisis and trying to recapture his lost youth. His mind was like a sewer pit. The evil in him didn't bother Annabelle in the slightest, but Douglas lacked any sense of refinement or a single interesting thought she could sense. He was a petty thug with delusions of grandeur, like Vinnie the vampire without the fangs. Annabelle grimaced and closed her mind to his thoughts, not caring if that would put her at a disadvantage.

"Greetings, Lady Annabelle, whose honored womb brings life to Hell." Douglas made a sweeping gesture with his arms and bowed low.

Annabelle considered telling him to shove it, but since he could now destroy her life just by picking up a phone and telling the wrong people her address, she decided to follow etiquette.

For the moment.

"And greetings to you, Master Crane, whose organization of Earth's Satanists makes it possible for Hell's greatness to expand even beyond its borders." She bowed as formality demanded, lowering herself just a little less than Douglas, inferior human that he was.

"Lady Annabelle, I'm honored that you've chosen to grace Iowa with your presence. I was so surprised to hear you'd taken up residence here! I thought only King Zagan had discovered the joys of life on Earth."

An obvious insult, since the joys of Earth were rarely found in poor suburbs with paint peeling in unison off every wall in the neighborhood and the scent of pee wafting up from most sewer drains. "Yes, well, I got the idea from him. But you know…" Smiling widely and tucking her hands behind her back to look cute and suggest innocence, Annabelle crept forward and lowered her voice as though sharing a secret. "I'm trying to surprise a few people. I hope I can count on you not to tell anyone I'm up here?"

Douglas's heart fluttered and his penis twitched, but Annabelle had done too good a job of dampening her allure. He could resist a dusty woman in baggy, unwashed sweats with fast-food grease clinging to her.

"Honored Lady, above all things I live to serve. Yet I'm afraid that I swore to report to Emperor Lucifer before anyone else and you know the consequences for disobeyal."

In a flash, Annabelle dropped her friendly pretense. Her smile became a scowl. "There is no such word as 'disobeyal,' you troglodyte." She thought of the guns hidden inside the house. "If I killed you now," she said, "someone who knew you'd come here would know I did it, right?"

Douglas, who did not lessen his pleasant façade one jot, smiled even wider so that he looked like a satisfied frog munching on a flea. Bingo. "O, most beauteous and splendid creature—"

"Shut up," Annabelle snapped. "Shut up, shut up, shut your mouth and do not finish that fake bullshit unless you want me to rip your jaw off. You obviously want something or you would have gone to the Emperor with my location already instead of waiting around to gift me with your presence like this. Just tell me what you're after. Now. Or I will kill you and damn the consequences."

Douglas sighed, his eyelids drooping. He looked almost orgasmic. "You are a true Lady of Hell, brilliant and brave. And…" Now he leaned in close to her, his smile so wide that it almost bisected his face. "…A true mother of Hell, as well."

Somewhere nearby, an owl hooted in an annoyed sort of way. *I know how you feel*, Annabelle thought before raising an eyebrow at Douglas.

When Annabelle didn't say anything, Douglas's smile wilted slightly. Annabelle wondered if he'd expected her to run into his arms, assuming he implied what she thought he implied.

Clearing his throat, Douglas pasted his smile back on and tried again.

"Your children have risen to such prominence, after all," he said. "With your noble status and beauty, how could they do otherwise?"

"You know, here on Earth we have a few half-demons and truly devoted humans wandering around. Just imagine what they could do if you were to mate with the *right man—*" here Douglas leaned so far forward that Annabelle could smell the stale cigarettes on his breath. Excitement opened his eyes wide enough that she could see a ring of white around the brown iris. "—And gave birth to a child with connections to Earth and the nobility of Hell?"

Annabelle felt she might explode with anger. She didn't know what her expression looked like, but Douglas backed quickly away after pulling his head out of his ass long enough to look at her.

Politics! Always politics! Everybody wanted power and influence and saw Annabelle as a rung on their ladder of success. How many more bargains would she have to strike, how many more compromises would she have to make, before she could have her own life?

Too angry and insulted to keep her temper, Annabelle's voice trembled when she spoke. It took all her control to keep from yelling.

"Master Crane, let me make this very clear. Even had I not made a promise to myself that I will never, ever have sex again with anyone I don't want to, which I have, I would never, in a thousand years, not even for my life, lower myself to having sex with an ugly, brainless, two-bit lackey like you."

Douglas was suddenly not smiling any longer, which made Annabelle feel like smiling again.

Until he spoke, anyway, his voice sharp and sullen. "But you're a succubus, a glorified demon whore. Aren't you supposed to want to bang whoever you can? Isn't it your job?"

It was indeed Annabelle's "job" to get pregnant whenever possible, but she wasn't sure where he got the idea she had to want to do it. "Hang on. You're not one of those morons who think that prostitutes and porn stars and all them go into that line of work because they enjoy sex, are you?"

Beginning to pout, Douglas snapped, "Well, why else would you sluts do it?"

Annabelle suddenly had a headache. Pinching the bridge of her nose between her right thumb and forefinger, she tried to keep the pounding feeling at the back of her head from bursting right through her skull. The image was clear in her head: her forehead would break wide open, splashing Douglas and his cheerfully colored t-shirt (and why wasn't he freezing?) with brain and bone. Hell, the shocked look on his face might be worth the pain.

"Of course, Douglas," she said aloud. "You've caught me. I'm really just an uncontrollable sex machine at heart. But I'm sad to say I'm having female troubles that prevent me from giving birth at this time. I'm here on Earth to hide in shame and seek treatment."

Annabelle's words dripped with sarcasm. She spoke off the top of her head and never thought Douglas might believe her. But when she opened her eyes she found him gaping at her. Annabelle imagined the creature from *Alien* popping out of his mouth and saying "Hiii!"

She lowered her head both to hide her laughter and to try to look embarrassed about her "barren womb."

"Really?" Douglas finally said.

"Oh yes," said Annabelle, inventing wildly. "I'm desperate! Sobbing each night away with the pain of my emptiness! My loneliness, which can only be cured by the touch of a man and the love of a child. There can be no other meaning to my life, no other path I can take to fulfillment!" Annabelle swooned, and the nearby owl chose to be helpful by hooting again.

"Well...um...yes, I mean...um..." said Douglas, backing up and looking increasingly uncomfortable.

"But now I have hope!" Annabelle cried, getting more into her role with each second. She put one hand to her heart and tossed her head back, looked at the moon with dewed eyes, and sighed as loudly as she could. "I have heard of a small group of sorcerers in the heart of Des Moines, specialists in demonic, um, biology. They're called the Brotherhood of the...of the Eel. You know, eels represent the penis in some cultures."

"Eels?" said Douglas, confused.

Actually, Annabelle couldn't think of any culture with that particular penis metaphor. "Yes," she said aloud. "In certain parts of Yemen."

Douglas nodded, putting one hand to his chin and looking deep in thought. "I always thought those people were a little weird."

"Right," said Annabelle, "but they're my last hope. I beg you not to take it from me. I want to enjoy sex and give Hell lots of little baby hell-spawn like any good demon woman would. Give me time to return to Hell with my head held high, instead of crawling with apologies!" She would have dropped to one knee and clasped her hands together in supplication for the full effect, but her pride didn't allow it. Instead, she settled for hugging herself and whipping up enough tears to make her eyes look wobbly and, hopefully, adorable. "After all, if it's new recruits you want, recruits with demonic blood, there are other deals we can work out."

It took Douglas a moment to catch up with her. Confusion, disgust, intrigue, irritation, and more confusion flew across his face. Eventually he landed back on intrigued.

"I imagine there would be," he said, predatory smile spreading back over his face.

Chapter

10

The lights in Jimmy's living room were dimmed low enough to make objects soften around the edges but remained bright enough that a person could keep from tripping over said objects. Jimmy had shut the windows against the winter cold and now sat beneath them in the large, padded chair in which Annabelle had once waited for him. He'd bought it for himself as a graduation present, feeling that all psychologists had to have an impressive chair to seat themselves in. How could a client take their doctor seriously if they sat on cheap velour cushions or something with stuffing leaking out of it?

Across from him sat Steve, as Jimmy insisted on calling him; there would be no running away from past identities or sins in his sessions. He lay back on Jimmy's couch, eyelids lowered and breathing even. Shadows darkened his face, but Jimmy could see his eyes moving rapidly behind the lids.

"Okay, Steve," said Jimmy, keeping his voice low and even. "Tell me where you are."

"I'm at home."

"And what do you see?"

"I see…a fireplace. With the red urn on top Grandma's ashes are kept in." Steve smiled, just slightly.

Jimmy nodded, recognizing the description of Steve's childhood home. "Is there a fire going?"

"Yes!" said Steve, sounding overjoyed. "I was outside in the snow, and I was freezing, but the fire's so warm, and I just ran over and put my hands right up to it, and I love the way the water fizzles on my hands!"

Jimmy grinned in spite of himself. "You enjoy snow, then?"

"Oh yeah! It's, like, the coolest thing ever!" Steve began fidgeting in place like a child longing to go play. "I can write my name in it or shove it down somebody's shirt to surprise them, or build snowmen or slide down hills covered in it...snow never gets boring. When you're done doing one thing, there's always something new to do."

"Do you think it represents starting over to you?" Jimmy asked. "Snow is white and pure; it appears and makes everything clean, covering up crap on the ground so suddenly the world looks fresh. It even smells fresher. Something in the air just seems invigorating when it's cold, especially when there's snow."

Steve went silent and still. It wasn't a nervous silence, but a pensive one, so Jimmy waited patiently and let him think.

"I dunno," Steve finally said. "But the snow always looks new to me, and that's really neat."

"Okay," said Jimmy making notes on the yellow pad in his lap. "So you've just come in from the snow, and what's happening?"

"Um...my mom just came in, and her eyes are all red, but she's smiling at me anyway and has soup for me." He paused, then said, "I hate it when she's sad."

Jimmy sat up straighter in his chair. Steve had never once mentioned his parents. "Is she sad often?"

"Yeah," said Steve. His voice grew smaller with each word he spoke. "She tries so hard, but I haven't seen her smile for real in years."

"Do you know why she's so sad?" Jimmy made a mental note to follow up on just what Steve's mother "tried so hard" at later. First he wanted to find out if Steve felt responsible for his mother's depression in childhood. The guilt could have a lot to do with the mess his adulthood turned into.

"Maybe," said Steve. He clenched his fists until the knuckles turned white and a twitch formed on the right side of his face. "Dad's been tired, and his skin looks all gray. And he's lost so much weight he's had to punch new holes in his belts. And his hair is all falling out, like in big ol' clumps. And I asked if he'd make a snowman with me a week ago, and he just stared at me and breathed all heavy, like it was hard for him to catch a breath.

"I thought he was invincible, you know? He was my dad. He could throw a baseball so far and worked all the time, and when he came home he'd smell like grass and the cologne Mom got him for Christmas. He was so big and I didn't think anything could hurt him…

"I don't want to see it!"

Jimmy scribbled more notes, reminding himself to ask later what "it" meant. Did Steve want to avoid seeing his father, or his father's weakness? Or maybe that his father's weakness meant the world wasn't as safe a place as child-Steve believed it to be? Probably all of the above.

With his head down, focused on his notes, Jimmy did not notice the lamp and phone on his desk beginning to shake.

"So now I'm outside 'cause I ran away, and I'm walking toward a park bench two blocks from my house. I'll sleep there…but the night is so huge and scary…" Steve began making soft keening noises, head tossing from side to side and fingers jerking violently. Behind Jimmy, the phone slammed into the wall and the lamp crashed from the desk. Then the desk began trembling, smacking into the wall and thumping against the ground. Jimmy's chair almost shook him out of it.

Leaping up, Jimmy took three long strides to get to Steve's side and knelt down beside him. The way the couch hovered above the ground made this difficult. "Steve!" he said. "Steve, it's okay."

"It's not okay, it's not okay, everything is wrong! The world is supposed to be one way, but if even a dad as strong as mine is so fragile, then the world isn't acting the way it's supposed to!"

That sounded like enough personal revelation for one day. Just letting Steve melt down without processing anything wasn't going to help anyone.

"Listen to me," said Jimmy, keeping all traces of emotion out of his voice. "I'm going to count to three, and when I finish, you're going to wake up. You'll remember everything you said here, but it will be only a memory. It's not happening to you now, and it can't hurt you. Do you understand?"

Whimpering and twisting, Steve managed to gasp, "Y-yes."

"All right, that's good. Here we go now, ready? One. Two. Three."

Steve's eyes snapped open. The pupils were wide and unfocused. "Annabelle?" he cried, stretching his arms out and waving them wildly around.

"No, Steve, it's me."

"Dr. Hamid?" said Steve. He drew his arms in towards his chest before dropping them into his lap.

"That's me," said Jimmy gently, smiling. "How're you feeling?"

Breathing gradually slowing to a normal rate, Steve leaned back into the pillows propping his head up and stared up at the ceiling. "Aside from the obvious?"

Jimmy straightened and walked over to the light switches, taking his time turning the lights up and returning to his chair so Steve could finish pulling himself together. "Obvious, subtle, whatever strikes you."

"It 'strikes' me that I'd forgotten my own dad died of cancer," said Steve, sounding very guilty.

"As you didn't remember anything when I met you just a few months ago, that's neither surprising nor shameful."

"No, I mean, I forgot about it even before I. Um. Died." Steve made a face. "It feels so weird saying that."

"Well, while you're my first patient to have actually returned from the dead, I can still say it's probably somewhat normal to feel what you've been through is odd," said Jimmy. Steve grinned and kept looking up at the ceiling.

"Thanks, but I don't mean I forgot it when I forgot everything else. Even when I was alive, on Earth, I forgot about it. I mean, I knew it had happened, but I never thought about it. Pushed it to the back of my mind like a…a disturbing letter that I'd crumpled and thrown in back of a closet. Never discussed it with girlfriends or friends. Not even Mom. We just went on like it had never happened and I…"

Steve paused to think again. Staring at him, Jimmy wondered what Hell was like for the dozenth time that evening alone. Here before him was a man who had seen the underworld. Did he know the truth about God and Heaven, too? Could he tell Jimmy the secrets of the universe, and where Jimmy was bound for after death?

Jimmy had yet to find the courage to ask. Given how his faith had lapsed, and how long he'd been questioning God and disobeying his father, a part of Jimmy was sure he was condemned to Hell. As curious as he felt about the afterlife and God, he didn't want to know if he was destined to fall into the fiery pit of torture and pain. And if there was no

God, Jimmy didn't think he wanted to know that either. Questioning the Almighty the way he had been was easy when there'd never been any chance of getting a concrete answer.

"I can't explain it," Steve finally said. Jimmy embraced the distraction with gratitude.

"I think maybe you already did," said Jimmy. "You told me about a month ago on my porch that you felt like the world had been painted in…in wrongness. Like that?"

"Yeah," said Steve. "The world was wrong, but I could never really figure out what was wrong or why it was wrong. Plus," he added, "it sounded like whining to put it that way. I didn't want people to think I was a whiner."

Right, because being a sadistic bully was much better. Jimmy covered his irritation and sadness by looking down and rubbing the back of his neck until Steve moved to grab the handkerchief sitting on the armrest of his chair. His shaking fingers could barely pick it up, but brushing it over his brow seemed to give him some comfort. Jimmy wondered how a body that drank no water could sweat. Habit, maybe.

"The world still scares me, you know," Steve said after putting the cloth down in his lap. "I walk outside and the noise is so big. Car engines are roaring and tree branches are rustling and feet are pounding against pavement and dogs are barking…it's just so loud, and I can't get away from it. I want to bury myself in a hole, you know?"

Jimmy couldn't help the brief thought that Steve would deserve it if someone else put him in a hole. Thankfully, thoughts like that occurred much less commonly than they had just weeks ago. He easily pushed the hostile idea aside. "And yet that's not what you're doing," he said aloud. "Didn't you even take the bus here today?"

Looking very proud of himself, Steve nodded. "And I'm taking it home, too!"

Then his smile wilted. "But it makes me so tired. I can go out for half an hour, and then I have to lie down for a day."

"That's to be expected," said Jimmy. "Integrating yourself back into society isn't something you can do just overnight."

The absurdity of the situation hit Jimmy suddenly. How did a man raised from the dead "integrate" himself into the world? Steve had no legal identity, which meant no way to get a good job or home. Besides, though he felt real enough to the touch, he didn't have a living body.

There had to be consequences for that, things Steve couldn't do or enjoy as a human would.

"Yeah, maybe," said Steve. He looked up at one of Jimmy's high windows, out towards the stars, and smiled. "Jeez, the idea of having a life is so exciting. Just going to work and bringing home money, or getting a beer with friends—I'd have to pretend to be drinking, but still—or going on a date. Maybe with Annabelle. All that stuff meant nothing before, but now I want it so damn badly. Except at the same time I don't want it, because I know I don't deserve it, and I feel guilty for getting this chance."

He looked back to Jimmy. "I dunno if I'll ever get the whole system."

"The 'system?'"

"Yeah. Punishments and rewards. Was six years in Hell enough penance or not? I'll never figure it out. But at least it's me I'm arguing with now when I try to get it all straight in my head."

"I'm glad," said Jimmy, realizing he meant it. "But be careful, because relapse is often part of recovery. It's sometimes common for trauma victims to see something that triggers flashbacks or attacks. If you have another panic attack or suddenly have trouble with your memories again or things get jumbled, don't lose hope. You've come a long way, and even sliding back a little won't beat you. Just be prepared."

Steve nodded and then looked at the clock miraculously still mounted atop the shaken desk. When Jimmy looked himself, he saw it was nearly nine p.m.

"Perfect timing," said Jimmy, standing up. "You sure you can get home okay?"

Steve, who looked exhausted, quickly widened his eyes and pasted a fake smile on his face to try and hide how tired he clearly was. "No problem!"

"Okay then," said Jimmy. "Have a good night."

Honestly, thought Jimmy as he warmed up his very late supper in his battered brown microwave, he didn't know how Steve could stand a bus ride of almost three hours. Jimmy considered himself fairly normal and yet even without Steve's issues he wasn't sure if he could endure being cramped in such a tiny space for that long, especially crowded with dozens of strangers.

He returned to the living room five minutes later, newly-warmed mac-and-cheese in one hand, and noticed the lamp Steve had shaken to the floor during his earlier psychic meltdown.

It was bent. The metal looked like someone had taken a hammer to it and beat it for an hour. Astonished, Jimmy put his dinner down and pulled the lamp close to examine it. Levitating objects was strange enough, but bending metal? A power like that would allow Steve to crush a person's skull with a stray thought.

A knock on his door interrupted Jimmy's thoughts. Staring at the lamp for one last second, too curious to put it down without a small shred of regret, Jimmy ran for the door. Steve stood on his front porch.

"Sorry," he said, looking genuinely embarrassed. A rush of freezing air and a few snowflakes came into the house with him. The wind moaned like a dying man, and Jimmy hastily ushered Steve inside and shut the door just to cut off the awful noise, wondering when it had started snowing. "But the bus is like a half-hour late. Can I use your phone to call Annabelle and see if she'll pick me up?"

"Sure," said Jimmy. "I'll call the...whatever the heck the bus operators are called nowadays and ask about the buses."

Jimmy had a sinking feeling in his gut that was immediately proven justified. The bus operator answered the phone with a "Hello" spoken in a tone that most people reserved to say "go to Hell" and informed Jimmy in a very rushed and irate voice that the number 157 bus, which served Runner Street, had crashed into a display of begonias thanks to the wind and snow (and whatever idiot had placed the flowers in the road). It would not be operating any further that evening. When she asked Jimmy if he had any other questions, her attitude made it clear that he had better not.

Hanging up his cell phone just in time to hear Steve say "Damn!" Jimmy turned and saw him slam the gray plastic of his home-phone receiver back into its cradle. Jimmy didn't know why Steve's aggression surprised him. True, Steve usually kept his head down and his voice low, but that didn't mean the anger that characterized his living history had disappeared.

"Voice message," said Steve, glowering at the phone. "She said she was going to be at the firing range today, but how long can she be there?"

"The firing range?" said Jimmy. "She has *guns*? There's an armed demon living less than a two-hour drive from me?"

"Second Amendment, Dr. Hamid," said Steve as though that closed the argument. "You get the bus people?"

"The 157 is down for the evening. Apparently it had a close encounter with a flower display."

"Shit," said Steve miserably, returning to his usual quiet speech and hunched posture. "I guess I'm walking. Do you have a map?"

"What about a cab?"

"Doctor, I don't even have the money to pay you this week. Annabelle used it getting the cell phone."

Jimmy bit his lip and pretended to look for a map in his phone book to kill time. Thinking of his mysteriously warped lamp, he wondered if it was a good idea to leave Steve wandering around in the dark for hours. Aside from the danger to Steve from muggers in the less-than-upstanding neighborhood of Renaissance Drive, the lamp suggested muggers might be in danger from Steve. If he panicked, he might even hurt innocent bystanders without meaning to.

"Listen," he said, not looking up from the phone book. "Why don't I lend you the taxi money, just this time. Pay me back when Annabelle gets paid."

"Hey, really?" said Steve, excited. Then his face fell. "No, I'd better not. Wouldn't they record my address when I gave it to them? Annabelle and I are trying to leave as little record of ourselves as possible."

"Steve, your address is already out there. You pay for water and electricity and now that new cell phone, don't you? And Annabelle had to give your address to her boss when she applied for work."

"I think she forged that one, since she started work before we got our place. Besides, that means I have to work even harder to keep our address secret from anyone else. Right now *they'd* really have to dig around to find us. But if Belial or somebody found us 'cause I was dumb enough to give our address out to some taxi dispatch, Annabelle would kill me."

To buy time (and avoid asking who the heck Belial was), Jimmy made Steve call Annabelle again and then again ten minutes later. Her voice mail came on both times.

As Steve remained adamant about avoiding taxis, Jimmy was left with three choices. He could let Steve walk home and risk his freezing to death or hurting someone. He could let Steve stay the evening on his couch and not get any sleep himself for fear of the Nazi psycho in his house. Or he could drive Steve home himself.

"Come on, Steve," he said, fishing through his desk drawer for his car keys. "I'll drive you."

Though Annabelle and Steve didn't live in the nicest suburb in Iowa, Jimmy thought their house was a sweet little place. A bit worn but sturdy and attractive, with green trim and a pretty if overgrown, lawn.

The lights were on, which annoyed Jimmy to no end. Steve had tried calling Annabelle's cell a dozen times on the way, only to keep getting that same damn voice message.

Well, Annabelle wouldn't get away with this. She might have gotten him to help Steve, but she had another thing coming if she thought she could inconvenience him this way. Besides, she was supposed to take care of Steve. Leaving him outside in a frigging snowstorm in the middle of the night was irresponsible and dangerous.

So, Jimmy pulled up to the curb, nearly ramming into the back of a battered truck because he slid so far on the wet road, which put him in an even worse temper. He slammed his door shut and stepped out into biting wind and a face full of snow. It was difficult to retain his dignity while spitting out mouthfuls of melting white slushy flakes, but he tried to look intimidating by stomping up the walkway. That plan backfired when he slipped in a patch of ice and landed on his ass.

Steve's face appeared right above his own, fighting mightily to keep from looking amused. "You okay there, Doctor?" Jimmy could barely hear him over the screaming wind.

"Shut it and help me up," said Jimmy. He smiled in spite of himself at the light in Steve's eyes, though.

The second he'd regained his footing, Annabelle came round front, brushing her hands against one another as though trying to wipe something messy from her gloves.

"There you are!" Steve cried. Jimmy turned so quickly he slipped again and wound up sprawled in Steve's arms.

Annabelle froze; Jimmy recognized the reaction of a child who'd been caught doing something naughty by her parents. She slowly, slowly turned around, gusts whipping her hair into black tendrils that blocked her eyes. At least, partially blocked them. Jimmy could still see how far they widened. But why? Was she shocked or scared?

"Hello," she said, smiling in a ridiculously bad attempt at looking casual. "Why are you—I mean what—I mean, it's great to see you, but—"

Jimmy scowled. Now he *knew* she was full of it.

"Where the heck have you been?" he asked, trying to straighten up. Steve finally grabbed him under the armpits and hauled him upright. "We've—thanks, Steve—we've been calling you for hours."

"Why?" she asked, her voice several octaves higher than normal. "The bus shouldn't have gotten you home for another half hour in this weather, Harry!"

Jimmy fought down the urge to tell her yet again to stop calling Steve "Harry." "It didn't occur to you that 'this weather' might throw the bus off? I had to drive him myself because you couldn't pick him up."

Suddenly, Annabelle got so angry Jimmy thought she might attack him. "How is it your job to drive your patients home? I didn't ask for your help, so get lost!"

"*What*? Would you rather I had him sleep over at my house, or should I have let him wander around the streets until dawn?"

The wind blew louder than ever, shrill wailing growing higher in tone until it sounded like the cry of a distressed baby. The sound so disturbed Jimmy that it scattered the thoughts in his head, leaving him stunned, shivering in place trying to absorb the noise.

Then, frowning and straining his ears, Jimmy realized that he heard a combination of noises. The wind wasn't just howling, there was really someone crying. Someone very nearby…

"Shit!" Annabelle rushed forward and grabbed Jimmy's shoulder, shaking him so that his teeth clacked together. He thought some of them might crack and fall from his head. Perhaps they would blend in with the snow, and he'd never find them again.

"Didn't you hear me?" she yelled from two inches away. "Get lost! Get your ass off my lawn! Go home!"

Head down in his usual submissive posture, Steve scooted forward until he was beside Annabelle and said, "Please! Please don't."

It was Annabelle's turn to hesitate. She loosened her grasp and turned from Steve to Jimmy, Steve to Jimmy, obviously trying to decide what to do. The wind fell quiet as she did, as though it followed her lead, and a sudden silence surrounded the small house. But then another cry rose into the still air, and another, and another, the sound of babies squalling with misery.

Steve, apparently as surprised as Jimmy, turned towards his house, where the wails came from. He said, "'Belle, is there a…a baby…in there?"

"No," said Jimmy. Rage grew inside of him, so strong that he initially didn't recognize it for what it was. Never in his life had he been so angry, not even at his father. "There's a lot of babies in there."

Then he shoved Annabelle, the first violent act of his life. He shoved her to the ground and enjoyed it when she impacted against the pavement and grunted with pain. Running past her to the front door, he found it unlocked and threw it open so hard it banged against the inside wall and left a dent. The kitchen/dining room area he stepped into had both a counter and a small table. Baby carriers of all colors and styles covered them both, each holding an infant. There were six in all—or six that he could see. God only knew what Annabelle had put in the other rooms in the house.

"What the hell is THIS?" Jimmy roared, voice growing louder with each emphasized word. He turned to find Annabelle trying to extricate herself from a snow drift, her face bright red with anger. Wind blew again, thwarting her first attempts to stand up.

"None of your damn business is what it is!" she yelled back.

Steve just gaped at her, too shocked to be afraid yet. Jimmy and Annabelle both ignored him.

"Oh, don't you dare try to shovel me that. Unless these babies are all yours, which they're not, I want to know exactly where they came from. Now!"

"How dare you give me orders! You useless little piss-ant!" Annabelle yanked her arm out of the snow, slid slightly, then stomped up to Jimmy and stuck one wet finger into his chest. "You've no idea of the trouble I'm in and have no right to judge. And I hope you know I won't hesitate to kill you if you put me or Harry in danger."

"He's not Harry!" Jimmy yelled, spittle flying from his mouth and splattering against Annabelle's face. "His name is Steve Silver, and your pathetic need to keep him dependent on you won't ever make him be 'Harry!' And kill me? Well, I guess that answers the question from the first night you broke into my home: *this* is the kind of lady you are."

Annabelle's jaw ground against the roof of her mouth. Jimmy knew she was going to attack him and that he should be terrified. But his anger burned like a gas fire, uncontainable and too strong to allow fear.

She whipped out one hand and wrapped her fingers around Jimmy's neck, lifting him off the ground and choking him. The world turned strange colors and spun before Jimmy's bulging eyes. The babies' cries became a morbid soundtrack to the insane visual tableau, an audio expression of Jimmy's agony and confusion.

Then something hit him in his middle and he crashed to the ground, a pair of arms cradling and protecting his head from impact. Jimmy inhaled Steve's jacket and smothered for the few seconds it took Steve to realize what was happening and free Jimmy's nose and mouth, though he didn't get up.

"Harry, damn it! Get out of the way!" Annabelle roared.

Steve's forehead rested against the ground next to the back of Jimmy's skull, and so his breath blew into Jimmy's ear. Even now, curiosity sent questions spinning through the back of Jimmy's mind. Did Steve need to breathe? Did he do it now from habit, knowing a regular human body would hyperventilate with fear? What was his breath made of?

"Annabelle, please!" Steve begged, keeping his eyes on the ground and his body above Jimmy's own. "Please!"

"Shit!" Annabelle stomped her foot into the floor in a show of impotent rage, and her boot went right through the tile. The babies screamed in distress and cold as snow blew in from the doorway. Steve squeezed his eyes shut, waiting for the bomb to fall, and tightened his arms around Jimmy. Jimmy, too busy trying to catch his breath to say anything, grabbed Steve's shoulders just to have something to hang onto. Shock from Steve's tackle had scattered his fury, now replaced by fear. Jimmy could barely keep from passing out as he waited.

"Shit," said Annabelle again, but this time she sounded tired. She pulled her foot from the floor and rubbed the sides of her head, collapsing into one of her kitchen chairs. "Harry, help the idiot up and get him a chair. I'll explain, Jimmy, and then we'll see what we're going to do."

Chapter

11

Ten minutes later Jimmy sat at Annabelle's kitchen table, rocking the only baby who refused to calm down on his own. He was a fidgety kid with huge, brown eyes squashed shut in discomfort and a mouth that looked big enough to swallow Jimmy whole. How the heck did such a tiny thing wind up with such a huge mouth and voice? Even Jimmy's sister, in the worst of her tirades, couldn't match this baby.

But finally, even this last stubborn wailer began settling down in Jimmy's arms. He grinned stupidly down at the kid, with feelings much too soppy to say aloud (or even admit to thinking) filling his chest. His mother had harassed him about getting married and giving her a grandchild from the moment he'd graduated college. When holding one that didn't shriek, he could see the appeal.

"Sure, wait until you try to change a diaper or your brat turns two and starts telling you it hates your guts." Annabelle plunked a glass of water down on the table hard enough that a few of the babies stirred. Jimmy tensed, waiting for the crying to begin again, but after a second they all quieted.

"That's all we've got," said Annabelle, returning to her seat. "Neither of us eats or drinks."

"I know," said Jimmy before taking a sip. All the yelling he'd done, to say nothing of the choking he'd received, had left his throat raw.

While his pride was grateful to the wind for concealing his screaming outrage from nearby neighbors, he half-wished they'd heard. Some of them might have called the police, who would have been useful since Jimmy had no hope of convincing Annabelle to let the babies go peacefully.

"Okay," said Annabelle, all business as she leaned towards him. Steve sunk into a shadow in one corner, obscured by darkness except for the blue glow of his eyes. It felt like being watched by a cat, Jimmy thought, distracting and a little creepy. He had to pull his attention back to Annabelle. "So, about a month ago, around when you and Harry had your fight over his past, my position—that is, my physical position, in this house—was discovered."

The baby in Jimmy's arms squirmed, so he rocked it gently for a few seconds before putting it back into its carrier. "By another...another demon?" Saying that word still made him feel silly.

"No, by Satanists. Not the fakes Anton LeVay gathered into his 'Church of Satan,' but real Satanists, the ones in contact with demons, who can curse people and make living things rot. All jockeying for their place in Hell's hierarchy, like any of the kings are going to give up their thrones to humans—"

"So this Satanist found you," said Jimmy before Annabelle could go off onto a tangent. He did not want to know any more about demons or Satanists than he had to. "And then?"

Annabelle scowled at him for interrupting her but returned to the topic after a second. "The little worm tried to get me to sleep with him."

"Why?" asked Jimmy.

Annabelle looked astonished. She burst out laughing and covered her mouth so the sound wouldn't wake the babies. "You are the first man who has ever seen me in person and then asked why someone would want to sleep with me."

"I've been trained to know that in a situation like this, a man who would try and use blackmail to force a woman into sex probably has power and control issues. A serial rapist, for example."

"That wouldn't surprise me," said Annabelle, "but in this case, his motives were political. Satanists want power, like all you humans, but more experienced ones know most demons won't just give them an honored place in Lucifer's court. The best way to ascend in the hierarchy is to have someone powerful on your side. Like a half-demon."

Jimmy's eyes widened. He looked to the six babies resting in their plastic carriers on the table and chairs, innocent of the fate Annabelle had planned for them. "He wants children to use like bargaining chips for power?" he asked, feeling like something slimy crawled up his throat and escaped through his mouth.

"A child from me would be an honor for any man or demon," said Annabelle, as though stating the sky was blue. "I'm a succubus, guaranteed to get pregnant any time I have sex; I don't have any non-fertile days and a twenty-four hour gestation period, so it's quick and easy to get a baby from me. I'm from a royal line, so my children are born with connections and advantages. And because half-demons are half-human, they can move through Hell and Earth easily, interacting with both worlds. That's exceedingly rare and prized. Most demons, except for succubi and incubi, have to use a portal to travel, plus a lot of power just to survive the trip, so you can see why creatures that move between the two as easily as you'd walk down the street would be valuable. I think there are maybe a dozen half-demons in the whole world, by which I mean your world *and* mine, who are of any use to Hell."

"Why so few?"

"They die," said Annabelle. "They age and die like humans—well, slower, but they're not immortal. And though their gifts are rare and valuable, their bodies are also more fragile than most demons."

"Easy to kill," said Jimmy, and Annabelle nodded.

"If you want to get technical, there are, oh, maybe a couple thousand humans with small strains of demon blood in them, but that doesn't mean as much. Their ties to Hell are weak, so we can't use them. Usually they go through their whole lives not knowing. It's at half-blood or more that they become useful."

Jimmy, disturbed by his own fascination, again had to force himself back into the conversation. Outrage made it easier to do. "So let me get this straight. This bastard wanted children, and you...just planned to give them to him?"

"Of course," said Annabelle, surprised by his surprise. "I give him kids; he lets me and Harry go. Simple."

"First of all, you said he wanted half-demon children. Second of all, everything else that's wrong with what you just said!" Jimmy's arms began waving through the air of their own volition, trying to express the frustration that no words were enough to get across.

In his corner, Steve stirred. The raised voices made him nervous.

Annabelle, not noticing his discomfort, grinned proudly. "Well, that idiot doesn't have to know these aren't demon children, does he? Half-demons don't usually show any signs of what they are till at least six or seven years old, and by then Harry and I will be long gone. Besides, I've kidnapped these kids from local mothers. With luck, the police will track them down, and Douggie will spend a lot of time in jail. He won't be able to track us or tell on us then. How would he explain keeping Harry and me a secret for so long?"

The smug look on Annabelle's face made Jimmy so angry he had to shut his eyes to block it out before he exploded in chunks of righteous Afghan flame.

"You're telling me," he said, eyes still shut, "that you kidnapped six babies from their mothers and planned to turn them over to this 'Douggie,' a baby-loving, blackmailing Satanist who might kill them?"

Annabelle heard the anger in Jimmy's voice, but it only served to irritate her. "Look, they're just babies. They've no personalities yet, no memories, no formed *brains*, even. And human mothers pop them out by the billions in this day and age. What's the big loss?"

"What's the big—" Again Jimmy had to cut himself off when he heard how loud his voice rose. "Aside from the trauma to their parents?"

Waving this idea away like a bad smell, Annabelle said, "I'm sure they'll mourn. So? They can always pop out another one if they want it, or adopt. It's hardly the end of their lives."

"You don't know that," Jimmy snarled, gripping the edge of his chair until the plastic creaked. "You make it sound like losing your car keys, but the suffering would be—! I know plenty of parents whose lives would be over, losing their children!" Jimmy hated how weak his arguments sounded. He knew he was right. It frustrated him to see Annabelle looking so much more composed and rational, to say nothing of smug, when her words were so vile.

"Then they'll die." Annabelle shrugged. "There's seven billion more of you to take their place. In a generation or two, no one will remember they ever lived."

Jimmy wanted to either scream or smash his fist through a window. "You don't just use children like things, damn it!"

It was one of the first truly surreal moments Jimmy had ever experienced (all of which had happened since meeting Annabelle). He stood in a run-down house with peeling purple wallpaper and flickering lights with exposed wires, facing down a succubus from Hell who could crush his bones into powder without the slightest exertion, trying to explain why it was bad to kidnap babies while a psychotic soul that started at loud noises hovered in the background. Jimmy just knew a dozen kangaroos were going to bound across the room in a minute.

"You humans do it all the damn time. You did it in this country up until recently: slavery, indentured servitude, arranged marriage without the consent of the children."

"Okay. Here, in modern-day America, you do not use children as bargaining chips. These babies are going back to their mothers now. *Right* now. Or I swear to everything I hold dear I will report you to cops and Satanists and the devil himself if he'll listen!"

Jimmy kept his voice a low hiss, but some of the babies started squirming uncomfortably anyway. Steve had almost folded himself into the corner.

"Idiot," snapped Annabelle contemptuously. "Douglas is going to be here any minute, don't you get it? I had everything set up. I finally found a night like this, with Harry away and weather that covered my actions, and then you had to bring him home early. I have to fork over the babies now or I'm in deep shit, to say nothing of the trouble Harry's in. Believe me, if you try to take us down that way, I *will* bring you with me."

"Don't you threaten me. You've proven very conclusively that you can't be allowed on this planet." Jimmy rose from his seat, too wound up to stay seated. "If my dead body is found on your floor, you're finished anyway. And believe me, if you don't turn those babies over to me with their names and addresses, right this goddamn second, your only choices will be to go down alone or bring me with you."

Sweat popping out on his brow, Jimmy tried to stare Annabelle down, tried not to think of how she could take his head off with a flick of her wrist. No luck. She read his thoughts and smiled, standing slowly and cracking her knuckles, playing on Jimmy's fear.

Jimmy tried to swallow and couldn't; his throat had gone dry. He waited for the deathblow to fall.

Instead, a knock shook the front door.

Annabelle spun away from Jimmy with a muffled curse.

"I'm guessing that's Douggie, then," said Jimmy. He heard himself speaking as if from very far away.

Annabelle grabbed two hunks of her hair and pulled, looking completely mad. She swore in a string of words that Jimmy figured would make him blush if he knew what language they were in. "If I kill you, I bring the law on me, since they know this is my house—to say nothing of the Wrath of Harry." In the corner, Steve shrank further under her fiery glare. "If I kill Doug, I'll bring Hell on me. If I hand over the babies, you'll turn me in to the law *and* Lucifer. Well you tell me, you meddling prick! Just what do I do?"

"You escape," said a female voice from just over Jimmy's shoulder. It was his turn to spin around. A stunning blonde leaned against the entrance from the kitchen to the hallway, a shit-eating grin plastered across her red lips as though she thoroughly enjoyed the chaos. "With the stylish SUV I've got waiting in the street behind the next yard."

Jimmy didn't recognize her, but judging by the shocked look on Steve's face, he did.

The way Annabelle cried, "Sam!" suggested she knew the blonde too.

Annabelle hadn't seen or felt Samantha teleport into the living room and grew instantly wary upon catching sight of her. She closed her mind to Sam's possible telepathic invasion and reached up to the shoulder holster she'd nestled the silver gun in, hidden under her baggy blue jacket. Even a demon would die if you splattered her brains against a wall.

"Who are you?" Jimmy asked, glaring at Samantha in that suspicious way he had, where with one stare he stripped a girl naked and made her feel like a lowly, inferior bit of scum. Did he even know how his self-righteous, holier-than-thou attitude hurt?

Of course, Samantha barely seemed to notice. She looked decadent as usual, wrapped in a snow-white rabbit-fur coat with a slinky red dress and diamond jewelry underneath. Annabelle could almost see Jimmy's dislike bouncing ineffectively off her.

"You may call me Samantha, darling. Sam, if you can keep the half-dozen little spawn on the table and chairs quiet. Now hurry up, we have an exciting escape to perpetrate."

"Hang on," said Annabelle when Sam straightened up and pulled diamond-encrusted sunglasses off with a flourish. "Sam...you're here!"

Harry had run to Annabelle's side and now shivered behind her, staring wide-eyed at Samantha and clearly trying not to panic. He jumped when Douglas knocked on the door again and yelled Annabelle's name.

"Oh my, am I? Well, let me just check." Samantha made a show of staring down at herself. "Yes, I do indeed appear to be here. But I won't be in a moment, and if you want to live, you probably want to come with." Throwing Annabelle a smile that had caused heart attacks on a dozen continents, Samantha twirled in a whirl of blonde hair and floral scent, moving to the back door.

She was stopped by Jimmy, a baby carrier in his arms.

"We're not leaving the babies," he said when Samantha blinked questioningly at him. She turned back to Annabelle, astonished.

"Is he serious?"

"Are you women succubi or not?" Jimmy snapped. "You're supposed to be mothers."

"Just because you shove the little discharges out doesn't mean you have to like them," said Samantha. "If you want the kids, you can carry them."

A loud series of thuds made the front door shake. "Don't think you can avoid us!" Douglas yelled. "You can't insult us like this! We're ready to tell the kings everything if you don't open this door!"

The thought of Lucifer appearing before her, crackling with anger and power, made a shiver run down Annabelle's whole body. "Shit. We have to get out of here." She grabbed two baby carriers, one in each hand, and rushed for the back door. Looking disgusted, Samantha picked up another as she would a dirty diaper, sniffed at Jimmy, and stalked after her, high heels clicking on the tile. Jimmy took a second carrier, and Harry took the last one in his shaking arms. His eyes were wide and red.

Leaping into the backyard, Annabelle slammed directly into the Satanist waiting for her. The impact forced him back a step, so he windmilled his arms to try and stay upright, kicking snow against the house. Crying out, Annabelle tried to focus through conflicting urges, all running through her brain at once and making her freeze with confusion: *grab your gun, don't drop the baby carriers, run, shut this guy up* —

The Satanist reached under his jacket and pulled out a gun. He swung it up and clicked off the safety.

Samantha ran by Annabelle in a blur of red and white, baby carrier in her left arm, right hand reaching out with the fingers curled into a claw. The Satanist opened his mouth to scream, to alert Douglas and whoever else waited in the front yard, but Samantha's hand wrapped around his throat before he could. A terrible snap filled the air and bloody bubbles spurted from his lips as he fell lifeless to the ground. The gun landed beside him like a dead animal, buried in weeds and snow.

"Oh my God!" Jimmy cried from the doorway. Harry shushed him through chattering teeth.

"What was that?" Annabelle heard someone say from the front door.

"Move it or lose it, Jimmy." She ran for the fence.

A single superhuman bound put Annabelle in the next-door neighbor's yard with two newly wakened, crying babies in her arms. Samantha landed beside her milliseconds later, and strained groans heralded Harry and Jimmy's attempts to clamor over the fence behind them.

Annabelle didn't know how they all made it through the neighbor's yard and onto the next street. Had she put the babies in her arms in the back seats of the black SUV Samantha motioned towards, then run back to help Harry and Jimmy across the fence? Had Samantha done it for her? She couldn't remember. Her blood roaring through her veins overwhelmed her senses and memory, driving her to further heights of panic with each second. They had to leave before the Satanists saw them, had to get away, get to safety, run run *run*!

Jimmy came last, sliding into shotgun with one of the baby carriers on his lap. Samantha threw the SUV into gear and was skidding down the road before he even shut the door, the oversized wheels shrieking as they tried to gain traction on the wet road. Then, to Annabelle's astonishment, she turned right, crossing Renaissance Drive and speeding past Douglas and three men he'd brought to collect his prizes.

"No!" Annabelle cried, too late; they'd seen Jimmy in the front seat and Harry in the back. She didn't know if the Satanists got a clear look, but if they recognized the two men and reported their identities to Lucifer or one of the kings, "disaster" would be the mildest word to describe the result.

Annabelle tried to think of solutions, and again the thought of calling her mother came to the front of her brain.

No! Annabelle squeezed her eyes shut and pressed the heels of her hands into them until sparks erased her mother's image. Calling *her* would mean consequences more severe than the lives of a few human babies.

She opened her eyes and watched Douglas and the others shrink with distance, becoming little dots in the rear window and then vanishing, out of range for Annabelle to check their thoughts. Annabelle sat slowly back in her seat, staring at the back of Sam's head and wishing she could read her friend's mind. Was it coincidence that Samantha chose to go right, or had she meant to show Harry and Jimmy to Douglas and his men?

"I tell you, darling, you wouldn't believe the uproar caused by your absence!" Samantha made a hard right onto the highway, making the SUV skid on two wheels before landing with a thump. The babies were inconsolable at this point, but she barely seemed to notice. "My word, but King Belial is furious. He swears he was tricked by you into transporting something illegally to Earth and has all sorts of ideas for how to punish you if he gets his hands on you again."

"Wait," said Annabelle through numb lips. "You mean they know I ran away?"

"Yes indeed. Queen Avaira 'accidentally' let slip it was you. Trade and diplomacy is at a standstill with every king accusing every other king of greasing the wheels to help one of Hell's few remaining succubi escape. I swear, every last conspiracy nut from the imps on up are sure your absence is a plot to tip the balance of Hell's leadership in somebody's direction. Exactly who, no one is sure, but everyone has a theory. My favorite is you running off with the illegitimate child of Choronzon in your womb." Samantha giggled.

"And the missing soul is a huge scandal." Samantha gestured vaguely towards Harry without looking at him. "Humans simply don't escape from Hell. This young man's disappearing act seems to have injured the pride of every demon from Emperor Lucifer to his slaves. They're all taking it personally. Oh, you should see them scream about how Hell is going to the dogs and there's no order or discipline anymore. They sound like old grannies unable to accept that their granddaughters have modern ideas about marriage. No one knows which human escaped with you, though, since more than a few souls have taken the chaos as an opportunity to hide. As far as anyone knows, a bunch of souls have just slipped through the cracks."

"Right, until you drove past Doug and his toadies. You gave them a look at these two!" Annabelle snapped.

"Did I? Oh well, darling, I make mistakes like anyone else."

Again Samantha jerked at the wheel, this time cutting off a huge truck with SAMSON'S DOUGHNUTS painted along its side. The truck beeped loud and long, and Sam cheerfully flipped the driver the bird before hitting the gas and leaving him far behind. Harry had to keep catching baby carriers as they rocked precariously in the back seat.

"We have to secure these things," said Jimmy.

"No one's stopping you," said Sam, pushing the gas pedal down even further. "By all means, go ahead. Myself, I need music." With a flick of her fingers she turned the radio on. It spit forth a rousing polka tune.

"Perfect!" said Samantha, turning the volume as high up as it would go.

Jimmy began to pray, occasionally interrupting himself with a mumbled, "This is so, so surreal. This is *so* surreal…"

A singer on the radio began to yodel just as Samantha took an exit so abruptly she nearly slammed into the concrete barrier between lanes.

"I love this car," she said fondly, patting the steering wheel. She drove full-tilt into a speed bump and the SUV flew three feet into the air before crashing down again.

"Sam!" Annabelle cried. She felt like every bone in her body had just been rearranged. In the front seat, Jimmy frantically tried to calm the baby in his lap. "Will you be—hey, did you cut your hair?"

"Why yes I did," said Samantha, throwing a smirk over her shoulder and nearly driving onto a lawn before turning back to the road. The squealing tires nearly drowned her words out. "I find it easier to have sex with an eight-legged man when I have hair only as low as my ass."

"Oh my," said Annabelle, trying to lean back and raise an eyebrow, though she wound up smooshed against the window instead when Samantha made a sharp left. "So—oof!—I take it I'm looking at the new Mrs. Bael?"

"The new *Queen* Bael," said Samantha, and though she didn't turn around again, Annabelle knew her smirk had widened. "I expect you to call me Your Highness from now on."

Annabelle snorted aloud, not at all surprised. Samantha had hit it off with Bael from the beginning, giving him just the right compliment when they'd met: "Why, Your Highness! I heard you had the legs of a spider, but never did I imagine they would be so wonderfully hairy and slender!"

Bael had puffed with pride, his cat head purring in pleasure. Stretching one dirty-rag gray leg out to Samantha and waggling the eyebrows on his human head like a dirty old man propositioning a teenage girl, he'd said, "Servants brush them every night. Want to feel?"

"Wait," said Jimmy suddenly. "You—Sam?—you say you cut your hair to the length of your, uh, rear?"

Samantha laughed. "This one's just adorable, 'Belle. Yes, sweetie, I did indeed, just a couple weeks ago."

"But your hair is only to your shoulders," Jimmy said. He squinted, leaning as close to Samantha as possible while rocking the baby carrier in his lap.

"Yes," Samantha agreed.

"So, what, you…cut it again?"

"No," said Samantha, and now she looked confused. "Why would I?"

"It's how they are, Dr. Hamid," said Harry quietly, his body as low in his seat as the laws of physics allowed. "Succubi and incubi, I mean. They're what you desire most. If you think shoulder-length hair is sexy, they'll have shoulder-length hair for you."

"So it's an illusion?" Now Jimmy looked nervous. He backed up and pressed himself against the SUV door.

"No," said Annabelle, "you don't understand. For you, she *has* shoulder-length hair. And C-cup breasts, and a height of 5'6 and a half, perfect for pulling against your own height."

"So she's not really five-foot-six? That's illusion, like I said."

"No!" said Annabelle impatiently. "Moron. You're so limited, all of you humans. In your tiny brains, you assume that because something is one way for you, what you see must be the only possible reality. Sam really has the form you see, just as she has another form for Bael, and another for Douglas back there, and one for herself. Each one is as real as the others."

"That's not possible," said Jimmy. "A person can't be two different things at once."

Samantha burst out laughing again, sandpaper against Annabelle's frayed nerves. The narrow human viewpoint was not as cute as Samantha thought. In another few millennia she would probably get as sick of it as Annabelle had.

"That's the problem with your whole ridiculous species," Annabelle grumbled. "There's so much outside your knowledge that you refuse to even acknowledge, let alone try to understand. You're so *small*."

"Yeah, I'd much rather be a soulless abomination like you," Jimmy snapped.

"Now that's not polite," said Samantha. The SUV closed in on downtown Des Moines with nausea-inducing speed, where traffic grew thicker by the second. Samantha began weaving between the lanes without ever using the brake, causing one vehicle after another to screech to a halt to avoid collision. "You'd better be nice to my friend, or I might change my mind about saving you."

"Right," said Jimmy, turning to glare out his window. "I might as well. My life is so messed up at this point there's not much lower I can go."

"Don't say that," said Harry, voice still quiet but now also earnest. "Trust me, there's always a lower place for you to be."

Chapter

12

"This is it?" Annabelle gaped at the Motel Four Samantha had just checked her, Jimmy, and Harry into. "This is the best you could afford, *Your Highness*?"

"No," said Samantha, self-satisfied look firmly in place. "I just wasn't willing to spend any more money on you."

The lobby was carpeted in a threadbare brown rug so thin and filthy that black and gray spots decorated whole sections and large holes threatened Samantha's high heels. The skeletal, yellowing old lady behind the counter glared at them, popping gum that she regularly, from the look of it, stuck under the desk or ground into the rug. Wind from the snowstorm outside blew in through a broken window someone had (poorly) taped over with plywood and duct tape, and the smell of rotting *something* diffused its way through the air. Annabelle grabbed her room key from Samantha and hurried outside before her clothes could absorb the odor. Fast-food grease stank badly enough.

In the parking lot, Harry and Jimmy sat shivering in the SUV, even through their jackets with the heat blasting. Annabelle opened Harry's door and handed him their key. "We're all in a room together. I don't think it's a good idea to be alone tonight, and Sam's too cheap for more anyway."

"Not with all these babies we're not," said Jimmy. "We have to get them back to their mothers. It's a miracle they survived everything that's happened so far, and even so, they should be taken to doctors to make sure they weren't shaken too hard."

"I agree, believe it or not," said Annabelle. She didn't care what happened to the babies, but her plan had been to frame Douglas for the kidnappings. Now if the police tracked the babies down, they might find her instead. Best to get rid of them, and doing it nicely would keep Jimmy from summoning up Choronzon or some other foul thing to eat her in revenge. "Sam, I need you to take these babies to their homes."

"That's funny," said Samantha.

"I take it appealing to her sense of loyalty wouldn't help," Jimmy said. A gust of wind made him shiver and draw back into the car. Harry continued hovering like a wide-eyed shadow in the back seat.

"All right," sighed Annabelle, as though about to make a great sacrifice. "Do this, and I've got a present for you." She gestured towards the diamond necklace hanging around Samantha's slender neck.

Samantha scoffed. "I'm royalty, sweetheart. I don't even have to buy jewelry anymore. CEOs and designers give me anything I want just so the rest of Hell will see me wearing it."

"Sure," said Annabelle. "But can they give you the custom made, one-of-a-kind jade and silver necklace made for me by Emperor Lǔ Wáng back in the 1650s? You know, the one you've been drooling over ever since you saw it fifty years ago and have tried to steal from me six times?"

Samantha's eyebrows rose behind her sunglasses, a sign she was thinking.

"You'd give me that necklace," she said flatly.

"What's wrong," said Annabelle, "don't you trust me?" She grinned cheekily and enjoyed the irritated glare Samantha shot her in response.

"Give me the necklace and I'll take the kids back."

"Not a chance. I'll give you the addresses, call the mothers tomorrow morning to make sure their children are back home, and then you can have it.

"Oh come on, Sam!" she continued when her friend looked unconvinced. "You can't think I'm dumb enough to stiff you. You're the only person left in Hell who's even remotely on my side. If you're hunting me too I'm screwed and we both know it. I need your help."

Samantha reacted just as Annabelle knew she would, lifting her chin and looking pleased by Annabelle's embarrassment. Yet her keen eyes continued scanning Annabelle's face and posture, looking for any sign of duplicity. Annabelle hoped she looked convincingly desperate.

"Well, what the heck," said Samantha. "If you back out on me, I'll just take the necklace anyway after you're caught and sent to Farfarello's pits."

A chill ran through Annabelle. She didn't try to hide it. The weakness would please Samantha, and she needed to keep Samantha happy.

An hour later Jimmy waited with Steve in the room of the new motel Annabelle had found them while she got Jimmy dinner from McDonalds.

"What's wrong with the place Sam got?" Jimmy had asked when Annabelle insisted they change locations. "Aside from the obvious, I mean."

"Are you very stupid or just trying to annoy me? You heard Sam talking. Please don't tell me you trust her to keep this location secret after all you heard. Hell, she might have pretended to save us just to lure us to that room."

So now Steve and Jimmy sat on a couple of ratty beds in a fourth-floor room just as crummy as the Motel Four room Sam had reserved for them. Jimmy's lamp flickered, engorging the shadow of a spider in the corner until it looked like a great dark beast hovered over the two men, waiting for them to fall asleep so it could break its fast.

The walls were bare, depressingly so in Jimmy's opinion. The longer he stared at them, the lonelier he felt. His imagination launched scenes onto the stretches of white wall like a projector onto a movie screen. He saw his mother and father praying, eating dinner at their faux-wood dining room table, watching a movie together as they did every Tuesday night. Crow's feet around his mother's eyes would deepen each time she smiled, while his father could grin widely enough to light up whole rooms.

And oh, his sister! Jimmy saw her studying in her room, hunched over her cluttered desk and reading a textbook with print so tiny it would have given Jimmy a headache just to look at it. She was so busy, always studying, and grew so annoyed if anyone interrupted her. But if Jimmy needed her, he knew she'd put the book aside.

"I think I'd better call my family," Jimmy said aloud. For some reason, saying the words scared him. By speaking, he felt obligated to follow through on his word.

His only hope was Steve talking him out of it. After all, the phone might be tapped. It was dangerous to both Jimmy and his family to call. Unfortunately Steve only nodded and said, "I understand. If I had any family alive, I'd want to call them too."

Now feeling guilty for dragging up more of Steve's painful memories, Jimmy pulled out his cell and dialed his sister's number. As usual, she would be essential in smoothing out relations between him and his parents. But to his astonishment, his mother, not his sister, picked up.

The wisest thing would have been to hang up, but Jimmy had never been very good at thinking on his feet. "Mom?" He blurted. "Why do you have Aaqila's phone?"

"Karim?" his mother's voice grew very wobbly...and then very loud. *"Oh, Karim!"*

Across the room, Steve jumped and gaped at the amazing volume of noise now coming from the phone. Jimmy shrugged helplessly at him. "Mom, it's okay—"

"It's been months since you called and we haven't heard a word! Your sister refuses to tell me a thing and I've left a dozen messages on your phone! I didn't even know you'd moved until Aaqila told me!"

"Why's she yelling like that?" Steve whispered.

"Because she's a mother," Jimmy whispered back just as his mother demanded to know if he was eating properly.

"Karim?" Jimmy heard his father's deeper, commanding voice in the background, laced with excitement. His guts began to squirm within him like a nest of live snakes. "Is that Karim? I heard you say Karim!"

"It's..." his mother hesitated, torn.

"Mom, no, please," Jimmy whispered. He collapsed back onto the bed, squeezing his eyes shut to try and block dizziness out. He was five years old again, helpless as waves of shame and fear drowned him. "Please!"

"It's not our Karim," said his mother. Jimmy could almost see the way she lowered her eyes, letting her long black hair hide her face so her husband wouldn't read her expression. "It's Karim from back in Santa Fe. Our old neighbor who always wore the Hawaiian shirts, remember? He has a question about...about what to get his wife for her next birthday."

"Ah." Disappointment replaced excitement in his father's voice. "Well, tell him hello."

"I will." Then, more quietly, "you have to talk to him sometime."

"I know," said Jimmy, though he didn't mean it. "Really, I just called to tell you I'm, um, going on a trip."

"Really? You haven't gone on a real vacation since high school, I think."

"Well, it's not really a vacation," said Jimmy. "It's more like a retreat for recently graduated psychologists, like me. You know, getting advice from our elders, making connections in case we need help later on down the line."

"You'll have someone watching over you way out there, then?" said his mother, a gentle, roundabout rebuke for how far away Jimmy lived, though she didn't know his exact location.

"I hope so," said Jimmy. "I'll be back in a week or so, but until then I'll be totally out of touch. My cell phone, too."

His mother tastefully avoided the obvious comment that Jimmy wasn't in touch even *with* his cell phone.

"Karim, you know, your father and I miss you. I accept that you have your own life and your own reasons for moving. But we'd like to see you sometimes."

There it was, the familiar guilt that had invaded every corner of Jimmy's childhood, seeking out every last trace of adult confidence and squelching it. Even now, it was so much a part of him that a simple, tactful statement like his mother's filled him with embarrassment and anger.

So he said the shortest phrase he could think of—"I know"—to keep his mother from hearing the catch in his throat. He swallowed and, in a steadier voice, went on before she could reply. "I miss you too. I gotta go."

"All right," she said, before quickly adding, "I love you," like she expected him to argue or cut her off.

Jimmy sucked in a breath, amazed at the tears behind his eyelids and the still-growing lump in his throat. Concentrating didn't make them go away, this time.

"Bye," he said and fumbled for the power button.

Bending over and putting his head between his knees, Jimmy gasped in air like a drowning man. Everything was wrong, the world was wrong, and he'd gotten lost in this terrible, constricting space where nothing was as it should be.

When a hand landed on his shoulder Jimmy's eyes flew open. He sat up too abruptly, knocking Steve's hand away. "I don't want to talk about it!"

"Okay," said Steve, his voice entirely too understanding.

"I mean it. There's nothing to say."

"All right, if that's what you—"

"And anyway," Jimmy snapped, "I have a right to be out here. I'm not the bad guy for refusing to let my dad's criticism derail my dreams."

Steve frowned, moving back to give Jimmy his space and sitting back down on his own bed.

"What?" said Jimmy.

"It's just…I mean, you're right, you're not the bad guy. But that sounds like a stock answer. Like you read it from a textbook or motivational speech."

"Yeah, well," said Jimmy. "Maybe if I say it to myself enough times I'll believe it eventually." He collapsed backward onto the bed again.

Steve let Jimmy stew in his silence, allowing him to calm down in his own way. Jimmy tried to clear his head of stress and concentrate on the "now": the coarse comforter beneath him, the cracks on the ceiling above, the vague thread of hip-hop music that crept in under the window from the parking lot below.

"So," said Jimmy once he thought himself calm enough to speak rationally. "Is there a God?"

Jimmy could almost hear Steve jerk in surprise. The question must have seemed random to him, though to Jimmy, it made perfect sense. In his head, his father and God were inextricably linked.

"I don't know," Steve said.

"What?" said Jimmy, sitting up so fast he grew dizzy. "But weren't you in Hell?"

"Well yeah, but it's not like I passed in front of any pearly gates first." Steve sat on the bed with his knees pulled up to his chest, looking more like a child than a grown man. "I died, and then I woke up roasting over a spit. And that was my reality until Annabelle found me and saved my life. My soul. Whatever. The point is, I didn't get any special knowledge just 'cause I died. All I can tell you is that Hell is a very real place and demons are as nasty as the Bible says."

"Hmph." Jimmy leaned back on his elbows and stared up at the ceiling again.

"Well, why does it matter so much?" asked Steve.

"Are you kidding? That's the ultimate question! Does God exist, why does He run the world the way He does, why do we suffer..."

"That's just the thing," said Steve. "If you knew for sure that God existed, what would you want to ask?"

That one was easy to answer; Jimmy had been thinking of questions like that since his childhood, even after he'd learned to stop asking them aloud because they made his father so angry. "Why the world's holy books all contradict each other. Did He mean to teach us through metaphor or by setting us up for a fight? Why did He create us all to need different things if He wanted us to follow the same path? Why did He make humans so prone to violence and misunderstanding and negativity?" Jimmy paused to wrack his brains. "And there's the usual. You know, why do good people suffer; why do we die; why are we here?"

Steve laughed, and then shook his head in apology when Jimmy glared at him. "It's just funny to hear questions as big as that asked like you'd ask someone to tell you the time. Anyway, though. So, if I told you there was a God, what would you do?"

A much more difficult question. Even if Steve had known there was a God, he probably wouldn't know how to contact Him. Jimmy would have to find God himself if he wanted to ask questions.

But would a search like that, one that would probably produce no results given how few supernatural beings lived on Earth according to Annabelle, a search that would take all of Jimmy's life, be worth the effort? To

Jimmy, a life lived without helping others wasn't worth living. If he gave up the work he'd been doing to bury himself in prayer and searching, that would take away from his life, not add to it.

"I guess my lifestyle wouldn't change," Jimmy said. "But still, knowing something like that changes things inside a person."

"You're saying you wouldn't be the same person if you knew for sure God existed?"

"Shoot, I don't know." Jimmy huffed.

"Well, what if I told you there's no God, then. Would that change your lifestyle?

"No," said Jimmy. "I've been working off that assumption for years, really. If there's no God, we as human beings have to help each other out, since we're all we've got."

"So if there is a God, you'll keep the life you have now, and if there's not a God, you'll keep the life you have now."

Jimmy blinked. "When you say it like that, it all sounds pretty simple."

"Maybe it is," said Steve.

Outside, the music grew louder and more insistent, refusing to be ignored.

Annabelle returned with McDonald's for Jimmy and a change of clothing for both men soon after. Jimmy opened the greasy plastic bag with distaste and wrinkled his nose at the smell.

"Why isn't there a receipt?"

"Don't start," said Annabelle. "I couldn't risk being seen, but I left money to cover everything just so you wouldn't bitch at me."

Steve looked at Annabelle and then back to Jimmy. He raised an eyebrow, reminding Jimmy that if he had questions to ask, he'd better ask them now. They might not have another patch of downtime for a while…if they ever did again.

Jimmy just unwrapped his cheeseburger and took a bite. His questions about God pressed at him like always, but he'd returned to being unsure if he wanted the answers after all.

The reality of Jimmy's dream amazed him. Though he somehow knew he was dreaming, he could feel the rough texture of the withered flowers adorning dozens of tables and shelves under the pads of his fingers, the carved detailing on the floor tiles with his feet. Windows showed him a fire blazing too brightly to see anything beyond it outside, yet the flames did not find their way inside to burn, or even warm, him. He shivered with cold in the luxurious dungeon of stone and tile that made the flesh of his naked body ripple with discomfort. Gloom oozed through the room with the cold, so that Jimmy could barely see his hand a foot in front of his face despite the roaring bonfire outside.

Hoping to find out where he was, Jimmy stuck his face flush against the window glass, cupping his hands around his eyes to block out the smothering dark of his prison and squinting his eyes to penetrate the painful brightness of the fire.

The strength of the fire made his eyes water, but they adjusted, and soon Jimmy could see vague shapes beyond the blaze. People, he realized, dozens of people danced behind the conflagration in a wild, bacchanalian festival.

Opening his mouth to call for help, Jimmy paused, words catching in his throat like a piece of meat too large to swallow, when he realized the people didn't dance beyond the fire. Rather, they writhed within it, somehow unable to escape, moaning and shrieking as they burned without dying, waving their limbs in futile bids to escape their perpetual agony.

Horrified, Jimmy lurched back from the window, slapping both hands over his mouth to muffle a scream. He welcomed the darkness that fell over his vision this time; he couldn't bear to see those grotesque, tortured figures any longer.

Bumping up against a wall of shelves, Jimmy knocked a few objects loose. They brushed against his naked back like fingers slapping his skin before wobbling back into place.

His breath thunderously loud in his ears, his hands numb, Jimmy reached for whatever he had dislodged and found leather-bound books. Except the leather felt strange, thicker and softer than normal, with hairs still attached that brushed against his palms.

Jimmy didn't want to see what he held in his hands. But in that strange way of dreams, his body walked against his will back to the window and the crackling fire on the other side of it, his sweaty hands just barely holding onto the thin, novelette-sized book. As he walked, he held the book farther and farther in front of him, so that when the fire illuminated it, it at first seemed to float in the darkness with no help from him.

As Jimmy had known the moment it brushed his back, the book was bound in human skin. Wrinkles on the cover shifted until a number of eyes, blue and green and brown, opened and stared up at him from between rolls of flesh and his own fingers. The book's eyes rolled madly, searching for what had taken it from its shelf.

Unable to hold back his shrieks this time, Jimmy flung the book away. Before it fell out of sight, the cover flew wide and a mouth within the pages opened and yelled—

A door flung violently on its hinges; light flooded the room. Jimmy whirled to see Annabelle and Steve enter his prison arm in arm, dressed for a formal party, each with a goblet of something alcoholic enough to sting Jimmy's nose.

Jimmy could barely recognize Steve, and it took him a moment to remember his patient had looked this way before being arrested. His head was shaved, and tattoos of Nazi paraphernalia crawled up his neck and the back of his skull. He sneered lasciviously at Annabelle, reaching around to pull one of her breasts from the low bodice of her gown. Jimmy winced at how hard Steve squeezed the tender flesh, but Annabelle only laughed and raised her goblet, spilling alcohol down Steve's throat and the sides of his face. It stained his shirt and hit the ground in great splashes of red that dyed stone and tile.

Jimmy feared his allies more than he had the wailing flesh-book and human bonfire combined. He could see a lit corridor beyond the door they'd entered from and willed himself to run for it. His body did not move.

"Oh shut up," said Annabelle to the still-yelling book. Handing Steve her drink, she flounced across the dungeon, reddened, exposed breasts bouncing with each step, and kicked the book with her pointed shoes.

Except it wasn't a book any longer, but a person, an emaciated old man with huge, extensive burns and lesions weeping pus onto the tiles. Steve laughed drunkenly at the old man's pain, sloshing wine all over the floor and almost falling on his rear.

"Kick him again!" he guffawed, sounding more and more like the screeching hyena with each passing second.

Annabelle grinned at him and obliged, one sharp toe digging into an open wound and impacting nerves and raw muscle beneath. The old man howled in agony, emptying his bladder onto the floor. Steve grabbed one of the bookcases to keep from falling as he doubled over with laughter.

Stop it! Jimmy wanted to yell, but his lips froze like the rest of him. Annabelle seemed to hear his thoughts, however, for she looked up at him. Her smile turned condescending.

Steve recovered himself enough to wobble over to her, handing her back her goblet before leaning down to grab the few wispy, white hairs remaining on the old man's head. He used them to jerk the burned and bruised head up, pulling most of the hair out in the process.

"Please," the old man sobbed, his bloody fingers scrabbling useless patterns in the urine and pus decorating the floor. "Please, please, please…"

Annabelle ignored him. She walked slowly toward Jimmy, studying him, as Steve smashed the old man's face into the tile, shattering his nose and sending a fresh wash of blood over the tiles.

"Stop?" she asked, halting only inches from Jimmy, that amused smile fixed on her face. She stood so close he felt the warmth of her skin. "Hypocrite! Aren't you here with us?"

Another thud as Steve slammed the old man's head down again, so that the man's pleas dissolved into thick, gargled gibberish.

"You know what we are. You saw Steve's police record, and you felt what I was the second we met. And yet here you remain."

Yanking the old man over onto his back and revealing a ruined mess with bloody bubbles streaming from the mound of cartilage and bone fragments that had once been a nose, Steve lowered his mouth to his victim's eyes. At first, Jimmy thought Steve kissed the old man, but then a grotesque sucking noise reached his ears as Steve inhaled an eyeball into his mouth.

Jimmy had hoped the old man unconscious by this point, but his screams proved him awake enough to suffer.

"Don't look away," said Annabelle, reaching out to stroke Jimmy's hair in a gentle, fond movement. She smelled wonderful, like lavender; Jimmy hated himself for noticing. "You helped us get this far, after all. We couldn't be here without you."

Jimmy awoke, his clothes stuck to him with sweat and his hair a wiry, tangled mass. His body ached for more sleep but he forced himself awake, slapping his cheeks and sitting up against the headboard. The stink of gore and waste and burned flesh wouldn't leave his nose however many times he told himself he'd been dreaming. Tears ran down his cheeks, and he gasped with fear and disgust. He clamped both hands over his mouth to keep from screaming, but the movement reminded him of his dream, so he muffled the noise into his pillow instead.

When he calmed enough to breathe normally, he was relieved to see no one else in the room. The door hung slightly ajar, so he assumed Harry or Annabelle sat just outside, but even the illusion of privacy comforted him. He didn't want them asking what was wrong when dream images of them continued playing behind his eyes, mocking him by refusing to fade away.

We couldn't be here without you...you know what we are...

The sight of the old man's smashed, eyeless face rose in Jimmy's mind, as clear in his vision as the motel television. He made it to the bathroom just before throwing up.

Chapter

13

Down in the motel lobby Annabelle sat in a creaking plastic chair that threatened to fall apart every time she moved. She pretended to watch the movie broadcast from the corner-mounted TV on one wall, but in reality, she scanned the minds of anyone who entered. For her own amusement, she kept a running tally of their thoughts: so far six people had been thinking about sex, nine about money (eight of those nine in negative terms), and four about marital problems (three had been easing said problems with affairs; the fourth wanted to have an affair of his own but worried he was too ugly). Another two had thought about movies they'd recently seen, one of which looked rather interesting. Annabelle decided that if she lived through the night, she would have to rent it.

Upstairs, Harry sat outside the door to their room, Annabelle's gun in his hands. She'd hated scaring him by giving the weapon to him, but if some demon bypassed her by climbing up a wall directly into Harry's room or something, he had to be able to protect himself. She really hated that he sat outside even the pitiful safety his room door offered, but he was going to protect "Dr. Hamid," by god, and wouldn't budge however she cajoled. She really, *really* hated that she hadn't thought to get her second gun when running from the house back on Renaissance Drive. She didn't dare teleport back to get it, either, as Douggie must have informed Hell of her old address by now. One gun would have to do, and Harry needed it to protect himself should anything get past her.

Though nothing would, Annabelle told herself firmly. She'd make sure nothing hostile made it out of this lobby alive.

So Annabelle sat in the lobby guarding Harry, who sat outside his room guarding Jimmy, who was probably sleeping like a baby with all that protection, the jerk. Annabelle spitefully decided she'd wake him by screaming "FIRE!" when it came time to leave.

About two hours after sitting down, Annabelle jumped to hear the front door opening, then blowing shut in the wind. She hadn't heard any thoughts approaching.

The surly desk teen grumbled a cursory greeting to whoever entered. He or she did not reply; Annabelle heard only light scuffling as the guest passed a credit card over the counter and signed papers.

Trying not to look too interested, fighting the urge to turn from the TV, Annabelle strained her telepathy, trying to feel something, anything from the stranger.

...Nothing. As far as Annabelle felt, a black hole had opened up around the front desk. She couldn't even read the mind of the teenager behind it any longer.

The guest was a demon, then. A powerful one.

"Room nineteen," said the teen through his cigarette. Metal and plastic jangled as he handed the demon his key.

"Thank you," said the demon. Then Annabelle heard a wet sound and a thump; she turned to see the teen lying dead over the desk, his head crushed beyond recognition. His still-lit cigarette fell to the rug with a bloody plop. Beside him stood his killer. All Annabelle could see was the back of broad, hunched shoulders covered by a long, old-fashioned raincoat and a pair of large black shoes sticking out from the bottom.

"Why give him your credit card and pay for a room before killing him?" Annabelle asked, leaning back in her seat and trying to look nonchalant, though her heart sped up and adrenaline poured into her system.

"I'd hoped to fool you. Get my room, lay low until you were off guard, then attack you," said the demon. "I figured out that was useless when you tried to crawl into my brain. You're very clever to keep an eye out for me this way." He turned to her and bowed.

He looked very human, with blond hair, brown eyes, and average height. A bit stockier than a normal person, a bit hunched over, but nothing outside the realm of physical possibility. Only the way he licked blood from his lips hinted at his inhumanity. Had he crushed the teen's head in his mouth?

"Nice credit card," was all Annabelle said aloud. "I'm honored that Hell would risk one of its few half-demons on little ol' me."

The half-demon raised an eyebrow. "I might be a demon who stole this card. This kid wasn't exactly careful about checking ID." He gestured towards the dead teen, then crossed the lobby to the front door, which he locked. Switching the "open" sign to "closed," he pulled the curtains shut over the glass.

"If you know about ID, you're a half-demon," said Annabelle. Keeping her muscles relaxed, she flickered her eyes around the lobby, looking for weapons, sizing up the space she had to work with. The TV she'd been half-watching had to weigh fifty pounds, and she could easily reach the tables and chairs set around it for potential TV viewers to sit in. Pens and keys behind the front desk could be used to stab him too, but she'd have to reach them first. Her hands itched for her guns, and she cursed Douglas all over again. "My illustrious countrymen make it a point of pride to *avoid* knowing anything about Earth."

"I'm an incubus, then. They come to the surface all the time, like you succubi."

Annabelle snickered cruelly. "You're too ugly, hunchback."

The half-demon stiffened, jerking to a stop for a moment before he finished closing the curtains.

"You're not trying to bribe me into letting you go," he noted, just the slightest trace of his anger audible in his voice as he turned back to her.

"I don't have anything to offer you," said Annabelle. "Besides, whoever sent you after me must have prepared you for that. No, I'll just kill you."

He stiffened again, his anger creeping more fully into his voice. "If it were that easy, they wouldn't have sent me."

"Maybe. But I can mana—"

He attacked. Leaping forward much more quickly than his stocky body should have allowed, his mouth opened…and opened…and opened. A tongue the thickness of climbing rope flew across the room and wrapped around Annabelle's arm. She screamed as his saliva began eating through her skin.

Yanking his head back, the half-demon pulled Annabelle off her feet; she landed on her front, all the breath flying out of her on impact. Her arm hurt so badly she almost passed out.

That tongue pulled back into the half-demon's mouth, reeling Annabelle in over the carpet, banging her into chairs and across filth that clung to her clothes and hair, making her gag at the odor. Like smelling salts, the stench cleared her fogged brain enough that she managed to grab a chair she slammed into. When the half-demon pulled her into range, she swung it at him.

She swung weakly from a poor angle, with no idea what part of her enemy she hit at, but the blow hit some part of him and made him retract his tongue when he yelled. The pain receding from her arm almost immediately, Annabelle's powerful healing abilities kicked in to soothe damaged flesh. Able to concentrate again, she teleported behind the front desk before the half-demon could grab her and crouched behind the counter, holding her breath to keep from making any noise.

"Oh you whore," the half-demon hissed, losing his temper completely. Annabelle heard him stomping around, searching for her, spitting out one curse after another, ranting threats and promising pain.

Annabelle bit her lip, trying to concentrate with fear scattering her thoughts. If she teleported out of the room, her enemy might be gone when she got back, and that would leave Harry vulnerable. If she reached for anything on the desk or moved too far from the counter, he might see her move.

The dead motel employee's lower body hung inches from Annabelle's face, his last, terror-inspired bladder and bowel movements sliding down his legs to soak the carpet. His pockets hung heavy with objects stuffed inside over the course of the evening, out of sight of the main floor where the half-demon banged about, shoving aside tables and demanding she come out.

Hand shaking, Annabelle grabbed the boy's pocket, unsure if the moisture she felt was his mess or her sweat. Trying not to make noise, she rifled inside: a tissue, newspaper clippings, keys—

The half-demon leapt onto the countertop with a roar from his black hole of a mouth. His tongue snapped out to wrap around Annabelle's torso, pulling her up and out into the open. Screaming, Annabelle grabbed onto the keys, fumbling to point one outward and aiming for his eyes. But he moved too quickly, held her too awkwardly, for her to gain any leverage.

"Get off me, you ugly freak!" she screamed and slashed down with one key. A bright red streak appeared on his face, and again his tongue loosened around her as he stumbled back in pain. However, he did not let go this time; Annabelle's shirt was fast dissolving under his acidic tongue.

Pulled helplessly around by his momentum, Annabelle caught sight of the television once again, now showing a black-and-white Cary Grant looking debonair in the same raincoat her enemy wore.

C'mon! Annabelle yelled at herself, *concentrate! You can do this, come on!*

Squeezing her eyes shut and forcing herself to picture the TV, she willed a teleport.

It worked. She materialized on top of the television, awkwardly hanging off it in the same way the dead teenager did from his desk. She heard the half-demon's angry yell and didn't have to turn to know he was coming for her.

Bracing her feet against the wall, Annabelle pulled. The TV came loose with electric sparks and pops, the force sending her flying back into a table then the ground. Her back screamed with pain; the holes in her shirt dripped with acid, rubbing into her flesh. The half-demon barreled for her before she could gather her senses, knocking furniture out of his way, face purple with rage.

One more time, you can do it, just once more—

Annabelle teleported again, right behind her enemy. She stood awkwardly and pain weakened her, but she still found strength enough to bring over fifty pounds of glass, plastic, and wires down over his head. The resultant crash must have been loud enough to wake dead people in cemeteries fifty miles away.

The half-demon's body stiffened as though indignant about being hit. Then it fell to the ground, the impact knocking the TV free so Annabelle could see he was well and truly dead.

Panting hard, Annabelle stumbled back to the counter and leaned against it, ripping her shirt off to get the acid away from her skin. She wanted to collapse, but didn't have much time. She could feel people in the nearest rooms, frightened by the screams and bangs, trying to decide what to do. Someone would call the police soon enough.

Burning the motel down would cover the evidence best, but Jimmy would never let her get away with putting uninvolved people in danger that way. As soon as he realized what she'd done, he'd come running back to save everyone or something equally stupid, bringing Harry with him.

Well, the only person who could identify her, the desk manager, was dead and she didn't see any cameras. She'd paid the bill with cash. Except for Jimmy's fingerprints in their room, nothing tied any of them to this motel, and the police had no reason to look for Jimmy. The only thing keeping this mess from appearing to be an average murder was the suspicious way the teen's head had been crushed and things an autopsy team would find in the half-demon's body that identified him as inhuman.

Well, as dead bodies were no longer living, she could probably teleport them with her somewhere. She'd never tried that, however, and teleporting such large objects, objects that had once been alive...could she do it?

No time like the present to find out. Annabelle dragged the teen's body over the counter, deciding to teleport with him first, as he'd been dead longer and his body was smaller. Closing her eyes and taking a deep breath through her mouth, Annabelle thought of the middle of the Dead Sea and willed a teleport.

Dawn peeked over the horizon when Jimmy saw Steve glance into their motel room. By that time, he sat awake and dressed in the corner chair, reading the complimentary Bible from the nightstand.

"You're awake," Steve said stupidly, pushing into the room. Jimmy saw a flash of silver, probably him tucking Annabelle's gun away.

Jimmy nodded curtly and said nothing. He didn't look up from the Bible, hoping Steve would take the hint and leave him alone.

No such luck. Walking closer Steve said, "Sure you can't get some more sleep? You've got bags under your eyes like big ol' bruises."

"I'm fine, Steve," Jimmy snapped, gripping the Bible so hard one of its delicate pages ripped. Then, before he could stop the words from slipping out: "And why wouldn't I be? I'm only tied up with demons and murderers who've ruined my life!"

Jimmy very much did not want to look at Steve's face. He didn't need to, knowing the wounded look that would be there. The guilt he felt for what he'd just said was bad enough...but he couldn't stop himself. One look made him want to punch himself in the jaw.

"That's...I don't..." Jimmy shut his eyes and put the Bible down to rub his aching forehead. "I'm sorry, Steve. That was cruel."

You know what we are.

"Shit." Jimmy bent over in his seat, head in his hands. He wanted to cry like a child, to whine things like, *I want to go home!* and *I want my Mommy!* He was damned, he knew it. Hell had laid claim on his soul for his part in Annabelle and Steve's horrible acts. Reminding himself that he'd stopped believing in God years ago didn't help.

"Dr. Hamid?" Steve hurried beside him and grabbed his shoulders. "What's wrong? Are you sick? Hurt? Scared? Of course you're scared, we're all terrified, stupid question, sorry, I just…can I help?"

Oddly, Steve's concerned babbling made Jimmy smile and eased his torment a little. Looking up, he saw Steve looking as earnest as a child, eyes wide and worried. Jimmy slowly sat up again, staring at Steve's face all the while.

"I have no idea what I'm doing," he finally said. "I never did, with you. Human beings are pretty predictable. We each like to think we're unique, and in some ways we are, but really we follow patterns, even in our differences. That's why psychology works. Looking at a thousand people who act one way in a situation, psychologists know that the next guy in that same situation will act pretty much the same way and feel a lot of the same things.

"But a lot of the things that make humans human…hormones and hunger and flesh connection…you don't have them. You're a soul, Steve. You're the very essence of humanity without the…the distractions our bodies and instincts create. But without those distractions, you're also highly…"

"Unpredictable?" Steve ventured when Jimmy fell silent.

"Yeah."

Steve walked over to Jimmy's bed and sat on it. Again, the two men faced each other, studied each other, trying to make sense of their own thoughts.

"It's not possible to rehabilitate a man like you," said Jimmy after a moment. "Psychologically working with…you know what you were, don't you?"

Steve nodded without looking away. Jimmy felt immensely proud of him, proud that Steve refused to minimize or hide from what he had been and the things he'd done. "I called myself twisted," he said. "The doctors said I had 'antisocial personality disorder'." He frowned. "Which I think means I'm a psychopath."

"Don't use the word 'psychopath'," said Jimmy, uncomfortable. "We haven't been allowed to use that word since 1980." He paused. "But, um, yes, that's about what that means. And there's no curing people with ASPD. Something in your conscience is just wired differently, and there's no rewiring someone to make them care about other people. Not something that can be taught, either. It's something a person does or does not do. And ASPDs don't do it. There's a lot of argument about whether you're born that way or raised into developing ASPD, but as far as 'curing' you, it can't be done, and that's just the end of the discussion.

"Except so much of you never entered the discussions." Jimmy smiled wryly and rubbed the back of his head unconsciously. "Never has any patient I've heard of been forced to literally become their victims. Never has any patient had so much of what makes us human stripped away. Your body, I mean."

"Does that make me more human or less?" Steve tried to joke, but just managed to sound depressed.

"Political correctness demands that I say both are equally special in their own way," said Jimmy. He was gratified when Steve cracked a smile. "Working with you tells me that you are absolutely, totally, 100% sorry for what you've done, to the point that guilt just about eats you alive. That's exceedingly rare, even in people with normal consciences. Most people find a way to brush off bad things they've done—at least consciously—by finding a way to blame the people they've hurt or convincing themselves they didn't really hurt anyone. If they're held accountable, they'll usually get uppity and complain that they're sorry already, so why is everyone being mean to them?"

"How could I," asked Steve, "when I was the people I hurt?"

Jimmy tried to nod, winced at the pain the movement caused, and rubbed his forehead again.

"Want some Aspirin?"

"Please."

Steve left for a moment for the vending machine while Jimmy poured himself a glass of water. His dream spoke the truth; he had known what Steve was. Yet Jimmy didn't believe in turning his back on people who needed help, especially people who truly wanted to better themselves. Picking and choosing who deserved his help and who didn't seemed wrong to him, morally as well as professionally. After all, Jimmy hadn't lived his patients' lives and could neither fully understand why they'd made the choices they had nor know for sure what he'd have done in their positions. Then again, Steve's case was so extreme, it made Jimmy doubt himself. If anyone deserved to be judged, Steve did.

The door opened. "They've only got Tylenol."

"Tylenol's fine." Jimmy turned in time to see a small package fly past his shoulder. Steve smothered a laugh.

"Yes, yes, I'm a crap catcher. I learned that after five years of being picked last for every baseball game, thanks." Jimmy picked the packet up and ripped it open, not noticing Steve's silence until he'd swallowed the medicine down. He shot Steve a curious look.

"Um." Steve shoved his hands into his jean pockets and scuffed the floor with one sneaker like a naughty child waiting to be punished. "On the same subject as before, kinda. I've had something I want to ask you, and I'd sorta like to get it out in case we all. You know. Get killed or something."

"How could I refuse the last wishes of a dying man?" Jimmy joked. Steve didn't smile this time.

"Saying I feel 'guilty' for what I did is…it just sounds so stupid. It's just not strong enough a word, right? But I guess it's the best one I've got. I feel really, really guilty, and I hate what I did, and I want to make it up to the people I hurt. And reading some stuff, the first step in that case is to apologize, right?"

Jimmy felt like he had when barreling down the highway, juggling baby carriages with polka music blasting in his ear seven or eight hours ago. "You…you want to find women you raped, and men you tortured and mutilated, and families whose relatives you killed to tell them you're sorry?"

"Bad idea?" Steve looked up from under the cover of his bangs with a strange mix of shame and hope on his face.

"I don't…I…wow." Jimmy leaned against the wall and blinked several times, trying to get the confused fog now buzzing around his head to clear. He moved back to his chair and sat down, thinking he shouldn't be so surprised when every offender wanted to be forgiven by somebody.

"Dr. Hamid?"

"Give me a minute."

"Okay," said Steve quickly.

Annabelle burst into the room, slamming their door into the wall. Jimmy dumped water into his lap and Steve whirled around with a yell; the lamp on the nightstand fell to the ground as though pushed.

Water soaked Annabelle's hair, pants, and sneakers; her shirt would doubtless have been soaked as well, had it not disappeared. What looked like a festering burn wound ran up her lower-right arm, and smaller, similar wounds dotted her bare belly.

She coughed and a small mouthful of brackish water splattered her chest. She stank so badly Jimmy wrinkled his nose even across the room.

"Holy—!" Steve gaped at her, obviously trying to think of what to do and too badly shocked to manage.

"We need to get out of here," Annabelle rasped, sounding like someone had dragged razor blades over her esophagus. "Now."

Annabelle woke up confused, not realizing she'd fallen asleep. Teleporting the first body put a viselike pressure on her, crushing her until she'd been sure she'd die. Falling into the Dead Sea and inhaling whole lungfuls of saltwater upon materializing panicked her so badly she hadn't been able to teleport to safety, but flailed around until sheer luck pushed her head above the surface. She almost hadn't taken the second body but stood in the lobby staring at it in terror, remembering the darkness and the confusion and the pain of drowning. Then someone's thoughts touched her, some meddling jerk who'd called the police and now hoped that they'd arrive soon.

Heck knew how she'd made it to the Dead Sea and back the second time, let alone climbed the stairs to her room; she kept blacking out, finding herself on the second floor, then on the staircase, finally dripping a puddle in front of her room door. And then...

Then she woke up naked in the motel room's cracked, yellowed bathtub. Harry's fingers massaged cheap courtesy shampoo through her hair in a soothing rhythm.

"We don't have time for this," she tried to snap, though she had a feeling she mumbled instead. She fell asleep again before Harry could respond.

Sirens alerted Jimmy to the police's arrival while Steve took care of Annabelle. He ran to the window where flashing red and blue lights almost blinded him.

Swearing internally, he jerked back. Had the cops seen him? If they'd seen him, they'd know he was guilty! The kidnapped babies and Steve's victims and the dead Satanist at Annabelle's house flashed through his head. Jimmy flattened himself against the wall, imagining life in jail where he would doubtlessly become the cupcake of a man named Meat Grinder who had too many tattoos and never showered.

No, the police could do worse than that. They could *call his father*. Jimmy's eyes widened and his toes curled in his sneakers at the very thought. He stuck his head between his legs and hyperventilated for several minutes.

His coat fell on his head. Squawking, Jimmy flailed, smacked into the wall, tangled himself in his sleeves, and finally tore the coat off to see Annabelle. She looked like half-recycled garbage, but at least she was conscious. She wore her wet jeans, and her dry jacket covered her shirtless upper body.

"Put that on," she said. "The police are going room to room, asking everyone to answer questions. We need to get out of here."

That sounded good to Jimmy, who couldn't get out quickly enough. He rushed so frantically that he tried to pull his jacket on three times before he managed, while Annabelle took her gun back from Steve.

The trio stepped out of their room at the exact instant a policeman stepped off the stairwell onto their floor and saw them. Steve physically had to hold Jimmy upright.

"Hello, officer," said Annabelle, not even pausing in her confident stride across the hall. It occurred to Jimmy later that, with her telepathy, she must have known the policeman had been about to step onto their floor. "Can I help you?"

"Yes ma'am, you can tell me what you're doing up so early with your pants all wet, for a start." The policeman eyed Annabelle up and down, his tone friendly, a bit flirtatious, but cautious. Jimmy concluded he knew how to do his job and miserably prepared for life in prison with daily letters containing ten-page lectures from his father.

"Sure." Annabelle reached the policeman and, without breaking stride, punched him. He fell back into the wall and then slid to the floor, unconscious.

"You...what...that's..." Jimmy did not resist as Steve half-carried him down the hall. They'd just assaulted a cop. In his mind, his father's ten-page letters bloomed into twenty pages. With illustrations.

"He's all right," said Annabelle, continuing on to the staircase. "Just unconscious. And he didn't see you, he was staring at me. C'mon, we'll get out the back while everyone's in their rooms or gathered in the lobby with the other cops."

"Where are we going?" Jimmy squeaked stupidly, staring at the cop until Steve shut the stairwell door behind him.

"Shopping."

The morning dawned clear and bright with air that sliced Annabelle's lungs when she breathed in. She felt giddy with anticipation and nerves. The danger following her and Harry, the brisk air, the travel and opportunities in front of her...the feelings built up and rattled around inside of her like a swarm of insects struggling to burst free.

The last favor Annabelle bribed out of Samantha before her friend returned to Bael's castle (with Annabelle's Chinese necklace around her throat) had been a rental car. Light blue, small, and electric with excellent gas mileage, it was much too sensible for Annabelle's taste. Though she'd been living in poverty and dressing in a cheap, slovenly way for months, giving up her most prized piece of jewelry to a demoness in a coat more expensive than her Earth house made Annabelle remember how fond of the high life she'd once been. A pang of nostalgia suddenly had her longing for a little red corvette that painted a swath on concrete or a sexy black motorcycle with an engine that announced her presence from miles away.

But she had to avoid being seen, and because Annabelle had a long way to drive and very little money, gas mileage was a pressing concern. She wanted to stop as few times as possible before reaching New York City.

Annabelle, Harry, and Jimmy drove most of the eleven-hundred-mile journey on I-80 Eastbound. Annabelle sped all the way, and for once, Jimmy didn't complain about the rule-breaking. His eagerness to finish with Annabelle's business and get away from her was a little insulting. True, she didn't want to attract him and made no effort to do so, but still. He should feel more of a pull towards her than he did, and for some reason he seemed even more eager to get away from her after waking up this morning. Being stuck in a tiny car for sixteen hours would not have been fun under the best of circumstances, but it was miserable with Jimmy demanding to know their exact destination, and if they'd reached it, every five minutes or so.

("Are we there yet?"

"No, Jimmy."

"Are we there yet?"

"No, Jimmy."

"Are we there yet?"

"Yes, Jimmy, yes! This uninterrupted stretch of road without so much as a tumbleweed blowing across it is New York City!")

Before leaving, Annabelle bought a new dress, cheap but sexy, tight, and white with a plunging neckline and cinched waist. She pulled her hair back into an elegant twist that left strands trailing over her shoulders here and there. The jet black was striking against the white of the dress and skin almost equally pale for the demon she dressed for. In an attempt to be attractive for the first time since escaping to Earth, Annabelle spent the last of her cash on stiletto heels and makeup. Annabelle didn't plan to break her promise not to have sex with anyone she didn't want to, but for this meeting, she needed to look like a succubus. Only as a demon would she gain anything now.

The winter wind blew through her old, ratty blue coat to assault her flesh, but she had no more money for another. She gritted her teeth when the freezing air stung the still-healing wound on her arm.

The trio arrived in New York City long after dark. The skyline was lit: white lights, yellow lights, blue lights from inside buildings and around windows, from streetlights, satellites, and strings of unretired Christmas decorations. They burned bright and steady or flickered like candle flames, some a firm color while others shifted rainbows against the black night. Annabelle smiled as the display slid over her car. She felt greeted to an outdoor temple, a sanctuary of welcome inviting her to relax and go wild at the same time.

Music blasted from a car that screeched to a stop beside Annabelle's at a red light. It had huge wheels with gold hubcaps that spun dizzyingly, and a sound system that made Annabelle's little car tremble.

"Hmph," Jimmy grumbled, covering his ears, "like the whole world wants to hear your crappy taste in music."

But the rhythm flowed through Annabelle, re-invigorating her tired limbs and making the decorative lights look twice as bright as before. When the stoplight turned green she slammed her foot down on the gas pedal and began weaving in-between cars, daring them to get in her way.

King Zagan's Earth residence stood in the financial district, a considerably darker, duller place compared to the neon spectacle of the entertainment district through which Annabelle entered New York. Zagan liked it that way, the colorless old curmudgeon. Money was the sun his world revolved around; modernity and beauty didn't even rank on his Scale of Things To Pay Attention To.

He lived in a three-story gated mansion that took nearly a block of Manhattan's Civic Center. From pillars to marble floors to grand staircases as wide as most people's bedrooms, Zagan had designed his home, his sanctuary, to be as palatial as possible in the modern cityscape. He wanted to make sure everyone knew at a glance that the owner was someone rich beyond most men's wildest fantasies, someone to envy and obey. Annabelle didn't know if the palace's proximity to St. Peter's Roman Cathedral was a coincidence or a deliberate irony.

Jimmy scowled when he caught sight of the place. Annabelle felt his disgust at the smugly opulent palace and jotted down a mental note to make fun of him about it later.

Annabelle pulled up to gold-plated front gates, wondered why they hadn't been stolen, and leaned far out her window to press the doorbell attached to the left support pillar. Seconds later, a camera on top swiveled towards her and a dull male voice spoke through a speaker above the doorbell.

"Mr. Zagan is not seeing anyone this late. We regret that you came all the way here for nothing."

"He'll see me," said Annabelle, craning her neck so the camera could get a good look at her.

"I'm sorry, ma'am, but he left strict instructions that no one was to disturb him."

"Where's the trouble in asking? Just tell him Lady Annabelle is here to see him, or have him take a look at whatever monitor you're watching me on. I guarantee he'll let me in."

"If you like, ma'am, I can take a message for you. He'll get it first thing tomorrow morning."

Annabelle sighed, thinking of shooting out the camera with the silver gun tucked under her jacket. "You're going to make me do this the hard way, aren't you."

"Ma'am, I must warn you that any further belligerence will force me to call the police."

Annabelle laughed aloud. Imagine, Zagan going to human policemen for aid!

She ducked back into the car and rolled the window up. "Brace yourselves."

"What?" said Jimmy, alarmed. Harry, who had been dozing, blinked awake when Annabelle put the little blue car into reverse and zoomed backwards into the street. A black Toyota twice her size braked with a loud squeal, crashing into a red truck in the next lane.

"Hey!" said Jimmy. "Watch out—"

Too late. Annabelle shoved the gas pedal as far down as it would go, leaving a trail of exhaust fumes behind her as she directed the car right at Zagan's golden gates. The drivers in the crashed cars jumped out and screamed at her as she peeled off. Annabelle laughed at them, even while she broke through the gates and onto Zagan's property.

Harry gripped his seat, frozen with terror. The sound of Jimmy screaming was music in Annabelle's ears, another stimulant introduced to her system in a night full of stimulation.

"Are you out of your damn mind? What's wrong with you? We're going to be arrested at the very least, you psycho!"

"Maybe you will be," said Annabelle, just to scare him. She jerked to a stop at the stairway leading up to the front door and pulled the keys from the ignition before ground security, all humans, came running towards her car. They all wore blue uniforms like imitation policemen and wielded Tasers and clubs. "But I have other plans."

Checking her boobs sat straight and high in her dress, Annabelle stepped out of the car feeling powerful. No, invincible. She threw the car keys to the closest guard on her way toward the front door. "Park that thing properly, will you? And you'll need to get someone to fix the gates and pay off those pissed off drivers."

The guard blinked at the keys he'd been given like he'd never seen any before while his co-workers exchanged confused and uneasy glances. They knew how to deal with thieves and aggressive male attackers, but no one had trained them for this situation.

Annabelle walked up the front stairway unmolested and kicked the heavy wood door open, making the hinges groan in protest when the lock snapped.

"Did you see that?"

"That's solid wood!"

"The locks...how could she just snap steel like that?"

The guards with sense hung back, but a few ran after Annabelle with clubs and Tasers at the ready. Jimmy quickly put himself between her and them with his arms up. "Trust me, guys. You don't want to do that."

When the guards grabbed him, he didn't fight. Annabelle rolled her eyes and thought, *What a wimp.*

She ignored the fuss behind her, even as she heard one of the guards ask for the police on a cell phone. This would all be over before they arrived.

A guard ran into Annabelle's path the moment she set foot in the marble-floored foyer. He pointed a small Colt revolver at her head. "Freeze!"

Annabelle knocked the revolver out of his hand before he finished the word, unwilling to give him a chance to blow out her brain or heart. Before the guard could recover, she grabbed his neck, slammed the front door closed with another kick, then bent the handle beyond repair with her free hand. Outside, guards began banging on the door, making demands they had to know she wouldn't listen to and creating an irritating racket that heightened Annabelle's excitement still further.

"King Zagan," she purred to the terrified, choking guard in her grip. "Tell me where he is. Now."

"I've never seen such a high-ranking demoness so lacking in manners," said a voice Annabelle recognized all too well. At the left side of the main foyer stairwell stood King Zagan, a shriveled little man with gray-tinged, rubbery flesh that only barely passed for human, even in the human business suit he wore. "Now let my guardsman go before you saddle me with paperwork and police attention by killing him."

The guard's eyes bulged from their sockets and bubbles spit from between his swollen lips. Annabelle shrugged and dropped him just as more guards came running down the foyer staircase, each with his own black gun.

Wondering how he could stand so many humans running loose in his palace, Annabelle sank into a deep bow at Zagan's feet. Her former captive hacked and gasped behind her.

The front door was shoved open, and the small army of guards burst through it. Jimmy and Harry stumbled in with them, restrained and bent over.

"Let him go," Annabelle snapped, straightening and pointing at the guard holding Harry's arms. He was clearly trying not to panic and not doing very well. One of the huge windows by the door shattered, spraying glass on the floor.

"It's all right," said Zagan, glancing with curiosity at the window and shuffling forwards a few steps. His voice sounded clogged, a sick old man's congested wheeze. "Let him go." The guards nodded and released Harry, who immediately stumbled to Annabelle's side. She put an arm around his trembling shoulders and glared at the guards. None of them noticed. They were all busy gaping at the window.

Annabelle worried about that too, though she kept her face neutral, hoping Zagan wouldn't realize Harry had shattered his window. She'd thought Harry could control his new abilities now. If fear still had him blowing things up (or whatever he did), he could seriously hurt himself or someone whose help Annabelle needed.

"I imagine you want the other one, too?" Zagan gestured toward Jimmy, his face inscrutable, as a proper nobleman's face should be.

"No, you can keep him locked up," said Annabelle. "And feel free to beat him a little."

Jimmy muttered something in Dari that didn't sound very flattering.

Eyes wide, Harry tugged on the sleeve of Annabelle's jacket and silently begged her to be kind.

Annabelle sighed. "Oh, very *well*. Let him go, then."

The guards looked at Zagan, who nodded, and complied. Jimmy fell to his knees and rubbed his wrists.

"Get back to your posts, all of you," Zagan commanded. He coughed, a thick, phlegmy sound. The guards all exchanged surprised glances; apparently their boss had never before changed his mind about wanting to be disturbed. Or anything else, Annabelle bet. "And you, Lady Annabelle. Come with me. Bring your pets if you must, as long as you can keep them quiet."

Jimmy began to splutter, so Annabelle raised her hand in a cease-and-desist motion and moved quickly to his side. "He's not trying to be rude," she whispered in his ear, hiding the communication by helping him up at the same time. "It's just that you're only a human."

Though he threw her a dirty look, Jimmy kept his mouth shut. Annabelle figured that was the best she could hope for. He could sulk all he wanted internally.

The trio walked after Zagan, leaving behind the marble entrance and entering a hallway lined in what looked like real gold. Jimmy was appalled by the excess, so Annabelle hurried to add, "Zagan's just royalty. This is how royalty is, whatever country you're in. Keep it together for now so we can get out of this alive."

To her relief, Jimmy again held his tongue.

The small group passed half-a-dozen closed doors before approaching an open one on the left side. It turned out to be a study, dark with no windows. Shelves covered most of the walls, crammed with books titled *Get Rich Quick!* and *How to Use the Stock Market to Your Advantage* and *How to Be Daniel Trunk: Seize Wealth and Crush Anyone Who Gets in Your Way.* A large desk sat near the far wall, with more bars of gold piled atop it than Annabelle could count.

Zagan moved behind his desk and sat down in the chair behind it, which had real jewels decorating every available inch. Annabelle had to fight to keep from grimacing at the tacky effect. It looked like some idiot gave a girl who dreamed of being a princess an unlimited budget and told her to use her imagination. Annabelle wanted to smash the ugly thing to pieces rather than look at it any longer.

"So," said Zagan, pausing to hack up more phlegm, which he spit into a gold spittoon behind his desk. "Jigoku's missing succubus graces me with her presence. Are you here to turn yourself in?"

"No," said Annabelle. "I'm hoping we can come to a mutually beneficial arrangement that will keep me free on Earth."

Zagan's hacking increased, growing louder until it became a painful sound. It took Annabelle a moment to realize he was laughing.

Jimmy looked deeply unhappy and mutely worried for the fate of his immortal soul. Annabelle covered her snicker with a cough.

"You succubi," said Zagan once he'd pulled himself under control. "I don't care what Emperor Lucifer decrees, I'm not stupid enough to marry. As though I'd share my resources with one of you! Always wanting jewels and expensive clothing and more servants. I'm not that desperate for an heir."

"Nor am I that desperate for your help," said Annabelle. She regretted it almost immediately when he leveled an angry glare at her.

We need his help, we need his help, don't be rude, we need his help…

Turning to the nearest bookshelf, Annabelle pretended to browse through the titles. In fact, she'd zeroed in on one the moment she'd entered the room: the Daniel Trunk book.

Ignoring the warning snarl from Zagan when she reached for it, Annabelle pulled the book free and said, "I've heard you're quite a fan." She put the book down carefully before Zagan, next to a diamond paperweight and an embossed pen with a golden clip.

Zagan smiled in a dopey, fannish sort of way, entirely unbecoming of a king. "Yes, one of the great geniuses of modern business. He creates and destroys laws and lives and gets away with it precisely by denying what he is: a modern-day monarch. Using money to influence politics in order to create more money, resulting in power over lives—it's genius, something the old powers rarely dreamed of. To have manipulated a system designed to work against royalty into producing a new type of royalty, think of the brilliance that took. Oh, Hell can learn from him!"

Annabelle kept her criticisms to herself. She didn't see what was so innovative about people with money finding ways to make more money. That was what the rich had always done. The entire French Revolution started over it, for Pete's sake.

"Well then. What do you think of a chance to work with him?"

Zagan's eyes widened, and his wrinkled, elephant-skin hands tightened reflexively on the edge of his desk. He stared down at the book and then up at Annabelle.

"Can you…can you really…?"

Annabelle fell back on her old ways with frightening ease. She smiled coquettishly, flipping a few loose strands of her hair back over one shoulder before leaning towards him, one hip propped on his desk. "Oh dear. Your Highness, I know it's been entirely too long since our last meeting, but have you really forgotten what I am? Why, here on Earth it's taken incredible effort just to dampen my effect on men, and even so, you wouldn't believe the offers I've had."

"Oh, I believe," said Zagan, running his eyes up and down Annabelle's body. For him, she had hair past her butt and breasts large enough to strain her dress and make her back ache. "And just what do you want in return for this business opportunity you're offering?"

"I'm not offering you a business opportunity," said Annabelle, crossing her arms. "I'm offering you the opportunity of a lifetime, and you know it. Your production studio is doing well, and your waste management company is taking off, but just imagine what the Trunk name would do. Actually, just imagine what a few tips or new contacts from him could do."

"You've done your research." A pungent odor hit Annabelle's nose when Zagan began sweating. The underarms of his two-thousand-dollar suit, almost identical to the suit Trunk wore on the cover of his book, grew dark and damp. He licked his lips, trying to get rid of the moisture beading his upper lip, as though he could hide his excitement that way.

Annabelle let him pretend. He'd be more malleable if she spared his dignity.

"Indeed I have," she said. "And all I want from you is a safe place for these two." She gestured to Harry and Jimmy, who started in their seats and exchanged confused glances.

"You want protection?"

"For them, yes. No one saw us coming here, Your Highness," by which Annabelle meant "no one important." Humans did not count. "I just want to keep it that way, to give these men a place to stay in secrecy and safety for a short time while I make long-term arrangements for them."

"Hmm." Zagan spared the men a brief glance, as he would any cargo, before turning back to Annabelle. She counted on his royal arrogance to keep him from asking too many questions about Jimmy or Harry. He shouldn't think of them as high-ranking enough to be worthy of scrutiny. "And are you expecting trouble, then? Is that why you need the help?"

"Oh no, Your Highness," she said. "I just don't want to take any chances."

"Really." The cynicism in Zagan's voice sent a chill through Annabelle. He stood up, gaze locked with her own, then shuffled past her to the men. He grabbed Jimmy's chin and forced the young man's face up, studying him intently. Zagan could not read minds as a succubus could, but he had some mean ability to see the truth of things, a talent that made him rich. Annabelle knew he looked into Jimmy to see if the rumors were true, if she'd really taken a human soul with her when she'd escaped Hell. In a moment, when he'd examined Jimmy's essence and found him human, Zagan would move on to Harry and discover what he was. Annabelle's heart leapt into her throat.

Abruptly, Zagan jerked back from Jimmy with a surprised and revolted noise, pulling his hand away like he'd been threatened. With a similar look of repulsion on his own face (and a string of obscenities rolling through his mind), Jimmy rubbed his chin as though trying to remove a stain.

"What kind of company are you keeping, Lady?" Zagan hissed, whirling on her so that flaps of gray skin wobbled over his lapels. "This boy's soul is barely human!"

Lowering her head with shame, Annabelle blushed. "I have no excuse, Your Majesty. But he...interests me."

"Hmph!" Zagan looked back to Jimmy, grimaced, and then turned to Harry. Again, Annabelle's pulse began thundering in her ears. No more distractions, their secret was up...

But Zagan only reached an inch or two towards Harry before throwing a nervous glance at Jimmy, shuddering with disgust, and dropping his hand. He turned back to his desk, leaving Harry to sag with relief.

Annabelle couldn't keep a tiny breath from escaping. She was going to buy Jimmy flowers. She was going to buy him a new house. She was personally going to find an angel to escort his soul to heaven. His soul, his disgustingly kind and generous soul, had repelled a king of Hell to the point where Zagan wasn't willing to even risk searching Harry's soul lest he find something similarly nauseating.

"Well," he grumbled, sitting down behind his desk again, "I can't see that a couple of humans will cause any trouble."

"Oh, Your Highness, thank yo—"

"IF."

Annabelle shut her mouth.

"If they agree to stay confined. I will place them in a suite of rooms where they'll have a bathroom, and meals will be brought up to them. They will not leave those rooms." He threw a glance at the two men that suggested he saw contagious fungus growing all over them.

"Of course, Your Majesty. Your fairness and wisdom astounds me."

Jimmy thought a sarcastic objection so loudly Annabelle knew he meant her to hear it.

"Damn right," Zagan said. "And I hope you don't think I'm going to be very patient waiting for you to fulfill your end of the bargain. You go ahead and go wherever you're going now, but I expect you back within a few days. And the moment you get back, I fully expect you to get to work on..." his eyes went soft and he sighed adoringly, looking back at the book on his desk. "...Daniel Trunk."

"Of course, Your Highness."

Zagan turned hard again. "It goes without saying that I'll have your pets watched as long as they're on my property. Also that *you're* going to pay off the cars you hit in front of my gates. And I assume I don't need to tell you what will happen to your men if you're not back in a reasonable amount of time, hmm?"

Annabelle swallowed, thinking of Harry going mad in imprisonment before some huge demon dragged him to a painful execution. "No, Your Majesty."

"All right, then." Zagan smiled and clapped his hands, rubbing them together. "Then you'd better get a move on, hadn't you?"

Annabelle bowed until her forehead nearly hit the floor.

It was miraculous that Jimmy managed to keep his mouth shut until they reached the rental car, the only place on Zagan's property that they could be sure wasn't bugged, under the pretext of getting non-existent luggage. His face kept moving from one emotion to the next, all tortured feelings that Annabelle didn't need to read his mind to guess the source of. He had literally just witnessed a deal with the Devil—or *a* devil, anyway. Though he no longer seemed to consider himself religious he had been raised that way and had to be, at the very least, confused and scared.

To Annabelle's surprise, she felt a bit sorry for him. It was never easy to be confused, frightened, and lost.

"Look," she whispered to him once they'd ducked into the car, she in the driver's seat and Jimmy shotgun, "we're really not that interested."

Jimmy blinked at her. "Huh?"

"Your soul. Hell isn't interested in it."

Jimmy looked at a loss for what to say.

"I know," whispered Harry comfortingly from the back seat. "That confused me, too."

"Oh come on," said Annabelle. "How many souls d'you think we have down there by now? You people just keep coming and coming and our birthrate keeps falling and falling with each succubus that dies. We just don't know what to do with all of you at this point. Besides, there are plenty of people with a little demon blood running around Earth now, so most humans are bound to get involved with a demon of some kind during their lives. Just being near demons isn't enough to get you damned."

"But you said—"

"I said there were a dozen or so half-bloods who were useful to Hell living up here right now. I also mentioned a few thousand people with lesser amounts of demon blood wandering around, remember? Plus half-bloods who have renounced their demonic sides. Do you know what our population numbers would look like if every poor schmuck who happened to get involved with a demon or part-demon wound up in Hell by default?"

"The Devil has a quota?" said Jimmy.

Annabelle sighed. "Never mind. Just…don't worry about your soul. You've maybe shown bad judgment in who you should help, but you haven't actually sinned. At all. Possibly in your whole life, being the sickening kind of do-gooder that you are. So just stay here and stay safe, since it's not sinful to keep yourself safe, especially when you're not hurting any other humans while *being* safe. Which you're not. So hang tight and relax. I'll be back as soon as I can, and you'll go to heaven in about seventy years when you die of natural causes with all the rest of the distastefully clean types that end up there."

Jimmy opened his mouth to reply, but Harry, leaning up from the backseat to grab Annabelle's shoulder, beat him to it. "'Belle, you didn't ask Zagan or Samantha for a long term solution. You're going to get more help, then?"

"Yup."

"But what do you have left to trade? You've worked so hard to make sure you don't have to sleep with anyone you don't want to."

Annabelle smiled, touched by his concern, and put a hand over his. "Oh, Harry. You're one of a kind."

She thought of Zagan's window, shattered when Harry went by, and grew worried.

"So who are you going to see, then?" Jimmy asked.

"King Belial, the King I traded with to get Harry and myself up here in the first place," Annabelle whispered, pretending to search for something in the empty glove compartment. Guards' eyes bored into her from around the car, ready to report any suspicious activity to Zagan.

"He's way up as far as power goes, so he'll know what's going on. Plus, he rules all the demons on Earth, except the ones here in Zagan's territory. And even Zagan had to trade with him to get up here."

"So this Belial will know what's going on and what to do about it," said Jimmy.

"Basically."

"Wait," said Harry, reaching up and grabbing Annabelle's arm. "Didn't Samantha say Belial's been blaming you publicly for some of the chaos down there?"

"Since his bitch of a wife told everyone I got to Earth using his portals, he didn't have much choice. He can still get in trouble with Lucifer, or our mother, for breaking the law."

"Mother?" asked Jimmy.

"Then he'll have to hurt you to keep that illusion up," Harry spoke over him.

"If I confront him in public, sure. But if I go to him privately, we might be able to come up with something," said Annabelle. "It's worth a try. Since our only other option is to run until someone or something catches up with us and kills us, I'd rather try and find a way to win."

"Or at least live," said Jimmy.

Annabelle grinned.

Harry didn't.

Chapter

14

Jimmy stared out of the largest window in Zagan's guest suite and thought about God.

He couldn't deny Steve's wisdom. Whether or not he believed in God, he loved his job and wanted to keep it. He believed in the importance of what he did and felt a calling to help people who had lost their way find life again.

But Jimmy also felt the desire to know God growing inside him again. Knowing whether there was a deity of some kind out there might not affect his life in the strictest sense, but Jimmy knew a person's viewpoint changed depending on his beliefs. A man who didn't believe in God could be as moral as a man who did, but nevertheless, the two men defined morality in different ways, took different paths to reach the same conclusion. So Jimmy wouldn't fool himself; if he decided God did indeed exist, that decision would change his life, even if the change wouldn't be flashy and obvious to those around him.

Sighing and shifting in his seat, Jimmy looked down, examining King Zagan's grounds. The thick trees, the green grass, the small pond on the eastern edge. How could such an evil creature have cultivated such a beautiful space? The inside of his mansion fit him better, looking as tacky as it did. The suite of rooms Zagan had given his guests looked like someone had picked the most expensive decorations they could, regardless of whether anything matched, and threw them randomly wherever they fit. The king-sized bed was covered by a maroon velvet comforter and accented with lace dangling from the canopy. Decorations included signed photos of Elvis, posters of Che Guevara, solid gold religious statues and delicate Ming vases.

Jimmy wondered if anyone had gone blind staying here overnight.

Steve sat shivering under Jimmy's arm. The two men had dragged a small blue couch over to the window to watch for Annabelle's return and now sat in front of it like baby birds waiting for mama to come back with food. Jimmy felt the last of his pride shrivel up and die.

Jimmy knew being in the house of a demon king had to be traumatic for Steve but had hoped he'd calm down after awhile. However, Steve instead acted more and more agitated as the hours passed. On the few occasions he managed to tear his eyes from the window they darted all over the room, looking for threats under every speck of dust and inside each drawer. The slightest noise made him jump and his shoulders were so tense they had to hurt. Eventually Jimmy had draped one arm over him, and Steve burrowed into his side as though his life depended on holding tight.

To live his whole life so afraid…Jimmy's heart swelled with pity. He remembered feeling terrible fear as a child during thunderstorms. He'd huddled under the covers, squealing with terror every time a flash of lighting bright enough to penetrate his thin comforter ripped through the sky. Sometimes, when his trembling and screaming woke her up, his sister would slide into bed with him and put one arm around his shoulders. He would cling to Aaqila as Steve clung to him now, trusting that she'd keep anything bad from happening.

Thinking of his sister led to thoughts of the rest of his family, which led Jimmy's mind straight back to God. He sighed in disgust at his lack of control but gave in, letting himself consider the problem that lay behind his every waking thought and sleeping dream.

The thing was, there wasn't any proof about God existing or not. Even if Annabelle flat-out told him that yes, God existed, she might be lying. A person didn't *see* God; they either felt Him or they didn't. In childhood, Jimmy had felt God's presence in almost everything he did, everything he saw and heard and read. He'd had some questions about God and His plans for the world, but he hadn't asked them because he was critical of God. Jimmy had just wanted to understand things.

His father hadn't seen it that way. Every lecture the old man gave, every time he yelled that Jimmy was going to Hell for blasphemy, every punishment where he locked Jimmy into his room to "think about what he'd just said," as though Jimmy's questions had been so repugnant he couldn't even look at his son, strengthened the wall of anger around Jimmy's heart. He tried to ask why he was being punished and scolded, only to be told that needing to ask only made the offense worse. Eventually, Jimmy realized his father was angry because he didn't have any answers to give and grew disdainful.

He began to associate faith with the ignorance he lived with, and anger became a constant companion, a barrier that kept Jimmy from feeling God any longer. He decided that he'd never felt God at all but had only deluded himself in childhood under his family's influence.

But now…

It wasn't just having a demon and a poltergeist popping into his life that was making Jimmy rethink his assumptions about the divine. He'd spent years away from home barely speaking to his family, especially his father. That period of rest and relatively low stress had helped ease the fury that defined Jimmy's teenage years. He'd made sure to avoid the topic of religion at all costs during that time, even in a purely academic sense, because the subject so pained and disturbed him.

Was he ready to tackle faith again? Not necessarily to accept the idea of God as true right off, but to ask if God was real and to be willing to explore the possibility? To pray without laughing scornfully at the idea that there might be someone listening?

"Steve," said Jimmy, staring out the window, "I've thought about your question. On forgiveness, I mean." Forgiveness and redemption, more than ghosts and demons, had been part of his faith as a child and linked naturally in his mind now.

Steve said nothing but tilted his head up and stared at Jimmy with too much intensity for comfort. Jimmy coped by continuing to stare out the window and not returning the look.

"Here's the thing," he said, squeezing Steve's shoulder, perhaps to give himself something to brace against. "I don't have a concrete answer for you because I have no experience in this sort of situation. I don't know if going to see your victims would traumatize them, because I've never studied anyone who's actually seen a ghost. I don't know if your intentions are purer than most people's, because I don't know what your lack of a physical self means for you. You know. Emotional self. Spiritual self. Understand?"

He glanced down at Steve long enough to see Steve nod. He couldn't read the other man's expression; he looked like a marble statue with blue fire burning behind the sculpted eyes. Again, Jimmy had to look away and fight down a shiver.

"So, I'll tell you what I do know," he said, staring out the window again without taking anything in. "Not as a psychologist. Just as a man.

"I know that making amends is a huge part of moving on from any past misdeeds. However, making amends is as much for the person who committed the wrong acts as it is for the one who was wronged; that way, the offender doesn't have to spend their lives feeling guilty. Much as I believe that you really feel sorry for what you did, Steve, at least part of the reason you want to be forgiven is because you want to stop feeling so guilty."

Steve stiffened but said nothing.

"That's normal enough. But if you're truly sorry for what you've done, you owe it to your victims to think of them before yourself." Jimmy took a deep breath, let it out slowly. What he had to say was cruel, but necessary. He remembered Steve slamming the phone down back at his house, face twisted with anger, and had to summon courage to go on.

"What you did wasn't just 'wrong,' Steve. It was heinous beyond all acceptable reason. It's not bad to want forgiveness, and it's great to make amends. But keep in mind at least some of the people you'd need to apologize to had nightmares of you every night you lived, and your death made them feel safe for the first time in years. So if what you're really doing is trying to ease your own conscience, thinking only of answers you want to hear and trying to get them at the cost of hurting your victims all over again, then there's no progress, certainly no compassion or redemption, in that."

Steve buried his head in Jimmy's shoulder and shook harder and harder with each word. Jimmy wanted to shoot himself for the pain he knew his words caused, wanted at least to apologize. However, this was one of the cases he'd just spoken about, one where his apology would be meant to soothe his own uneasy conscience and help Steve not at all.

Instead he asked, "Should I stop?"

"No," Steve replied immediately, and though he still trembled, he spoke clearly.

Jimmy waged an internal debate with his conscience for a few seconds, then decided that Steve had to choose for himself what he could handle. Making decisions for him like Annabelle did wouldn't help.

"I've only got one more thing to say anyway," Jimmy said, squeezing Steve's shoulder again, this time in comfort. "Just that…whatever you decide to do, remember that they're not obligated to forgive you. Whatever you try, however sincere you are, even if you work your butt off for years with the best intentions, your victims don't owe you anything. And it's not just possible, but probable, that they won't ever forgive you."

Steve made no reply, and Jimmy didn't say any more. He just kept staring out the window, not seeing anything past his own thoughts despite the lightening sky over Zagan's grounds. Long minutes passed and Steve's trembling eased. He relaxed his grip around Jimmy's middle.

Jimmy almost felt ready to ask if Steve felt okay when the sound of an approaching engine made both men straighten on the couch. By now it was nearly five in the morning, and though cars rumbled down the street in front of Zagan's palace, this was the first one that turned into the drive and approached the gates. It was a truck, old and beaten but very sturdy with huge, thick wheels and an unmuffled engine.

"They want us to know they're coming," said Steve, his voice high with panic. He squeezed Jimmy almost hard enough to crack a few ribs, then yanked his shrink down as he tried to curl into a ball. He pulled his knees up and hunched his shoulders down until only his wide, tear-filled eyes were visible over them. "They're coming for us and they want us to be afraid!"

Just as Annabelle's car had done hours before, the truck rammed into Zagan's newly-fixed gates and barreled for the front door. Jimmy could see three huge, dark forms crouched in the truck bed, and another two sitting in the front seats. The truck moved too quickly for him to make out any details.

"Oh, God," Jimmy whispered, not spotting the irony of his words as he extricated himself from Steve to press against the window. His attention focused completely on the truck painting a green blur across the drive, spitting oil and smoke that sizzled where it landed on concrete and grass alike.

The truck leapt with a roar and zoomed up the stairs until it reached the front doors and plowed right through.

Steve twisted the edge of his sweater. His voice was sandpaper dragged from his throat. *"They followed us!"*

From the first floor, Jimmy heard the roar of gunshots, one after the other, until he couldn't tell how many guns were being fired at once.

Fear froze his limbs to the ground for a long moment, so that he heard every scream and grunt from the floor below. Who was winning? On that note, who were the bad guys? Were the men in that truck demons, or more Satanists, or an enemy of Zagan's that just had really bad timing?

It took Jimmy a moment to realize he wasn't the only one paralyzed with fear. Steve had collapsed to the ground in a fetal position, trembling and shaking and whimpering in the throes of a breakdown. Watching him, Jimmy didn't feel pity as he normally did. Rather, the sheer ridiculousness of the situation hit him. Here was Steve, a man who'd built his life on violence, trembling like a baby. Which left Jimmy, who didn't even know how to make a fist properly, in the position of protecting them both.

He burst out laughing, a high, wild sound that made Steve curl into himself even more tightly. The laughter consumed Jimmy, and he was unable to stop. The professional part of him diagnosed himself with hysteria, then wondered if taking certain drugs felt like this, like being separated from his body while it jerked with spasms of helpless laughter. He fell to the ground with a thump and started slapping himself, afraid he wouldn't even be able to control his bladder if he didn't stop.

From almost directly below, a large object—a body?—slammed into the ceiling, making the floor beneath Steve shake. Someone started screaming in pain, so loudly he could be heard even above the gunfire and battle cries. Then, as abruptly as the scream began, it stopped. Jimmy's imagination supplied dozens of scenarios showing him just how the man might have been silenced, each more gruesome than the last. He stopped laughing.

Sitting up, Jimmy crawled over to Steve and grabbed one of his arms. "Steve?" he said as gently as possible given his lack of breath and growing panic. "Steve, come on, get up!"

"They'll take me back," Steve whispered. Objects began shaking all around the suite: pictures bumped into the wall, furniture danced over the floor. "I'll have to go back and they'll dip me in oil and peel off my fingernails and put me back in all those bodies where I'll feel the things I did again and again and again..."

It was like listening to a skipping record. "*Again and again and again and again...*"

"Listen to me!" Jimmy grabbed the front of Steve's sweatshirt and pulled him up, trying to force Steve to face him. "Look at me. We have to get out of here. Once whatever's down there gets past the guards it'll come for us. We don't want to be here when that happens."

Though Steve said nothing, he looked like he could understand what Jimmy said. After a moment, he gave the slightest nod before his head went back to rolling helplessly like a baby's.

Jimmy stood up so slowly he wanted to yell at himself to hurry up. He had to, though; if he pushed Steve too far, the other man might shut down completely. Walking at a snail's pace still meant going a lot more quickly than dragging Steve down the hall would. Thankfully, Steve followed Jimmy's lead, allowing himself to be helped to his feet and then led to the door.

Though having taken Steve that far, Jimmy froze with his left hand clutching Steve's and his free right hand on the gold-plated door handle. What if leaving these rooms was a bad idea? Their suite had plenty of places to hide: just this room offered closets and cabinets and drawers as deep as Jimmy's bed at home was tall. Besides, it had been hours, and Annabelle could return at any moment to rescue them.

But the gunshots from below grew fewer and farther between each second, the yells fading into groans of pain that eventually weakened into the worst noise of all, silence. The attackers downstairs would come soon and tear this suite apart. Besides, whenever Annabelle showed up she would search as long necessary, to find her "Harry." She even had Jimmy's cell phone number to locate them with.

Slowly, Jimmy forced himself to turn the handle, his fears fighting him all the way. Steve's psychic tantrum had broken the lock, so it opened. The click it made sounded like a guillotine blade sliding home.

Jimmy and Steve's suite was right next to the front stairway. A single look down would have given Jimmy a good view of whatever was attacking, but that would give their enemies a chance to see him, too. Deciding he couldn't take the risk, Jimmy turned the other way and hurried, Steve's hand clasped firmly in his own.

Though Jimmy had only managed a quick glance around the hallway when one of Zagan's guards shepherded him into the guest suite hours ago, he was fairly sure the hallway didn't stop at the back wall, but connected to another adjacent hallway leading left. Jimmy hoped he'd find a stairway there that would lead to a back entrance.

Looking from side to side, constantly peering over his shoulder and expecting to see horror movie monsters leaping at him, Jimmy pushed on. Doors on each side tempted him, demanding that Jimmy open them and see what waited inside. *The key to salvation lies inside of me,* one whispered. Another told him, *This is the perfect place to hide, dark and quiet.*

Maybe, Jimmy thought. *But if the things downstairs can hear my thoughts like Annabelle can, or feel my soul like Zagan did, it won't make any difference.*

About three-fourths of the way to the end of the hall, a door lay open. The microsecond-long glance Jimmy had in passing showed him blinking video monitors and spinning chairs that still moved, telling him people had been sitting in them just seconds ago. Then he passed it and reached the end of the hallway, turning left into what he'd thought to be a hallway, and almost ran into a closed door.

"Oh please," Jimmy whispered. His hands had sweat so much he was surprised Steve could still hold on. "Please, please be a stairway!"

Jimmy grabbed the handle, round and brass and cool to the touch, and pulled.

It was a broom closet. Jimmy's jaw dropped, astonished at how bad his luck was. He kicked aside plastic buckets and bottles of bleach, trying to find the stairway he so desperately needed, the stairway that had to be there somewhere. The world couldn't be so cruel a place that it had trapped him this way!

Steve squeaked and pointed back the way they'd come. They stood too far away to see the front stairway on the other end of the hall, but the footsteps clomping up towards the second floor made deafening thumps, miniature claps of thunder echoing from blood-red carpeting to white ceiling plaster.

There was no time to think, even to consider thinking. Jimmy grabbed Steve's hand, turned back, and ran to the open door he'd gone by a second ago with its monitors and wheeled chairs. The steps grew louder on the stairway, and something green appeared over the top, with spikes protruding high into the air and glistening even in the dim light. The open doorway was so far, *too* far. Jimmy knew he'd never make it, the demon would see him and cut him down before he could reach the door—

Then Jimmy's body dived into the room, Steve falling with him, their hands still connected and now glued together with sweat. Jimmy twisted in midair with strength born from terror and grabbed the edge of the door, slamming it shut. It occurred to him too late that the noise might alert their approaching attackers. His only hope was that the door echoed loudly enough that anyone outside couldn't tell where the noise came from, or softly enough that the marching footfalls would obscure it. Though Jimmy doubted it would do any good to lock the door, he locked it anyway. Then he turned to look at the room he'd entered, trying not to hope for too much. The disappointment he'd felt at the broom closet seconds ago had almost crushed him. He'd almost wanted to lie down and let his enemies kill him just to end the awful mix of suspense and distress. To be disappointed again might kill him anyway.

As Jimmy had expected, he'd landed in a room the security guards used to monitor the grounds. Wires strung through the room in bunches of blue and yellow and red and black, accentuating the flickering TV screens and all the equipment that kept what looked like every room, hallway, and broom closet of Zagan's vast estate under surveillance.

Steve skittered under a small table supporting a dozen television monitors, wrapping himself in a cocoon of wires and shadow. After a moment, all Jimmy could see were two blue irises, peering out like miniature flashlights from the dark.

Jimmy supposed that if he had to hide instead of escape, this room offered the best place to do it. He had a clear view of the hallway outside on one of the monitors and would see anyone trying to come inside. At the moment, he saw nothing. The hallway and stairway were empty.

So where had the green thing ascending the staircase gone? Jimmy frowned and scanned the many monitors in front of him, trying to figure out which rooms and areas he recognized, only to stop short when he reached the monitor showing him the first floor entryway.

"Oh my God," he whispered. His body went numb. "Oh my God."

He looked at a scene straight out of the war movies he'd loved as a young boy. Bodies lay strewn over the marble floor and stairway, some whole, most in pieces. Jimmy's imagination filled in what his senses couldn't, until he smelled the stench of entrails brought to air and heard the screams that no one was left alive to yell.

Jimmy collapsed into one of the spinning chairs, his attention focused completely on the entryway. He didn't see the figure that crept up to his door, though it was clearly visible on the hallway monitor and its shadow loomed large beneath the door.

"Aah..." Steve gasped, pointing at the menacing shadow from his hiding place and trying desperately to pull together the courage to warn Jimmy. "*Aaaaaah...*"

The door was ripped off its hinges with a crash of splitting wood and the screech of rent metal, revealing a nightmare to the two men inside. It was a sickly swamp-green, covered in horns and eyes and mouths with more teeth than Jimmy could count. Bloody saliva fell from those mouths, hungering for something the dismembered men downstairs hadn't been able to satisfy.

The TV monitors blinked, then faded, leaving just two words flickering across every one:

disappear he

r

e

Then they blacked out.

The demon leapt into the room and barreled right for Steve, ignoring Jimmy completely, and began ripping at the wires of Steve's cocoon. Electricity crackled and sparks flew through the air.

Steve screamed.

Staring at the horrific creature made every doubt that had plagued Jimmy since meeting Annabelle fly up into his face. Annabelle said Hell wasn't interested in his soul, but she was a demon—of course she'd say whatever was needed, to gain his trust. What if God did exist, and by helping a soul condemned to Hell, He took offense? What if, in helping Steve, Jimmy destroyed the eternal chances for his soul, damning himself to the fire for a cruel and pathetic man who'd built his life on hating Jimmy and people like him?

But when Steve twisted out from behind the fallen monitors and equipment, scooting backwards on his rear and sobbing with terror as the demon advanced on him, knocking equipment from its path, those doubts left Jimmy just as quickly. A man was in front of him, afraid and in pain. That was all Jimmy ever really needed to know.

With his own version of a battle cry, Jimmy stood up on his chair and leapt onto the demon's hunched, scaly back. It straightened and flailed, trying to pull Jimmy off, as Jimmy wrapped his arms around its neck and squeezed as tightly as he could.

Turning, the demon jumped backwards, smashing Jimmy's body into the wall. The shock vibrated through him, and he'd released the demon before he even realized he'd moved. His body slid down the wall and collapsed on the floor, unable to move.

The demon turned on him. One hand, adorned with claws as long as Jimmy's forearm, came down upon Jimmy, and he wanted to escape but couldn't—

Then—

There wasn't any pain. Jimmy didn't feel a thing. The claws were coming towards him and then they were not, and he couldn't figure out where they had gone. He followed the demon's arm with his eyes, his gaze traveling down past all the chattering little mouths and rolling, bloodshot eyeballs set into the demon's flesh until he saw that the demon's thick claws had stabbed him and now protruded from his chest. Confused, Jimmy stared down at his chest, trying to understand why he didn't feel anything with such huge, deadly things skewering him like chicken on a kebab.

Wow, he thought absently. *Look at all that blood.*

The demon laughed even as two warm and human arms, Steve's arms, wrapped around Jimmy from the side and held him close. It looked so odd, seeing a man without liquid inside of him crying. Crying without tears would be like an action movie without blood; it would look silly, unrealistic. Did Steve's sense of showmanship override whatever biology kept his body together?

However the tears came about, Jimmy knew Steve's grief to be real. It touched him deeply that Steve sat beside him and tried to comfort him now, at the end. He could have run away or tried to hide but had not, and Jimmy could have burst with pride. He would have applauded if he could have felt his arms.

Look how far you've come! he said, except he didn't say it, because his mouth had stopped working.

The room grew darker and darker. Cotton had been shoved into Jimmy's ears so that he couldn't hear the demon laughing or Steve crying. For some reason, static from the TV monitors filled his mind instead, growing louder and louder until static became his whole world, the only thing in Jimmy's head after his vision gave out and he could no longer feel Steve holding him.

Then the static went silent, too.

Chapter

15

On the night before Annabelle, Harry, and Jimmy traveled to New York City, when Annabelle gave Harry her gun, Harry pulled her aside before she went down to the lobby. It was three a.m., and Jimmy had finally gone to sleep sprawled across his bed, snoring so loudly the furniture next door probably shook.

"He's going to be in so much trouble if he ever gets married," Annabelle sighed, imagining a pretty woman kicking Jimmy out of bed. Harry smiled at her, then gestured for her to go with him. He shut the door as quietly as he could, not that it mattered. Jimmy would have slept through a small riot breaking out under the bed.

The hallway was narrow but deserted, good enough for what Annabelle knew would be a very serious conversation. Annabelle leaned up against the wall and crossed her arms, waiting for Harry to begin.

His posture exuded submission and he spoke quietly, non-threateningly. Everything about him suggested he prepared to beg, except...well, there was no one sign that pointed Annabelle to a new, steely resolve in Harry. But it was there, as visible to her as the brown of his hair.

"I want you...I *ask* you to be nice to Dr. Hamid," Harry corrected himself.

"I am being nice to him," said Annabelle. "I took him with us, didn't I?"

Harry shook his head. "You are not," he said. "You're making fun of him and teasing him and calling him names. More importantly, I don't think you have any plans to help him after all this is over."

"Help him? Why on earth would I want to help him?"

"Because he's a good guy who deserves the help."

"He's a sucker, Harry! Like I've been telling him, and you, since we met. He knows I'm taking advantage of him, and he's doing it anyway. He doesn't expect my help."

Lowering his head, Harry said, "'Belle, what makes him a sucker?"

"Helping people for no reason, with no reward? Giving up so much of his life for someone he doesn't even know?"

"Well…" a fine tremor entered Harry's voice. What he planned to say made him nervous. "Isn't that what you did for me?"

Annabelle stood with a jerk and Harry flinched back from her, making her feel instantly guilty. She forced herself to relax, keeping her hands in plain sight.

"It's not the same," she said.

"Okay," said Harry, but Annabelle knew he humored her. "But 'Belle, you're here because the world you knew was a certain way and you didn't like it, so you decided to change things for yourself. Dr. Hamid is the way he is for the same reason; he didn't like things back home, so he left and is trying to make something better. When I was alive, I was too stupid to realize the…the status quo was all wrong, and I was part of a system that was wrong, until someone forced me to see the truth."

Finally, Harry raised his eyes again and Annabelle felt herself melt into them. She grew annoyed, because the moment she met Harry's gaze, she knew that she would help Jimmy. Even if she refused to accept herself as a sucker of Jimmy's caliber, if Harry wanted her to help, then she would.

For that, she hated herself. And Harry for turning her into such an idiot.

"You and Jimmy are different from me," Harry continued. "Don't you see how similar you and he are? You both saw something wrong and you left it behind, went to find something more. You're feeling your way along, trying to find lives that have meaning for you, and screwing up sometimes. But the guts you two have, to question everything, to act on your feelings, to help stupider people like me find our way too...can't you see it?"

"He and I are nothing alike," Annabelle snapped. Harry flinched again, and again she pulled herself back to show him she was no threat. She held back because she loved him, but more, she thought bitterly, she held back because she'd become a sucker who couldn't bring herself to hurt Harry, however much he might deserve it.

Now, less than a day later, Annabelle had returned to Hell for the very same reason.

She materialized directly in Belial's bedroom without announcing herself first, an offense for which even she could be killed. However, if what Samantha said was true and Belial had told everyone she'd tricked him into opening a portal for her, he probably wouldn't want her coming to his door as though they were friends.

Besides, Annabelle could create another advantage for herself staying hidden: if Belial wouldn't help her of his own volition, she'd blackmail him by threatening to reveal that she, not Avaira, had given birth to his heir.

Belial's dark blue room looked less magical and more oppressive to Annabelle this time. The thought that she would die here came to her, and she couldn't make it go away. Everything became a threat. Staring down at the carpet, she saw herself falling into it like the surface of an ocean, being submerged and drowning underneath fiber waves.

The arrival of sheer terror in the form of Avaira saved Annabelle from such dark thoughts. Then shock forced away the terror, because Avaira was *humming*. Her red eyes were soft and only for the little bundle cradled gently in two of her arms. Two other arms fussed at the blanket swaddling that tiny bundle. It had to be the baby.

This couldn't be Avaira, General-Queen Avaira, cooing at the tiny, helpless creature in her arms. The slayer of a thousand demons did not sing to a baby, or stroke his cheeks, or stare at him as though he was the only important thing in the universe.

Then Avaira caught sight of the intruder in her bedroom, and she joined Annabelle in shock.

"What..." Avaira spluttered, "what...you...how..." She shook her head, stiff white hair flapping round her face, and clutched her baby so tightly it began to fuss against her chest. "You can't stay here!"

Avaira advanced on Annabelle, so Annabelle backed away, keeping her hands up and trying to make sense of the fact that Avaira didn't look violent, so much as…concerned in a panicked sort of way. Her jumbled thoughts, leaking from under her powerful shields but impossible to pick apart the way they ran together, showed Annabelle that same concern.

"Don't you understand? You have to leave! Now!" Avaira caught up to Annabelle and grabbed her arms with her remaining free hands. She looked frantically about as though some great danger lurked under the bed or in the closet; enemies that only she could see hid everywhere, waiting to strike.

For Annabelle, reality had been turned on its ear. Avaira, a maternal sort in this strange new universe, apparently meant to protect her from something hiding behind the curtains.

A shield slammed down around Avaira's thoughts, courtesy of her husband. When Belial walked in, everything made sense again. Avaira must have thought being nice to Annabelle would make her leave, thus keeping her and Belial from meeting again. She just didn't want Annabelle seeing her husband.

"Hmph!" sniffed Annabelle, pulling her arms free.

Avaira looked horrified, red eyes flicking between Annabelle and Belial. Finally, bending into a bow, Avaira tip-toed up to her husband, clutching their baby to her chest. She reminded Annabelle irresistibly of Harry begging her to help Jimmy.

"My Lord," said Avaira, voice cracking, "my Lord, please. She…she gave me a son. My Lord, she gave us a son!"

"I know, Avaira." Belial smiled benevolently and stroked Avaira's hair, as a man would comfort his dog. "You're a good wife. But if Lady Annabelle came all the way back here, knowing how much danger she'd be in, it would be abominably rude for me to just send her away."

Though Annabelle couldn't see Avaira's face, the Queen's sagging shoulders told of her defeat clearly enough.

"As you wish, my Lord," Avaira said. She sounded as though her heart had broken, and she kept her head down as she retreated toward the doorway, baby almost completely covered by four arms wrapped around it. Belial smiled fondly after her for a moment before looking at Annabelle.

The second he turned away from Avaira, the Queen lifted her head just the slightest inch, enough for her hair to move back and reveal her mouth and a corner of one wide, desperate eye. She looked to Annabelle one last time, trying with all her might to convey urgency with her expression.

Run, she mouthed, and then she ducked out the door.

Annabelle wanted to laugh Avaira's behavior off as lunatic jealousy but felt too uneasy and confused for that. Annabelle looked back to Belial, who still smiled at her as though having a wanted felon appear in the middle of his bedroom was a mildly pleasant occurrence. His eyes were so different from Harry's, despite being such a similar shade of blue. Harry's were expressive and usually kind, while Belial's were like blue chips of glass, revealing nothing and making Annabelle feel cold just looking at them.

"Well now," said Belial. "It's lovely seeing you again, Lady Annabelle. Welcome to my home."

In the absence of understanding, Annabelle fell back on practiced manners. She bowed low and said, "The honor is all mine, Your Majesty. I apologize for intruding on you so rudely but felt the situation was urgent enough to warrant the indiscretion."

"Yes, I've heard that you've run into your fair share of trouble up on Earth," said Belial. He motioned her towards an armchair in the corner, blue velvet with wooden arms, and poured her a glass of wine.

Annabelle accepted the glass graciously but did not drink.

Belial's castle sounded like a livelier place than before. Annabelle could hear the usual bustle of courtly life from beyond Belial's open door. Servants called to one another, people walked by alone and in groups, music played in the distance. The smell of cooking food reached Annabelle's nose, as did the scent of flowers. She could see neither flowers nor food, which meant that the flowers were plentiful and the kitchen kept very busy indeed for the smell to reach so far. The first floor of Belial's castle had to be filled with steam and boiling meat, while flowers probably decorated most of the walls outside Belial's room for the fragrance to hit Annabelle's olfactory senses so strongly. Perhaps a special occasion was coming up? Or maybe Belial's followers were still celebrating the new security they had with a healthy young prince to guarantee succession and prevent attacks from would-be conquering kings.

"You could call it trouble." Annabelle smiled and pretended to take a sip of her wine. The gun hidden beneath her ratty green jacket brushed against her side and comforted her. "And I'm afraid I'll need your help to get out of it."

"Yes, I thought you might." Belial rubbed his chin thoughtfully. "You know, I just might have something that would do the trick for you. Excuse me; I'll need to have the hallway cleared so no one will see you."

Belial walked outside. Annabelle craned her neck to see him go, and noticed that when he stepped from his room, a dozen heads turned to look at him as though he'd materialized out of thin air. He'd probably put an illusion on the doorway, preventing anyone outside from seeing anyone inside. That was powerful magic, and even having seen feats of power from him before, Annabelle was impressed. Belial hadn't become a king by being weak.

The small group in front of Belial's door nodded at his words, though Annabelle couldn't hear what anyone said. She had no way to see into Belial's mind, or the minds of those around him, with his shields in place. If she probed for weaknesses he'd know she meant to read his mind, and her life wouldn't be worth a single human soul then.

The group hurried away and Belial walked back inside.

"I can't help but notice just how eager you are to keep me hidden," said Annabelle, swirling her wine around in her glass. "I mean, of course I don't believe those awful rumors about how you've been smearing my character, but it does make a girl wonder."

She expected Belial to deny it with his usual friendly look, and hoped to read something in his body language that told her the truth. To her surprise, the smile fell from Belial's face. He looked almost ashamed.

"Ah well, I can't say I don't deserve that," he said. "The truth is, people are angry at you, and if my name is associated with yours, I and mine will be in a lot of trouble."

Looking out the window, Belial shook his head. "It's a shameful thing. But I had to choose between you and me, and I chose you to take the fall."

Damned if Annabelle didn't find herself sympathizing. That was politics, like it or leave it, and men like Belial who thirsted for power couldn't just leave. Not two centuries ago, Annabelle had been the same way.

"With luck, though," he said, attempting to put his usual, amiable face back on and partially succeeding, "I can help you find a place to be safe without compromising my own safety. Unless I'm very much mistaken, you're looking for a place to live in obscurity, just like you tried to find wherever on Earth you were living, yes?"

Annabelle nodded. "That, and I need a couple of troublemakers taken off my tail."

"If they're nobody important, that shouldn't be a problem either. Come with me." Smile pasted back on, Belial spread his arms as though welcoming Annabelle to some great event and ushered her out the door.

Flowers did indeed decorate the hallway, strung around every available post, bit of furniture, and crack in the stone walls. Thousands of lilies, roses, daisies, carnations, caliphs, tulips, bluebells…they seemed randomly strewn about, as though someone had walked down the hall throwing them everywhere. The display was almost enough to distract Annabelle from noticing how all of Belial's demons had disappeared; she couldn't hear a thing, not even distantly.

"Avaira has been rather festive since the birth of our son," said Belial, clearly amused as he kicked a caliph aside. Annabelle tried to keep from showing her surprise. To be so happy over a child! She couldn't understand it.

The hallway led to a spiral stone stairway. Belial and Annabelle climbed in silence, Annabelle ready for an attack. Nothing happened, so she was left thrumming with anticipation and nerves as they stepped off onto the highest floor of the castle and into a small, bare room with two guards standing motionless, one on each side of the door. Huge, ugly brutes, one with an extra, toothy face protruding from his belly, the other with tentacles undulating gently from his back, they wore full dress armor though no one could see them here.

No one but me, thought Annabelle, and for some reason her uneasiness doubled.

The room inside was bare save for a crystal ball in one corner. It rested in a slab of stone carved to look like a clawed hand rising from the floor.

Gesturing to the ball, Annabelle asked, "Is there someone you need to speak with, then?"

"No, but someone is going to be contacting me soon, so I want to be nearby. Besides, this is the best room in the castle for privacy, spelled to be impenetrable to even the most powerful prying minds."

Annabelle went as far as the doorway and then stopped, her instincts telling her to be wary. Belial seemed to accept her decision, as he didn't try to convince or force her further inside—though the two guards ruined the concept of "privacy" completely. Why make such a point of clearing all his subjects away, but let these two stay?

"Now then, Douglas and his men won't be difficult to take care of. Satanists aren't nearly as important as they think they are, poor things. What will be more difficult is getting you to a place where you won't be bothered again," Belial pretended to wipe a streak of non-existent dust off the crystal ball.

"I can't say Douggie is all that deluded. He seems almost desperate to raise his profile, actually."

"With babies, yes. It's all about the children, isn't it? Politics can't survive without new blood, even among creatures as long-lived as we. So babies are born to parents who have their lives all planned out. Maybe when we talk about 'destiny,' we don't mean it in the mystical, karmic sense. Instead, we're talking about the actions that *must* be taken by all living creatures in order to be politically and socially successful. To deny that predetermined set of actions is to be shut out from society and ruined in one's career."

"But who predetermines those actions?" said Annabelle, her rebellious streak urging her on even as her cautious side, that now sounded a lot like Jimmy, screamed at her to shut up.

"Like I said, the parents. Just like it is my son's destiny to be King, decided by you, who gave him to me, and I, who will raise him. It's no choice of his own, and yet our decisions will determine his whole future. Just like being born a succubus determined your life. Just like Emperor Lucifer choosing me to fill my position, determined mine."

For the first time in six millennia, Annabelle thought about all the millions of children she'd had and given away. It was true, she'd set them on paths that most would never have the strength to deviate from, if they even had the intelligence to consider trying to change their lives, or the desire to do so. How responsible did that make her for their choices and for how their choices had shaped Hell?

Annabelle began chewing on her thumbnail as her thoughts grew more and more confused. Then, bursting up from her subconscious to bring her train of thought to a screeching halt, came this terrifying thought: *I never told Belial about Douglas or the babies!*

The crystal ball began to shine, growing so bright that Annabelle had to shield her eyes for a moment before it dimmed to a more reasonable level. When she looked again, Zagan's face filled the ball's surface. He was sweating with anger and fear. His eyes, distorted by the ball's round surface, bugged out like bloodshot golf balls.

"This is an outrage, Belial!" he shrieked. Annabelle heard the unmistakable sounds of violence from somewhere out of the crystal ball's sight. Someone fired a gun, and Zagan jumped high with a gasp before whirling back to face Belial again. "I demand you call your men back at once, or it will be war between us!"

"Your thirty legions against my eighty?" said Belial, smiling as cordially at Zagan as he had at Annabelle. "I believe I can manage, but I appreciate the warning."

Annabelle had gone from confused to reeling. Her first, panicked impulse was to teleport away, back to Zagan's mansion. She had to get away from Belial and his smooth lies and pasted-on smile, to find Harry and take him to safety. She stopped herself, remembering that she couldn't teleport Harry with her, so she had no way of saving Harry by going to him. Rather, she had to make Belial stop his attack from where she stood.

Before Annabelle could move for her gun, the guards outside the doorway grabbed her, pinning her arms behind her back and forcing her to the ground. She heard the door slam behind her, stone grating painfully against stone.

"Ah," said Belial, glancing down at her. "Just a moment, King Zagan. Lady Annabelle, I advise you not to try and teleport or phase out of this room. It's reinforced to prevent that, and you'll be injured."

"Bastard!" Annabelle shrieked. "How *dare* you!" The guard on her left struck her across the back of her head with his armored glove. Through a haze of stars and a whining noise in her ears, she heard Belial scold her for her language.

"King Zagan," he said once he'd finished his lecture, "I'll contact you again when I'm done here. If you're still alive, feel free to engage me in negotiations at that time."

The crystal ball went blank.

Annabelle coughed a wad of bloody saliva onto the floor. "You sent Douglas Crane after me. That's how he knew where I was."

"Yes, I was hoping he'd take care of you," Belial sighed. His nonchalance astounded her, even though it was no different from how he always acted. Still, to act so casual now! How could he when it was her life at stake! "After all, if you gave him the babies he'd wanted, you would have angered everyone who worried about how much power half-demon babies gave a lowly human. The search for you would have turned into a full-blown, no-expense-spared manhunt, and you and Douglas would both have been dead within a week."

"And if I didn't give him the babies," Annabelle said grimly, barely able to keep her head an inch from the floor with one guard's hand on the back of her skull, "he would have killed me, or had someone else kill me, so no one would know he planned to rival the nobility of Hell." She laughed, though doing so made her head spin. A line of bloody drool fell from her lips. "Everyone's too cowardly to kill me themselves. My death sentence would have been passed around to every potential executioner in Hell before anyone had the guts to do anything about me."

"Yes, well, you coming home has kept me from having to worry about that part," said Belial.

"Was it even Avaira who really attacked me the first time I came here? Was she the one who told everyone I'd run away?" Annabelle asked. "Or did you order her to do those things too?"

"Don't be ridiculous," said Belial, but just what Annabelle was being ridiculous about, he didn't say.

What could she do? Annabelle couldn't threaten him with punishment for killing a succubus, because no one would ever find out he'd done it. She couldn't threaten to hurt him herself, pinned down and unable to teleport. There wasn't even anyone to avenge her. Even if Samantha had rescued Annabelle from Douglas and his men out of affection or the goodness of her heart, she'd still made sure no one saw her doing it. She'd never be willing to stick out her neck.

Then again, no one said Annabelle had to tell the truth.

"You'll regret this, Belial!" Annabelle hissed. "I took up with a...a...religious man on Earth. A powerful religious figure!"

"How pious can he be if he associates with you?" said Belial.

Good point.

"He thinks I'm an angel," Annabelle invented. "And he knows where I am, and if I don't come back, he has, um, powers, holy powers, that will make you sorry!"

Belial raised one perfectly plucked eyebrow. "And where is this paragon of virtue now? Lighting up a temple somewhere?"

"Like I'm going to tell you." Annabelle smirked, trying to look much more confident than she felt.

"I see. He wouldn't be one of the men you dropped off at King Zagan's Earth residence before coming to visit, would he?"

And *bang!* Just like that all of Annabelle's hopes disappeared, leaving an aching emptiness behind. She gasped with the agony of it, like a hole punched through her chest that left her weak and shaking. This was it, the end, an end she'd never really believed would come.

"It seems so," said Belial. "Well, why don't we just have a look through Zagan's palace? You let me know if you see your holy man anywhere."

The crystal ball flared to life once more, showing Annabelle the front entrance of Zagan's mansion, that massive marble staircase. Bodies were strewn around like leaves fallen from a tree. Blood soaked the ground so thickly that it looked like the dead floated in a shallow red river.

The killers had gone, so the crystal ball's view moved on. As it went, the image spread beyond the crystal ball itself, soon covering the entire far stone wall so that Annabelle could see every claw mark made against Zagan's walls.

The crystal ball's projected vision moved upstairs, looking for the misery of new victims to put on display for Belial's mockery. On the left was the suite Jimmy and Harry had been in when Annabelle left them. The door hung open, exposing the empty room. Seeing it, Annabelle found herself capable of feeling even worse than she already did. She began to heave, her gut begging to be unloaded. When the view moved on and the projection wall showed her a twisted, bent door with blood trickling from the side, she vomited for real. The mess splattered her face and ran down to her clothes. One guard laughed and shoved her face in it before yanking her head back up to see the view projected on Belial's wall again.

"Oh dear," said Belial, studying the projection. "If this is your holy man, you're not going to be pleased."

Annabelle shook and gagged with terror, squeezing her eyes shut. It was Harry, she knew it. Belial saw Harry projected onto the wall, saw him being tortured somehow, saw him being ruined and driven back to the madness she'd worked so hard to save him from.

Noises came from the projection, grunts from one unfamiliar voice and sobs from another familiar one. Annabelle had heard Harry sob that way nearly every night for months.

Annabelle had to look. She couldn't not; she couldn't hear Harry in pain and turn away. Slowly, fighting herself for every inch, Annabelle raised her head until she could just barely see the projected image on the wall, blurry through her hair and lines of blood and vomit dripping into her eyes. She made out two figures, one with dark skin and black hair, the other with pale skin and light brown hair that dangled in front of his eyes.

Unable to stop herself any longer, Annabelle looked right at the terrible wall, where Jimmy lay limp and covered in blood. Only Harry's arms kept him from the floor. Harry's devastation was plain in every line of his face, his grief deep enough that he didn't even notice the blood staining his skin and clothes. He fumbled with Jimmy's body, holding one hand down against the huge wound in Jimmy's chest in a fruitless attempt to staunch the bleeding, trying to lower him to the ground without dropping him.

"Noooo..." he keened, voice high and full of grief. "Oh, no..."

A demon hovered beside them, its claws caked in bits of flesh and gobs of congealing blood. It rumbled deep in its chest and advanced forward, flicking its fingers out, then curling them in again.

Annabelle screamed, but Harry saw nothing but Jimmy. There was nothing to stop the demon from running him through.

Except the demon stopped moving. He began looking all around the room, a shocked expression making his ugly face comical and ruining the frightening impression he'd given only seconds ago.

"What in Lucifer's kingdom is that?" Belial whispered, and for the first time ever, Annabelle heard confusion in his voice.

Beyond the huddled forms of Jimmy and Harry, a few unbroken TV monitors sizzled with static. Most had been crushed or broken, some completely split apart, and now lay in pieces on the ground in an orgy of wires and glass and sparks. They trembled, slightly at first, then more violently. The plastic casings banged together hard enough to crack further; the desk they sat on began to bump and smash its way across the room until it hit a wall and clattered to the ground.

Memories flashed one after the other before Annabelle's eyes. Harry's locked door, mangled and hanging from its hinges when Annabelle arrived home from work, despite being double-thick, locked, and reinforced. The endless parade of cups and dishes that turned up shattered without anyone touching them. The window in Zagan's mansion that broke just as Harry went by.

"What is he?" said Belial, eyes growing wide. He swallowed audibly and tugged on the white collar of his robes as though it had grown too tight. Belial watched his assassin stumble round, struggling to keep its balance as the shaking increased. "Lady Annabelle, what is that thing?"

Harry grew luminescent, light shooting from his every pore and illuminating the room until the few monitors still working looked dim by comparison. His sobs increased and grew into cries; the light intensified until Annabelle could barely see.

Harry *screamed*, and his light grew so bright Annabelle might have been staring at the surface of the sun. Power exploded from him, ripples of force that tore through everything they touched. The demon assassin flew back and dissolved into millions of particles that swirled around the room. The television monitors, the table, the walls; they were exploded and destroyed in the wave of grief that rent Harry's heart in two.

Belial cried out, and if Annabelle had any regrets, it was that her fear for Harry kept her from enjoying his shock the way she wanted to. He touched the crystal ball and its view pulled back until the stone wall showed the front of Zagan's mansion.

Rumbling and groaning, the palace began to collapse, gravity and momentum finishing the job Harry's power had begun. Annabelle envisioned Harry's body buried under tons of plaster and wood and screamed. She began to struggle and, amazingly, broke free. Her guards, as affected by the sight of Harry's power as she, had loosened their grip in their distraction.

Still shrieking like a madwoman, Annabelle grabbed the gun waiting under her jacket, pointed it at the first head she saw, and fired. The demon with two faces fell, waving its arms as though trying to stave off Annabelle's second shot. It failed, and she blew the head in its belly to bits with her next, point-blank shot.

A muscular tentacle wrapped round her neck, the embedded suction cups pulling at Annabelle's flesh.

"Blasphemer!" the tentacled demon snarled. "Traitor! Human weapons, you brought human weapons *here!*"

Pulling the trigger felt enormously, beatifically powerful. Annabelle focused all her rage into the little round bit of metal that turned a powerful tentacle into a bloody stump with a single shot. She fired again, not sure if she was yelling or laughing by now, and loved the way the guard's head turned into a shower of bone fragments and bits of brain. The gore baptized her, blowing away and replacing the vomit on her front.

When she turned to Belial, she found him pressed up against the back wall, staring at her with wide eyes full of fear and loathing. Yet he remained a true king and did not scream or beg.

Though it ached from the gun's recoil, Annabelle kept her arm up, barrel pointed straight at Belial's golden head. She felt strong enough to maintain the stance all day, and watching Belial squirm might have been worth trying.

The wall projection showed Annabelle the ruins of Zagan's mansion, with nothing moving but trails of dust.

"Get help, Belial," she said. "Get your legions up there and dig them out, or so help me I'll paint the wall with your brain!"

But no, Annabelle realized, looking closer at Belial's face. The tightness of his mouth, the furrow of his brow; these were not signs of fear as she'd hoped, but of anger. He lowered his head as a bull will lower its head to charge, rather than as a gesture of shame.

"You think," Belial said, "you really think that you, a whore masquerading as a noblewoman, can point your little piece of tin at the greatest king of all Hell and see him surrender?"

Belial spoke a word that Annabelle didn't recognize; six thousand years of life made her too young to know it. But she could feel power, old and strong, bursting from it even as her body was raised above the floor and tossed across the room like a weightless doll. Belial's power slammed her into the wall with enough force to shatter a human spine.

Pressure against her front kept Annabelle up against the wall, unable to twitch so much as a finger. Her bones groaned with strain, warning her they would soon shatter, and her flesh rippled over her muscles, sliding towards the wall in grotesque waves. Annabelle shut her eyes, but knew her eyeballs were about to burst or sink back into her brain.

The gun had flown from her hand to land somewhere she couldn't see, not that she could have fired it anyway. Annabelle knew she was about to die if she didn't escape from Belial's magic, but since she couldn't teleport from the room…

Of course, Belial had never told her she couldn't teleport *inside* the room. She couldn't leave it, but could she move to another spot within it?

Though Belial had promised her pain if she tried to teleport, Annabelle hardly had anything to lose now. Unable even to take a breath to steady herself or open her eyes to spot where to land, Annabelle thought of the crystal ball in the corner and ordered her body to shift.

Relief came immediately. Never had just *being*, just standing and breathing and supporting her body with her own two feet, been such an ecstatically wonderful sensation.

Annabelle perched on the crystal ball like a bird of prey, sighting Belial and pouncing on him before he realized where she'd gone. The move had no grace, but was effective; his head hit the ground with a crack that Annabelle found enormously satisfying. She looked for her gun while Belial tried to pull himself together and found it against the wall she'd been trapped on. Rolling off him to grab it, Annabelle leapt to her feet and forced the barrel into Belial's mouth before he could say another spell.

Annabelle's breathing sounded obscenely loud in her ears, but her grip was steady enough.

"Belial," she hissed. Bits of the King's dead guards dripped from her front onto his white robes. "You're going to get help for my friends, and you're going to get it now." Trying to think of a way to keep Belial quiet while still letting him up and get the help she'd ordered, Annabelle glanced at the crystal ball's projection to see the collapsed mansion one last time—and froze.

Harry's head and shoulders appeared above the rubble, and though his figure looked tiny on the wall, Annabelle could see him frantically pushing debris aside to dig himself out. The moment his arms were free, Harry reached down and pulled Jimmy up with him. Limp and covered in gold dust from one of Zagan's expensive trinkets, Jimmy looked like nothing so much as an expensive, oversize child's toy.

For whatever reason, Harry didn't use his new-found telekinesis to free himself. Perhaps he was too tired or worried he couldn't control it. Either way, he just kept scooping away piles of nails and plaster and metal until his and Jimmy's bodies came free.

Annabelle turned back to Belial, glaring at her over her gun barrel. What could she do? Harry obviously still needed her help, but now that his situation wasn't so desperate or hopeless, she had no reason to involve Belial.

Yet just leaving the king alive to come after her would be an equally stupid thing to do. Almost as stupid as killing him and bringing the wrath of Hell down on herself would be.

Biting her lip, Annabelle focused on Belial, though she didn't really see him any longer. Harry needed help. He was still too fragile to take on a crisis like this by himself. Belial had seen Harry and could track him down again if Annabelle left him alive.

Pulling the trigger both thrilled and terrified her. It was an insane act of defiance she hadn't considered in even the lowest moments when she'd considered calling her mother. It sealed her fate. Belial lay dead on the stone floor with his brain splattered to all four walls, but Annabelle knew she might as well have turned the gun on herself. She was dead now, too. Annabelle felt her consciousness split in half, so that half of her panicked while the other half calmed, accepting the situation with relief. No more running. No more fear or uncertainty. She had one last task to perform and then death could come for her.

Dropping the gun with its single remaining bullet onto the ground—she had no more use for it—Annabelle jumped back onto the crystal ball and then into the ceiling, letting her body travel through the rock and out into sulfuric open air. Then she teleported up into the earth itself, traveling toward the surface where Harry waited for her, letting the good, rich soil embrace her one last time.

Chapter

16

Jimmy knew he should be terrified. He hated heights. Always had, since as far back as he could remember. Airplanes provided a particular kind of torture. Whenever forced into one of those hellish steel death traps, Jimmy inevitably spent the flight flattened against his seat hyperventilating, hands gripping the handles hard enough to make his knuckles ache for days. Images of the engines failing and the plane falling like…well, like several tons of metal and flammable gasoline that would crash into the ground and explode in fiery death ran through his head for hours before and after the flight itself took place.

The only pleasant flight Jimmy could ever remember having was one he took with his father twenty years before. He hadn't wanted to go, but his father had been so proud of getting his pilot's license, and Jimmy still hoped that if he did what his father said, he could win his love. When they reached cruising altitude, the most amazing thing had happened; Jimmy's father saw his son's fear and spoke gently, explaining all the strange sounds the plane made. He told Jimmy everything he did to the plane before he did it, explained away all the strange clunks and bangs and groans so they became normal parts of flying.

Don't you make strange sounds in a normal day, Karim? Don't you break wind after eating, or yell when you stumble, or make uncomfortable noises when you run into walls?

Jimmy, relaxed in an airplane seat for the first and only time of his life, giggled and saw the oncoming blue sky as full of possibility and hope. He saw the sun lighting up the sky with color as it set, oranges and reds and pink hues. A lake shimmered below like smooth blue glass, a cool contrast to the magnificent, fiery sky. All of God's glory spread out before the plane for Jimmy to experience in that moment: the beauty of His world, the love of Jimmy's father, and the conquering of a terrible fear. Then and there Jimmy realized, though he was too young to put such beatific transcendence into words or even fully understand his feelings, the depth and profundity of his connection to God. The greatness around him humbled him, stunned him, and yet made him feel wonderfully free. It was the cheesiest, sappiest, happiest moment of his life until then. Above all things he had felt loved, and he'd assumed he'd never forget that feeling.

Except he had. Jimmy had forgotten the plane and the love and the transcendence faster than he'd believed it possible to forget anything.

Now that moment came back to him. Jimmy felt warm and safe, relaxed in his seat in a way he never felt on an airplane. Looking around, he recognized the control panel as the one his father had operated all those years ago. There, by a panel of switches, he saw the same deep scratch he'd noticed twenty years ago (*Oh my God!* he'd shrieked, *the plane is damaged! We're going to crash!*). The door had the same loose handle (*Oh my God! The door is broken! We're going to die!*), the underside of his seat the same wad of gum (*Oh my God! This plane is old! It won't work and we'll fall apart at thirty-five million feet!*).

Someone sat beside him, someone he loved who loved him back, strongly enough that Jimmy could feel it like a physical force. From the corner of his eye he could see the vague figure of a pilot, but when Jimmy turned his head the pilot's image slipped away like a fading dream. However much he squinted or widened his eyes, however hard he craned his neck, he couldn't get a good look.

Giving up, Jimmy slumped back into his seat, just letting himself bask in comfort and affection like a baby resting in its mother's arms.

How strange. He'd spent his life pushing and fighting to help others, reaching out to give anyone and everyone a chance at a satisfaction that he himself had only felt for the barest moment twenty years ago, and he hadn't even realized it.

Jimmy began to laugh at the shroud of misery that covered his own life; he'd grown so accustomed to it he'd stopped noticing it. Why was it so important to him to help every bleeding heart and sob story that crossed his path? Had he started believing that no one was ever nice to anyone, so he had to make up for that lack? Or had he hoped, somewhere in his sad, pathetic little soul, that if he gave enough, someone might someday give back so he could rediscover this moment on the plane?

He was laughing, and then he was crying, burying his head in his hands, desperately ashamed of his weakness.

The pilot was not ashamed of him, did not blame him for his confusion or his fear.

The creation is as God's family; for its sustenance is from Him: therefore, the most beloved unto God is the person who does good to God's family.

Jimmy knew the quote. He'd read it a thousand, a *hundred-thousand* times in his youth when trying to grasp at his slipping faith, trying to remind himself of what he believed in. Could he have been reading it the wrong way, with his life in the wrong place for him to understand it? The impact the quote had on him in childhood went away as his faith in his father went away, yet now, hearing it again for the first time in so many years, it resonated anew.

Jimmy put his right hand to his heart. It felt full with joy, and love, and the promise of tomorrow. When a loud thump sounded right in front of him, he barely noticed it over the peace in his soul.

Opening his eyes, Jimmy saw Annabelle crouched on the plane's nose, wildly out of place against the cloudless sky in her ridiculous skin-tight dress with her hair blowing all over. He grinned at the sight of her—he would have grinned at the sight of the devil himself, the way he felt now—wondering how she stayed upright.

Behind her, the sun still shone so brightly Jimmy knew he should be blind staring into it, but he didn't feel any discomfort.

Annabelle reached for him, her fingertips stopping just short of the plane's front window. Her eyes were wild.

"Take my hand!" she yelled, voice perfectly audible over the wind, the engine, and through the thick windshield plastic.

Jimmy blinked at her, confused. He couldn't think of a single reason she'd ask him something like that, though he suspected she had a good reason. He wanted to stay where he was, in this warm and happy place, and knew breaking the window to touch Annabelle would spoil that.

He glanced towards the pilot, but didn't receive any advice.

Looking back up at Annabelle's earnest, frantic expression, Jimmy decided he didn't have any reason not to take her hand. It wasn't like he hated her. In fact, though he hated admitting it to himself, he could relate to her in many ways—an unpleasant realization, given what a raging, annoying bitch she was. And, of course, the "evil" thing.

"Take my hand!" she cried again, shaking her arm as though Jimmy might have forgotten it was there.

"I..." Jimmy hesitated. The more he stared at that smooth, graceful hand, the more important it felt that he take it. The sky behind her grew brighter and brighter, and somehow Jimmy knew he had to make a choice, to stay in his seat or take her hand, but what did that choice mean? Why did he have to choose? Why so quickly? Why was Annabelle even here with him, wherever "here" was?

She looked desperate. She kept jabbing her hand forward, insisting with and without words that he take it. It was important to her that he do so. Perhaps, being the type of person that Jimmy was, nothing else mattered.

He reached for her. His arm went through the windowpane plastic as though it didn't exist; he grabbed Annabelle's proffered hand and then felt pain. Agony ran through his body, centering just below his heart, where blood ran freely from a huge hole.

Jimmy screamed. He squeezed his eyes shut and scrabbled at his chest with his right hand, squeezing Annabelle's with the left.

"It's all right," she told him, transmitting reassurance with a squeeze of her hand. He couldn't see her any longer as the world darkened around him, but he recognized her voice. "It's all right, I've got you. Just hold on..."

When Jimmy opened his eyes again the plane had disappeared, along with the bright sky. In its place Jimmy saw dawn edging over the New York horizon. He lay on the ground with stones poking his back, his head and shoulders cradled on Steve's lap. Annabelle knelt beside him, her hand still clutching his own. She looked exhausted.

"You did it!" Steve cried. Jimmy winced at the volume. His head hurt, along with the rest of him.

"What...where..."

"You were stabbed. A lot," said Annabelle. She let his hand go and slumped back; when she raised one arm to push a tangled lump of hair out of her eyes, it trembled with fatigue. She coughed dust from her throat.

"You healed me?" asked Jimmy, dumfounded. He looked down, ignoring the soreness of his joints as he pushed the strands of his shredded shirt aside and examined his chest. The wound remained, but looked weeks old. "You can heal?"

Annabelle still had the strength to give him a withering look. "I'm a mother," she said and left it at that.

Harry gently helped Jimmy roll on his side and gripped his shoulders as Jimmy vomited on the ground. Annabelle leaned back on her hands and stared up at the sky, trying to fight off the need for sleep. She had too many things to do still to be tired and couldn't take more than a moment to rest here. After the show Harry had just put on with his powers, police and firemen would be en route. No way Zagan would stick around to take any responsibility, the weasel.

People were beginning to gather at the edges of the mansion, so Annabelle hunched over and tried to hide as much of Jimmy and Harry from view as she could. She got a face full of debris and hacked.

"We need to get out of here before I get permanent sinus damage," she said between coughs. "And Jimmy needs a hospital."

"What?" said Jimmy. "I'm not healed?"

"I gave you a patch, but it's been centuries since I've used that sort of magic on anyone so I don't know how well I did. Besides, even if I didn't make any mistakes, you've still lost a dangerous amount of blood."

"So what do we do?" Harry whispered. He was scared but composed, staring up at Annabelle with childlike trust.

Annabelle scooped Jimmy into her arms and lifted him into the air. He cried, "Too fast!" and tipped his head just before vomiting again.

"Sorry," said Annabelle, "but we don't have much time, and I don't know how to fix you. I need to get you to a hospital, fast. Harry, float a cell phone over here so we can call an ambulance—"

"Are you kidding?" Jimmy said, sitting up halfway before collapsing against Annabelle again. "Do you know how much ambulances cost?"

"You're more worried about your paycheck than your life?"

"If I spend the rest of my life in debt and my insurance drops me for being too expensive, my life'll be at risk again anyway."

"Of all the—! Fine, I'll carry you myself. Hang onto me."

Jimmy squeaked, "What?" just as Harry said, "You're...you're leaving me alone?"

Turning to face him, Annabelle smiled, letting all of her affection show. It was so frightening to love someone this much, and yet she couldn't stop and didn't really want to. "Just for a few minutes, Harry, I promise. We're close to New York Downtown Hospital, so I just need to drop him off at the Emergency Room before his wound reopens or something."

She knelt down, trying not to jostle Jimmy, to meet Harry's shaded eyes. "Can you make it? I'll come running right back to you, I swear."

Harry nodded, but he nodded many times very quickly, as though trying not to tremble or seize up. Annabelle felt like some sort of heart-eating ice woman, making him look like that.

You've turned him into a doll for your comfort.

Annabelle knew now that Jimmy had spoken the truth. Harry was not a doll, and with all the powers of Hell about to come after her in force, he had to learn to stand on his own as a man right away.

"You're all right," she told him, though she was really reassuring herself. "You'll be fine. You just need to run into...um..." she looked around and saw the lights of the city to her left. "To Sylvie's, the health food restaurant two blocks that way." Annabelle pointed. "Right on the corner. All you have to do is walk down this street for two blocks, and it's right there, huge, with one of the neon letters busted. You wait there for me; hide from these nosy idiots and the police there. You're just someone having dinner—or if you can't manage that, pretend you have stomach problems and hide in the bathroom until I get back. I swear I'll come back, Harry."

"I believe you," he whispered. "I'll wait. Please take care of him."

Jimmy grumbled something inaudible, words laced with pain.

"I will," Annabelle promised, standing back up (Jimmy swallowed heavily). "And then I'll come back. I'll come back!"

She turned and ran, kicking off her stiletto heels so she could go faster, wishing she could teleport with another living thing so she didn't have to leave Harry even though she knew it was for his sake as much as Jimmy's that she do so.

He can do this, she told herself, though the idea that he could was as painful to Annabelle as the idea that he couldn't. She put her head down and ran faster, enjoying the way exertion heated her body, fighting off the winter cold. She was strong enough to fight the cold weather, and she could fight off this new cold in her heart, too.

Hours later Annabelle hovered over Jimmy and Harry, watching them sleep.

That Harry could sleep at all had come as a surprise, but then again, she still suspected his "coma" back at her house in Hell when she'd first rescued him had really been an exhausted sleep. Anyway, Annabelle understood by now that there was a whole lot she didn't know about being a poltergeist. And what else could he be but a poltergeist? A dead soul not passing on yet not transparent and helpless like a ghost...that was the definition she'd always heard. She'd never known of any confirmed cases of poltergeist sightings on Earth, which made sense, because she'd never heard a confirmed report of a soul escaping from Hell, either. If escaping from the afterlife turned a soul into a poltergeist like she suspected, Hell's kings would go to all lengths to guard the secret. Every ambitious schmo would be stealing the damned away if they knew they could create such a powerful creature by smuggling a soul up to Earth.

Harry looked so peaceful in sleep, all his worry lines smoothed away, brown bangs tangling in his eyelashes and tickling his nose. Annabelle reached out and pushed them out of the way, smiling as his nose crinkled and then relaxed.

His body didn't look nearly as comfortable. True, the hospital chair he sat in was padded, but it was also narrow with stuffing trailing out onto the floor. Harry had bent himself into a strange angle just to fit.

Despite the IV in his arm, Jimmy looked a lot more comfortable lying in a hospital bed. Annabelle knew he'd be fine even before the desk nurse told her his condition had stabilized. Suckers were easy to take advantage of, but it took more than a falling building to kill one. They always came back to irritate you again.

Annabelle realized she was glad Jimmy had pulled through and didn't quite know why. He wasn't her friend. She didn't love him. And yet...

"I tell you, darling, you're one of a kind." Samantha stood in the doorway, her smug face eerily shadowed in the hospital's dim lighting, her black silk clothes fading into the dark. "You've created chaos in Hell without losing a single one of your little harem."

"Amazing how you knew I was here," said Annabelle, unsurprised to see her friend. "Just like you knew my address back in Iowa."

"What kind of friend would I be if I didn't keep up with you? Anyway—" Samantha pulled a roll of money out of one silk-lined pocket and tossed it to Annabelle. "—Come on. We have to get out of here within about, oh, the next thirty seconds if you want to live."

Annabelle stared at the fat roll of thousand dollar bills with mixed feelings. For most of her life it would have amounted to pocket change, but now it meant freedom, the freedom she'd given up so much to find. Oh, how she wanted that freedom.

Sighing heavily, wanting to cry, Annabelle tossed the money back. "Thanks, but I've got it covered. That's a lot of cash, though, and trouble. You must love me after all, huh?"

It was a joke, so Annabelle in no way expected Samantha's reaction.

"Oh, you've no idea!" Striding forward with her arms wide, Samantha scooped Annabelle into a hug, spinning her around so that their hair, light and dark, wove patterns against the yellow walls and stale hospital air. "That money is all thanks to you. Bael and I would still be broke if you weren't such a thoughtless little spitfire!"

"What?" Annabelle jerked out of Samantha's grasp just as her friend dipped her backwards tango-style, and fell on her rear.

"Hides it well, doesn't he?" Samantha brushed back dangly black pearl earrings and smiled. "But with Belial in control of the only known portal to Earth, the second-largest army in Hell, and a seasoned battle vixen for his general, there was just no stopping him. He was monopolizing this ridiculous amount of resources."

"Crap." Belial had been Hell's ascendant king since before Annabelle's birth, but she'd been out of the loop for so many years that she hadn't realized just how powerful he'd become.

Pieces came together in Annabelle's mind. That explained why Bael had been so keen to marry Sam, so far below his station. Even more than an heir, he'd desperately needed a pathway to Earth to gain new allies and resources.

"And now, thanks to you, Belial's money and resources are ours!" Sam laughed, clapping her hands like a child given a particularly succulent piece of candy. "Brilliant!"

"I bet," said Annabelle, standing and brushing off her butt. "You've been spying on me, right? You knew the second I blew Belial's head off, so you had time to take over his castle and the portal to Earth before anyone else knew what was happening, let alone had time to make a move."

"By Lucifer's holy horns, I knew just making sure you could roam free would cause chaos I could use to my advantage, but 'Belle! All my major problems in one stroke! No one but you, darling." Samantha shook her head as though amused by a mischievous child. "Well, there's still one small problem: we're in the regrettable position of having to kill the troops that don't take oaths of loyalty to Bael. Most of Belial's men are coming along, though. The real loss is going to be General-Queen Avaira. All that talent and battle experience! But oh well, better dead then against us."

Sam pushed back her coat sleeve to check the huge Rolex on her wrist. "Speaking of dead, there's going to be dozens of soldiers and assassins arriving about now to kill you for killing Belial and destroying his empire. However you're planning to escape, you'd better hurry."

"I will. But first, Sam, it sounds like you owe me a favor—and in lieu of your money, I want something else."

"Oh?" Samantha hid her caution well, but Annabelle knew her well enough to see it. She took one last look at Harry's sleeping form, but quickly turned to the floor instead because seeing him hurt too much.

She'd already placed a note on Jimmy's bedside tray explaining her decision, leaving him to decide how much he wanted to share with Harry. The paper she'd borrowed from the hospital lauded the benefits of the medicine Effexor across the top, something Annabelle found wonderfully ironic since it was an antidepressant and Jimmy a shrink. Maybe he'd think she was criticizing him.

"I dunno if you did it on purpose, and I'm not asking, but thanks to your driving back in Des Moines, Douglas Crane and his cronies saw these two." Annabelle gestured to Harry and Jimmy. "So he—Douglas, not these two—and anyone he talked with about these men have to die. And Harry here needs to be erased from Hell's records before our illustrious kings calm down enough to start looking for missing souls."

"What a pain!" Samantha whined. "I'll have to go looking through stuffy old records to find him. Is his name really Harry, then?"

"Yes, but he'll be recorded under 'Steve Silver'." Annabelle hated giving Samantha his name, but there was hardly anything to lose. She already knew Harry's face, so she had enough information to hurt him if she wanted to.

"All right," Sam agreed. "Then we're even."

Annabelle nodded, lacking the energy to pretend she disliked the bargain they'd made. Harry's life was worth her own any day. "Now I have running for my life to do." Looking up and meeting Samantha's light blue eyes, so much lighter and yet so much colder than Harry's, she said, "Thanks, Sam. I mean it."

Samantha laughed uncomfortably at the sincere words. Duplicity she could handle, but honesty? She hadn't been exposed to enough of it to know what do. "Don't be such a sap. It's just…politics. Just another deal."

"Sure," said Annabelle. "I'd better go."

Samantha nodded, the smile sliding off her face. She hesitated visibly, something uncertain flickering into her eyes as she looked at the floor, mumbled, "Take care," and vanished.

Desperately wishing she could do the same, Annabelle turned for one last look at Harry, a sweet torture she couldn't deny herself. Then she left the room, shutting the door behind her. She walked down the sterile, white hall and used the stairs instead of the elevator, unsure if she was buying time to calm herself down, or just being cowardly and hoping a solution would drop on her head before she got outside.

The hospital was a bright and busy place, but the stairwell was dim, painted brown with scuffed rubber lining the dirty stairs. Annabelle met no one on her walk down. It felt like she'd fallen into a tunnel, vaguely similar to when she sunk into the earth: as though she might never reach the end, and spend the rest of her life going down and down and down…but eventually she reached a metal door with a huge sign reading EXIT in bold red letters.

The winter air outside cooled, but did not refresh, Annabelle when she stepped out into the rear parking lot. It faced a ditch rather than a street, and the smell alone made her want to run away. Even with streetlights, hospital lights, and the muffled sounds of traffic from the other side of the building, Annabelle felt isolated. A vague aura of menace lingered round the lot like nausea after a head wound.

Turning and craning her head, Annabelle could just make out some of the buildings on the other side of the hospital's main structure. Everything looked so gray and tasteless from the ground, showing none of the brilliance of the skyline from above.

Scrabbling noises came from the ditch, the noise Annabelle had been waiting for. She turned just in time to see Avaira's white head and red eyes appear over the edge, followed by three arms that hoisted the General-Queen to the surface.

Death had come, and Annabelle found she didn't fear it. In her heart, she felt the sacrifice she planned to make was right, absolutely, unequivocally, ineffably right. Was this how Jimmy felt all the time, knowing he did the morally correct thing? If so, she understood what made him so willing to endure life as a sucker. Now that she had become a sucker too, she found that the sacrifices involved meant next to nothing compared to the reward of this feeling.

She held her ground, again kicking off her heeled shoes, which Harry had thoughtfully picked up when she'd first discarded them at the remains of Zagan's palace, so she could stand steady. She braced herself for a familiar explosion of rage from Avaira, but Avaira showed no sign of theatrics. She simply walked across the parking lot, almost as slowly as Annabelle had walked down the hospital stairs moments ago. Her eyes were dull, her posture defeated.

Annabelle only knew what everyone in Hell knew about Avaira: that she'd been a lowly slave until Belial made her his bride (the scandal had been huge). No one but the two of them knew all the details, but Annabelle didn't need them to know that Belial had been Avaira's whole life. She didn't understand why anyone would be willing to make another living creature, let alone a demon king, become their world, but Avaira had done so. As far as Annabelle could tell, as far as Hell's gossip line knew, Avaira had lived only for her husband.

And now he was dead.

A sword flew into the ground at Annabelle's feet point-first, making her gasp and step back. Her head snapped up again to see Avaira holding an identical sword in one hand. It was a simple tool, without ornamentation. Studying the plain, well-used weapon, with an edge sharp enough to cut a man in half and dents from previous battles running up and down its length, anyone could see it had no function but to kill.

"You gave me my son," said Avaira, her voice as dead as her eyes. "You have the right to die quickly and with honor."

"'Gave'?" Had the baby died too? Annabelle's inner peace disappeared, leaving her confused once again. So much for using her instinct for "the right thing" to guide her. Was there a right thing to do for a woman like Avaira who'd just lost everything?

She could only go forward with her original plan. She couldn't decide what to do for Avaira; she had no right, and no resources, to start helping others. Annabelle could buy Harry and Jimmy's safety with her death. That had to be enough.

Annabelle pulled the sword from the ground without a word. It had been centuries since she'd used one, but since she just had to die to make her plan work, that didn't matter much. The smartest thing would be to refuse the sword and just let Avaira get things over with.

But Annabelle could never just let things happen. Fighting fate took her from Hell months ago, and even now that she planned to accept fate, she couldn't throw aside her nature to do it. No, she'd die swinging. She was incapable of doing anything else.

So, Annabelle held the blade at the ready and waited for Avaira to attack.

"Holy Excedrin, Batman, who's tap dancing on my skull?" Jimmy tried to reach one hand up to his throbbing head (which had to be at least twice its normal size) but had no idea if he actually managed to do it. He rapidly ascended from a black void of chemical-induced unconsciousness, but that blackness overlapped with his waking view of the hospital room and left him disoriented, unsure of all his senses.

Steve's face flew into his vision, his expression anxious yet joyful. "Dr. Hamid! Oh thank God."

"Not so loud," Jimmy groaned. "Do I have my hand? I mean, is it still attached to my arm? Actually, is everything still here below my neck, or is my head just floating in a pickle jar somewhere? Because I can't feel anything."

"No, all your parts are connected. I think. I mean, all the parts I can see. There are a few things I'd rather not look at to make sure."

It was a statement sure to panic Jimmy, except the feeling flowed back through his limbs as Steve babbled. Though that included a fresh wave of pain, Jimmy's relief was strong enough to make the discomfort worth it. He raised his right arm only to feel a tugging at the joint, an IV.

"Wow," he said.

"Yeah, your blood loss was dramatic. That's the word the doctor used: dramatic. I just had this image of your blood putting on some sort of Shakespeare play in stupid costumes when he said that."

Of course, that image flew into Jimmy's head, making him laugh, which was painful in a whole different and terrible way. "Oh, Steve, please pick a different time to be funny, okay?"

"Sorry. You feel pretty crap then, huh."

"I think this is how Jesus must have felt when nailed to the cross," Jimmy agreed. He looked gingerly around the room, an average, tacky hospital room with its antiseptic smell, yellow-painted walls, limp curtains, and a TV mounted in one corner. Through the tiny window in his closed door he saw nurses, doctors, and orderlies running around fast enough to be slapstick comedians desperate to make a tough audience laugh. At least, it looked that way. Jimmy couldn't tell for sure with his door closed; he really just saw blurs of color rushing past.

He realized he and Steve were alone in the room. "So where's Satan's bride?"

"I'm not sure. I guess she's out talking with the doctors."

"She didn't tell you when she left?"

"No, it's just...I think I fell asleep." Steve grinned. "I guess even dead souls get exhausted enough to sleep sometimes. I was a terrified wreck, and sitting at that snooty yuppie restaurant for almost an hour didn't help. You should've seen the way people kept looking at me, especially since I had 'Belle's heels on the seat next to me."

"You did incredibly well for yourself," said Jimmy, unable to help feeling a little pride, however much he reminded himself that Steve deserved the credit for this victory. "Remembering a little detail like bringing Annabelle's shoes to her when so frightened yourself is no little thing."

Steve looked like he'd just been crowned king of Earth but grew concerned again when Jimmy coughed.

"Hang on, I'll get you some water." He reached toward the table beside Jimmy's bed to do just that, then frowned. "Hey, you've got a letter here."

"What?" Jimmy turned too fast, winced when the room spun around, and saw the paper with his name on it once his vision leveled out.

He picked it up and saw the miniature advertisement for an anti-depressant across the top.

Very funny, Annabelle.

While Steve poured him a cup of water, Jimmy scanned through the letter. Because he had trouble absorbing the information, he read it again more carefully. Then a third time, hoping he'd missed something. When he decided he hadn't, he slowly put the letter down in his lap, wondering what to think.

"What is it?" Steve asked.

"Steve, I...I don't know how to tell you this." Jimmy cursed Annabelle in his head. She had to leave him this one last unpleasant task, hadn't she? Couldn't tell Steve herself that she wouldn't be coming back. No, leave it to good ol' Jimmy to break Steve's heart!

"Doc, you're scaring me. Just tell me —"

The world imploded.

A huge, invisible hand pressed Jimmy deep into his mattress, leaving him fighting for each breath through half-flattened lungs. Steve fell—no, he was shoved—to the ground. The cheap plant in Jimmy's windowsill began to turn brown and crumble away, the window glass to groan in its frame. Power had turned the air into a solid, malevolent thing trying to crush anything that lived.

Annabelle was a powerful demon with telepathy, teleportation abilities, strength, healing abilities, illusionary powers (Jimmy refused to accept her earlier explanation for the way her appearance changed) and who knew what else. Being near her still felt nothing like this. What awesome, terrifying creature from Hell could emit so much spiritual pressure without even being in Jimmy's room?

Oh, Annabelle, Jimmy thought. *Who've you offended* now?

Everything happened so fast.

Avaira was on Annabelle, a streak of white lightning against the night sky, beautiful in her own deadly way save for the overwhelming grief in her eyes. Her sword came down faster than Annabelle could see, and only instinct brought Annabelle's sword up in a block. She moved sloppily, ashamed to see just how out of practice she was; no noblewoman should let her skills atrophy so terribly. The impact sent a jolt of pain up her right arm, weakening it and letting Avaira's sword slide along Annabelle's blade towards her body in a shower of sparks and sharp edges.

The sword pierced Annabelle's shoulder; she leapt back with a scream. Blood spurted from the wound, and the sword pulling out sent a fresh wave of agony along her nerves. Everyone in Hell, *everyone*, feared Avaira, and rightfully so. To think that with her heart not in their fight, her mind and senses deadened by grief, the General-Queen still had such speed and skill!

Annabelle dropped to the ground to avoid a wide swing, then leapt up to try and take advantage of Avaira's exposed middle. Before she made it halfway to her feet Avaira stabbed down, penetrating deep into Annabelle's left thigh.

Her leg went dead, and Annabelle collapsed onto the ground. She fell hard, and when her arm struck the ground her sword flew from her hand and skidded across the parking lot. Annabelle thought it wanted to get away from her before her weakness got it killed, too.

But ah, her weakness was no shame now, for however sloppy her death was, it bought the lives of a man she loved and a man she grudgingly respected. Annabelle shut her eyes as Avaira raised her sword in a quick and graceful arc, unable to keep fear away, yet ready for the end…

(What happened to demons after death, anyway, wondered a tiny voice that sounded much like Jimmy? No one knew, for demons did not return to Hell when killed. Did they cease to exist, like the Atheists believed? Did they get a second chance in Heaven? Were they reborn into new demon baby bodies?)

Footsteps. Lots and lots of footsteps, growing in number and volume with each passing second, marching in unison and finally echoing around the parking lot like gunshots.

Annabelle's eyes snapped open and she saw that Avaira had lowered her sword. The General-Queen gaped in shock at something to her left. When Annabelle turned, she saw why: Belial's—no, Bael's—gate to Hell was open, and dozens of demon soldiers, bearing the crests of all the kings of Hell save Belial and Zagan on their decorative armor, marched out into the parking lot.

Glancing up through the hospital windows with her eyes and mind, Annabelle found people moving normally through the halls, not apparently feeling any distress or confusion unrelated to the illnesses and injuries of patients. Some demon had bespelled the place then.

"No!" Avaira shrieked, showing a spark of life and feeling for the first time. "She's mine!"

"General-Queen Avaira," said a blue-scaled demon wearing a helm that hid his face and distorted his voice, "you are under arrest for disobeying the will of the united Kings of Hell. Drop your sword and step away from Lady Annabelle. Lady Annabelle, you are under arrest for the murder of King Belial. Both of you step over here, hands in plain sight, mouths closed. Now."

Annabelle's nails scraped at the pavement in fear. If they took her to Hell and tortured her...what if she gave Harry away? Again, the image of her mother rose in the back of her mind. *Call her,* a terrified voice in back of Annabelle's head whispered, *call her, she'll save you...*

The miniature demon army surrounded her and Avaira, every soldier with a sword drawn, claws at the ready, or arrows pointed their way. The irony amazed Annabelle. This had to be the first act of cooperation between Hell's kings in centuries. How did trying to live her own life lead to a revolution?

"You think you have authority over me?" Avaira roared. More than a few soldiers shrank back. "None command me save my Lord and Master. With him dead I acknowledge no authority except my own judgment!"

"Some soldiers of Belial's agreed with you," said the same blue-scaled demon, who had not flinched before her temper, "and decided they would rather follow you than King Bael. They have all lost their heads. No one will save you, General-Queen."

"Save me?" Avaira spit on the ground. The pavement sizzled where it struck. "I need no rescue from traitors like you!"

With that, she leapt straight into the formation of soldiers, sword raised high and fangs bared. The blue demon's head rolled to the ground before he could so much as lift his spear. Every stroke of Avaira's sword resulted in another dead body on the ground, and half a dozen demons had fallen before anyone moved. Apparently, the army had assumed that even Avaira wasn't crazy enough to take them all on.

For a moment, Annabelle thought Avaira might even win. But sheer numbers were against her, and as live and dead bodies piled atop her, she began sinking under the weight.

Annabelle looked around for the sword she'd dropped. She had to kill herself, right now, before the army pulled itself together enough to capture her.

A blow to the back of her head smashed Annabelle's chin into the ground with a crunch. Annabelle gasped with pain and realized she should have just teleported away, but her mind had been so completely focused on dying that escaping hadn't occurred to her. She tried to concentrate enough to teleport now, but her head spun and her jaw, arm, and leg all screamed with pain. Blood soaked her hair and filled her mouth, choking her; she couldn't even pull together the concentration to fight back as two guards stretched her arms behind her back and put heavy, magical manacles on her, disrupting the little thought she had left and stealing her ability to teleport. The guards weighed down on her as they did with Avaira, and however hard Annabelle tried to kick, move her arms, or teleport, nothing would move.

"Where's the missing soul?" A large demon with thick horns called in a voice obviously accustomed to being answered. Annabelle froze.

"Not in this parking lot, sir, but I can sense it nearby."

"Go find it." All the soldiers except two, who kept watch over Avaira and Annabelle's battered bodies, moved to obey.

Annabelle's soul screamed. This wasn't how it was supposed to be!

The soldiers swarmed toward the hospital like a hive of angry bees, weapons ready and psychics at the front to weed Harry out from the crowd inside.

Biting down on a scream resulted in a pathetic squeal escaping Annabelle's mouth. Her mind raced so quickly she was sure it would explode from her skull; she couldn't understand half of her garbled, panicked thoughts let alone come up with a plan. She had no hope of beating even one soldier of the royal army, not through fighting or seduction or treachery.

No, Annabelle had only one chance, one wildly insane long-shot: she could call upon a very special demon. A demon so powerful, so dangerous, that asking her for help was more foolish than letting the army have their way with her and the hospital.

Annabelle thought of the guards finding Harry, or worse, torturing her until *she* gave them Harry, and knew she had to try.

As the psychics approached the hospital's back door, Annabelle opened her mouth, spit out a mouthful of blood, and screamed: "MOTHER!"

For a second, a single beat of Annabelle's heart, nothing.

And then...

Power.

Pure power washed over the parking lot and hospital, spillover from a creature so old and strong that simply by existing it brought lesser creatures to submission.

As far as Annabelle knew, only four beings in creation could emit so much energy so casually. The first was supposedly God, though as Annabelle had never met God, she couldn't be sure.

The second was Choronzon, the living shadow.

The third was Lucifer.

The fourth...

Slowly turning her head, ignoring the pain that ripped through her immobilized shoulders and abused skull at even that simple move, Annabelle looked over the heads of the makeshift army. All of the soldiers fell to their knees, if they hadn't already been forced there by the swell of spiritual might emanating from the slender figure that materialized in front of Bael's portal: Lady Lilith, Mother of Hell. She glided towards the army, an ethereal, terrifying figure. The army trembled before her.

"That. Is. Enough." said Lilith.

Chapter

17

To Annabelle, Lady Lilith was a mother above all else, so she saw a beautiful woman in her forties with dark, luxurious hair and wide green eyes approach. This evening Lilith had draped her long limbs in purple silks that moved when she did, clinging to some places and obscuring others, making a person looking at her long to see what was underneath. Diamonds hung over her forehead, attached to a string that laced through her hair, both holding and decorating an elaborate style. She walked slowly forward, jewels tinkling as she turned her head left and right to observe the scene around her, an unreadable expression on her regal visage.

As Annabelle had hoped, no one, not the Captain or the psychics, dared speak to Lady Lilith, not even to mention a missing soul. Save for a few cries of, "Lady Lilith!" and "Honorable Mother!" the parking lot went silent.

"Why, I must be losing my vision in my old age," said Lady Lilith, each word a crack of thunder. "I could swear I'm watching two honorable soldiers of Hell, my proud descendants, manhandling my daughter!"

Annabelle's captors let go, inadvertently dropping her to the ground. Bowing apologies—they didn't dare say even "sorry" aloud— they pulled her back to her feet, unlocking her manacles and brushing her off in their eagerness to please.

The moment they backed away, heads so low they could barely walk, Annabelle fell to her knees like all the others before the Mother of Hell, she who held ultimate authority even without land of her own or an army under her command. Those in the hospital had to be in pain by now. Annabelle hoped no one would come to the windows and look directly at Lilith. Her monstrous beauty could drive humans mad or turn them into slaves with a single glance.

Lilith went to Annabelle and put one hand on her shoulder. A violent shock of pain ran through Annabelle's body, like she'd been branded with a hot iron. "Dearest Annabelle. You've caused a great deal of trouble for everyone, haven't you?"

Annabelle bowed lower, her forehead touching the ground.

"Your youthful exuberance is to be expected," said Lilith, "and I'm sure all this drama you're involved in seems very important to you. But you have responsibilities and crimes to face up to, and it's high time you came home and did just that."

Biting her lip, not daring to say a word, Annabelle glanced back at the hospital, looking for help she knew would never come. In a second-floor window she saw a dark and familiar face, one full of grief and worry, which almost made her heart stop. Annabelle shut her eyes, begging the vision to disappear by the time she opened them again, but it did not: Harry stood behind the window, finger pads and nose pressed up against the glass, eyes wide and focused on her.

Annabelle quickly looked away, letting her hair fall before her eyes to hide the fear in them. *Human? Did you see a human? No, I didn't see a human, you must be imagining things...*

Why did Harry have to watch her be brought low this way? It was too cruel, to both of them!

That wasn't Annabelle's only problem, either. When she glanced at Lady Lilith, she was horrified to see her mother staring up at the window as well, right at Harry. Annabelle, like all other demons, had to do what Lilith said. Defiance was not only impossible, but unthinkable. Would fate be so terrible as to make Annabelle watch Harry's death?

Apparently not. When Lilith looked down again, her eyes had softened.

"Emotions are tempting things," she said, stroking Annabelle's cheek. Annabelle bit her tongue until it bled to keep from screaming. "And I know something of losing oneself to the moment. In the end, when both parties go their separate ways wiser than they were before, they should find no shame in their adventures together and many lessons that enrich their future lives. But make no mistake: young people making an adventure of their lives, lost in love for each other, must part eventually. Painful though it is, in time, it's for the best."

Lilith knelt down and gently raised her daughter's chin until they stared right at each other. Fear nearly made Annabelle pass out.

"You will face punishment for your crimes," said Lilith, stern once again. "Severe punishment, so agonizing and lengthy you will beg for death. That, too, will be for the best. Because when it is over your honor will be returned to you. You will again be a true lady of Hell, beloved and respected for the new lives you bear."

Could her adventure end like this, in despair? Could the freedom Annabelle fought so hard for be taken from her without a whimper of protest? For a few short months Annabelle had had her own life, and really believed no one could make her a slave again.

Now, looking into Lilith's eyes made Annabelle tiny, a powerless speck of dust to be brushed aside at her mother's will. Here was true helplessness, true hopelessness, the kind that metal bars and prison walls couldn't force on someone.

Annabelle bowed her head in submission, thinking of Harry and hoping he wouldn't judge her too harshly. Lilith had allowed her to save him, even if she also planned to force Annabelle to break all the other promises she'd made to herself. There would be rape, daily rape and constant pregnancy and pain with no time for rest or healing until Annabelle's soul and body shattered.

But Harry would be free. As long as Harry was free, a part of Annabelle would be too.

Annabelle risked one last glance up at the hospital window. Her eyes met Harry's for the briefest second and she thought, *I love you* as hard as she could. She wasn't worried he would do something stupid like run down to the parking lot and try and save her, not really. He'd come a long way, but no creature living or dead had the strength or courage to take on Lilith. Annabelle only feared that he wouldn't understand why she was leaving him with no explanation and barely a glance.

Her last look at Harry reassured her. In that last glance, Annabelle had seen, and believed, that Harry loved her, too.

Roughly a month ago, Harry and Annabelle sat behind their little Iowa house, staring up at the stars in silence and enjoying a rare moment of peace.

As the evening wore on, rather than growing more relaxed, Harry grew more and more wound up. Not in a bad way. Annabelle thought he seemed pensive.

"What are you thinking?" she asked.

"I'm wondering about the nature of the human soul," he said.

Annabelle groaned. "You're not going to start asking me about God, are you?"

Harry glanced over at her, surprised. "You've met God? I mean, you were born to a demon mother and lived in Hell your whole life. When did you meet God?"

"You don't just meet God," said Annabelle. "At least, that's what I've heard. That would be like meeting Bill Gates just because you work at Microsoft."

"Right," said Harry. "Anyway, I'm not thinking about God, I'm thinking about human souls. I'm here, right? You carried me here, and I'm solid, except I don't have a body like humans have a body.

"Now, if you go by some schools of thought, souls go elsewhere when they die. That's what I did when I died, so that makes sense. It's just, if Hell's where bad people go, then what about good people? You told me there's a Heaven, but where is it?"

Annabelle shrugged. "Hell is underground, so maybe Heaven is up."

"Yeah, but I've been reading about that in some of those books you got me, and 'up' doesn't have any meaning in space; it only means something in a place where there's gravity. Plus, up where? Carl Sagan said our galaxy has, like, a hundred million stars. Plus, there's a hundred million galaxies, and each one also has a hundred million stars. The Mormons say one of those stars is closest to God, a place called Kolob, but where is it? And how do souls know how to get there?"

"Maybe Heaven isn't a physical place, then," said Annabelle, deciding she'd have to be more choosy about the books she brought home from now on.

"Sure, that's a lot like some of the ideas in Hinduism and Buddhism: our soul exists on after we're gone. But in that case, where are they all? Do souls blend with the air?"

Now Annabelle was intrigued, if skeptical. She waved one hand back and forth, just feeling the air whoosh past, and wondered if it really was just air after all. "I only saw the souls in Hell," she admitted. "Souls that don't go to Hell, I've never spoken to them. Well, except for some ghosts here on Earth, but ghosts don't count, since they didn't go anywhere. I guess the things you're talking about could be right here, hovering around us in a different way. I can't read any thoughts out here except for yours, but there are non-human creatures I can't sense. The creatures you're talking about might have different minds than living humans do."

"Sure." Steve lowered his voice and leaned towards Annabelle as if imparting a secret. "Sometimes I've felt like I'm being watched when no one is looking at me."

"Everyone has."

"So maybe everyone's feeling something that's all around, all the time. I have to wonder, could I be part of that? I mean, I'm technically dead." Harry raised his hands in front of his face and rotated them, staring so intently that Annabelle wondered if he could see every cell forming him. "Could I just choose to dissolve into thin air, to become part of whatever it is I'm talking about, and exist in a whole different way? If I just learned to let go of this body…"

"Do you want to do that? What if there is no spiritual world except for Hell, and you just disappear? If you even manage to change yourself at all?" Annabelle feared that idea. She grew annoyed at her fear, and at Harry for making her afraid.

"I think there is, though. Another spiritual world of some kind." Harry stared up at the stars again. "Have you ever been in a crowd for some kind of exciting event—a concert, a church service, a baseball game? And then, together, everyone's watching something that moves them at the same time, so you feel that the guy next to you is moved just like you, and then everyone in the crowd can feel each other, and so everyone gets more excited because they can just sense the excitement of everyone, and it carries them off, emotionally. Just looking at another person doesn't do that. It's something you feel. You feel what they feel."

"You think that's a spiritual thing, then?" Annabelle asked. She put great skepticism into her voice, because she preferred mocking these ideas to actually thinking about them. If she took them seriously, she might have to accept the idea that Harry would move beyond her reach someday.

"Yeah," said Harry, oblivious to her scorn. "It's like people being joined in something beyond just the experience itself. Souls touch."

"You know," said Annabelle, "that might just be human beings being human beings. You're social creatures, so of course you'll be affected by each other's moods."

"Sure, but why are we affected? What makes a single consciousness into mass consciousness? Scientists might find the exact part of the brain that lights up when one person joins with other people someday, but that doesn't make the experience itself any less...well, at the risk of sounding like a girl who likes pink too much, any less magical. It happens, even in my pathetic life. I've felt it, felt a whole crowd become a single creature sharing one thought, one emotion. It's really something." Harry turned to Annabelle and smiled, carried away by his own romantic ideas. "There's something there. Maybe I don't know what 'it' is, if it's a single God, or a trillion souls floating through the air to form something vast and ineffable. But maybe someday I'll be ready to join it...if I earn the right."

Depression washed over Annabelle. She did not like the thought of Harry moving on without her or changing into something that she'd no longer be able to identify as her Harry. That he sounded so happy about it only made it worse.

Yet his words made sense. Hadn't she come to Earth to try and make something of herself that she couldn't while tied to Hell? She'd been desperate to change, and change she had, though not in any way she'd expected.

Now, a month later in the parking lot of New York Downtown Hospital, Annabelle needed all her self-control to keep from looking at Harry again. If the soldiers saw him, they might be less merciful than Lilith. Eyes on the ground, Annabelle thought of that day, of her sadness at the idea of Harry leaving her behind, and of the irony that it was her leaving him.

This is your chance, Harry, she thought, wishing he could read her mind. *Now you're free of all expectations, of retaliation, and of my jealousy. Find the higher plane you're looking for, on another planet, in the sky, or right here if you're right and the air is more than it seems. Your future, your happiness, is out there waiting for you, and nothing is left to stop you from finding it now.*

Desperately sad and euphoric at the same time, Annabelle took Lilith's outstretched hand and rose to her feet, keeping her head submissively lowered. She didn't say a word, refusing to show her enemies any weakness. They could take her freedom away, but the changes she'd made to herself were hers, and Hell couldn't have them.

The pride in her sacrifice was there, new pride to replace the vanishing pride she'd felt over having control of her own life. Annabelle had used that pride to sustain herself over long, lean months on Earth with Harry. Now that her life belonged to Hell again, that pride crumbled away. It rotted like fruit left on the ground through autumn as Annabelle thought of what she'd be made to do back "home."

She did not fear pain. Several centuries ago, when her boredom actively began to hurt her, Annabelle started exploring pain and the limits of her body's tolerance. She had driven herself to madness and welcomed the insanity because she'd never been mad before.

This would be more than pain. Her brethren would use, humiliate, and worst of all, *bore* her until freedom and love faded from her mind, reduced to the vaguest memory. Eventually, Annabelle knew she would doubt she'd ever been free at all.

Annabelle squared her shoulders and walked toward the gate to Hell, still open and sending a million colors of light around the parking lot, without showing any sign of her suffering. Whatever her fickle memories would tell her later on, Annabelle had been free, and Harry would remain free thanks to her efforts. That would have to be enough.

Before her, the gate to Hell crackled, hungry for bodies and souls to suck down to the underworld.

Annabelle obliged it.

Jimmy's mother shrieked so loudly that Jimmy had to hold the hospital phone receiver a foot away from his ear to keep from going deaf.

"Mom, Mom, it's okay—"

"Okay? *Okay*? When you've heard a building collapses across town, you're okay. When it falls down next to you, you might be okay. When it falls on your head and puts you in the hospital, *you don't get to say you're okay*!"

Jimmy now thoroughly regretted calling home. He'd just been so scared after that last wave of power had almost crushed him. To have felt God for the first time in years, to have had some of his emotional wounds healed, only to die without even trying to patch things up with his parents would be too cruel an irony.

It figured that the first thing he'd come up against was the reason he'd left home in the first place. One of the reasons, anyway.

"Look, Mom, seriously," Jimmy said. "I'm—ow!" Turning too quickly to talk into the phone, Jimmy upset his stab wounds.

"'Ow?'" His mother's voice raised about six octaves. "What do you mean, 'ow'?"

"It's not...I mean..." Jimmy squirmed in his hospital bed. "I'm just a little sore from where some, um, support beams stabbed me. But it's fine, everything's been cleaned—"

Again, Jimmy had to jerk the receiver far away from his ear. "This is because you haven't been eating your vegetables!"

"No, I—what?"

"I told you, you need to keep a balanced diet, but no, you go and live off McDonald's grease!"

Jimmy blushed. That was actually true.

"And the next thing you know your body turns useless and your head's all sluggish, so you do ridiculous things like run off for days at a time on shady dealings and invite collapsing buildings onto your head!"

"Okay, Mom. MOM!"

She lowered her voice but began sobbing about what a terrible mother she was in Dari so quickly and quietly that Jimmy couldn't keep up.

"Mom. I called to say I'd like to come home for a visit."

The sobbing stopped. Imagining the look on his mother's face was enough to put Jimmy back in a good mood, or as good a mood as he could be in when feeling so anxious, tired, and sore.

"When?" she asked.

"Pretty much as soon as I get out of here. Is that too little notice?"

"No!" she burst out. "You know how much we want to see you. Oh darling, why don't I come up? I just know those awful doctors don't really have a clue how to heal someone. I'll fly up and then we'll come back down to Albuquerque together."

Jimmy smiled. What a mom thing to say. "Thanks, but like I said, my wounds aren't anything serious. I'll be resting in my own bed tomorrow and down to see you in a few days."

"Wow," said his mother. "I think I've been overloaded. My brain seems to have short-circuited."

"Boy, do I know that feeling." Steve walked back into the room then, and Jimmy didn't need his psychology training to see how upset his patient was. "Ah, the doctor just walked in."

"You let me talk to him! I'll tell him how to take care of you properly!"

"Um. Much as I'm sure he'd benefit from your experience, he's a little too busy not letting people die. I'll call you tomorrow, okay?" Jimmy hung up before his mother could ask for a way to contact him. "Steve?"

Steve slumped against the wall across from Jimmy's bed, his forehead resting against the ugly yellow surface. "Gone."

"Damn." Jimmy collapsed back against his pillows, assuming that meant Annabelle was dead. What could he do now? Were demons going to keep coming after them both? "I'm so sorry, Steve."

"Thanks, Dr. Hamid." Steve's voice sounded dull, but he straightened and walked across the room, more to do something than to get anywhere. "Christ. What do I do now?"

"If you're asking me instead of just wondering aloud, Annabelle left some ideas behind in her letter."

"What?" Steve jerked around. "Does she say how to get down to Hell?"

Jimmy frowned, confused. "Why would you want to do that? Won't you be captured pretty much immediately once the records get straightened out and the, uh, authorities realize you're gone?"

"Well I can't just leave her down there."

"Leave who?" asked Jimmy, feeling more and more like the conversation had fallen into an alternate reality.

"The Wicked Witch of the friggin' West. Annabelle, of course!"

It was the first time Steve had snapped at him that Jimmy could remember. Jimmy was torn between confusion, nervousness at the show of temper, and elation that Steve had grown comfortable enough to show how he actually felt.

Confusion won out. "But...when demons die...Annabelle said they don't go back to Hell. Or, their souls don't. If they have souls, I'm not too clear on that."

The air conditioner under the window kicked in, another bizarre occurrence in a night full of them. Whose idea was it to have the damn thing going in winter? Jimmy shivered and wrapped his blankets tighter round his neck. For a moment, he didn't notice that Steve now looked just as bewildered as Jimmy felt. "What are you talking about?"

"What are *you* talking about?"

"I'm talking about saving Annabelle!" Steve gestured wildly with his arms.

"Wait. You mean she's alive?" Jimmy reached over towards the wobbly table at his bedside, knocked Annabelle's letter over when he tried to grab it, and almost fell out of bed trying to get it up from the floor.

"Her letter says something else?" The letter flew up from the floor as though grabbed by a strong gust of wind, right into Steve's hands. "She went out there expecting to die?" Steve's voice rose until he reminded Jimmy of his mother. Steam suddenly exploded out of the radiator underneath the window. "What the hell was she thinking?"

"Um," said Jimmy, hoping to derail Steve's train of thought before he completely lost it. "So, she's alive, then?"

"She sure is. And she's even more out of her mind than I thought if she thinks I'm not going after her." Harry glared at the radiator, which stilled again.

Jimmy hesitated. "You know...she put ideas for where you could go in that letter because she hoped you'd move on with your life."

Steve gave Jimmy a scathing look, for about a second. Then his shoulders sagged and he looked at the ground in his familiar, passive way.

"I know it's a bad idea," he mumbled. "I only have the abilities I do because I'm an unnatural thing in this world. Back in Hell, I'll be powerless again.

"But shit, Doctor," Steve shivered and hugged himself. "How am I supposed to make a life for myself up here knowing she's down there enduring God knows what? I mean, haven't I been seeing you because I already have enough to feel guilty about?"

"Yeah," said Jimmy. If Steve was sticking to his guns even after losing the attitude, he really had to mean what he said. "All right, I see your point. Still, at the very least, you know you can't do anything without more information. You don't know anything about Hell, do you? Your viewpoint was, uh, a little limited while you were there."

"Tactful as always," said Steve.

"That's me, the soul of diplomacy. Which will be good, helpful for introducing you to some of the people on that list." Jimmy gestured to the letter still in Steve's hands. "Did you read it all the way through? She listed a couple people—or demons, I'm not sure which—who can help you get control of these interesting new powers of yours. Maybe they'll know something about how to get back into Hell also."

"Or can at least direct me to someone who knows. And much as I hate waiting, I know I have to have a plan before storming into territory that turns me into quivering jelly." Steve ran one hand through his hair and then rubbed the back of his neck, a nervous gesture that Jimmy recognized well. "But I *am* going after her."

Jimmy didn't doubt that for a second. He poured himself some water from the plastic pitcher by his bed. Raising the cup as though making a toast, he said, "Once more into the breach, my friend," and drained the cup dry.

THE END...
MAYBE